EMMA PUTS MY PHONE DOWN, AN UNEASY look on her face. "Where are you, Sutton?" she asks aloud in a nervous whisper, as if she knows I'm close.

I wish I could send her a message from beyond the grave: *I'm here. And this is how I died.* Only when I died, my memory died, too. All I know in my heart, in my *bones*, is that someone killed me. And that same someone is watching Emma as closely as I am.

Does this scare me? Yes. But through Emma, I've been given a chance to uncover what happened in those final moments before I took my last breath. And the more I discover about who I was and the secrets I kept, the more I realize how much danger surrounds my long-lost twin.

My enemies are everywhere. And sometimes, those we least suspect turn out to be our biggest threats.

BOOKS BY SARA SHEPARD

Pretty Little Liars
Flawless
Perfect
Unbelievable
Wicked
Killer
Heartless
Wanted
Twisted
Ruthless
Stunning

Pretty Little Secrets

The Lying Game
Never Have I Ever
Two Truths and a Lie
Hide and Seek

NEVER HAVE I EVER

A LYING GAME NOVEL

BY

SARA SHEPARD

HARPER TEEN

An Imprint of HarperCollinsPublishers

HarperTeen is an imprint of HarperCollins Publishers.

Never Have I Ever
Copyright © 2011 by Alloy Entertainment and Sara Shepard
All rights reserved. Printed in the United States of America. No part
of this book may be used or reproduced in any manner whatsoever
without written permission except in the case of brief quotations
embodied in critical articles and reviews. For information address
HarperCollins Children's Books, a division of HarperCollins Publishers,
10 East 53rd Street, New York, NY 10022.
www.epicreads.com

Produced by Alloy Entertainment
151 West 26th Street, New York, NY 10001

Library of Congress Cataloging-in-Publication Data

Shepard, Sara, 1977–
    Never have I ever : a Lying game novel / by Sara Shepard. — 1st ed.
        p.   cm. — (Lying game ; [2])
    Summary: Sutton Mercer watches from the afterlife as her long-lost
twin sister, Emma Paxton, continues to pretend to be her in order to iden-
tify Sutton's killer.
    ISBN 978-0-06-186973-0 (pbk.)
    [1. Twins—Fiction. 2. Sisters—Fiction. 3. Murder—Fiction.
4. Dead—Fiction.   5. Mystery and detective stories.]   I. Title.
PZ7.S54324Ne   2012   2011022941
[Fic]—dc23   CIP
                                                              AC

Design by Liz Dresner

13 14 15 16   LP/RRDH   10 9 8 7 6 5 4 3 2
❖
First paperback edition, 2012

The pure and simple truth is rarely pure and never simple.

—OSCAR WILDE

PROLOGUE

LIFE AFTER DEATH

It's the little things you miss when you die. The feel of sliding into bed when you're exhausted, the clean scent in the Arizona air after a storm during monsoon season, the flutter in your stomach when you see your crush walking down the hall. My killer took all those things away from me just before my eighteenth birthday.

And because of fate—and a threat from my murderer—my long-lost twin sister, Emma Paxton, stepped into my life.

When I died two weeks ago, I popped into Emma's world, a world that was about as different from mine as you could get. From that very first moment I saw what

Emma saw, went where she went . . . and watched. I watched as Emma reached out to me on Facebook and as someone posing as me told her to visit. I watched as Emma traveled to Tucson, cautiously hopeful about our reunion. I watched as my friends tackled Emma, thinking she was me, and brought her to a party. I stood beside her when she got the note that said I was dead, warning her that if she didn't continue to pretend to be me, that if she told anyone who she really was, she'd be dead, too.

I watch today as Emma pulls on my favorite thin white tee and swipes my shimmery NARS blush onto her high cheekbones. I can say nothing as she slides into the skinny jeans I used to live in on weekends and sorts through my cherrywood jewelry box for my favorite silver locket, the one that sends rainbow prisms around the room when it catches the light. And I sit silently by as Emma sends a text confirming brunch plans with my best friends, Charlotte and Madeline, even though I would've worded it differently. Still, Emma has the basics of me down cold—almost no one has noticed she isn't me.

Emma puts my phone down, an uneasy look on her face. "Where are you, Sutton?" she asks aloud in a nervous whisper, as if she knows I'm close.

I wish I could send her a message from beyond the grave: *I'm here. And this is how I died.* Only when I died, my memory died, too. I have glimpses here and there of who

I used to be, but only a few solid, fleshed-out moments have bobbed to the surface. My death is as much a mystery to me as it is to Emma. All I know in my heart, in my *bones*, is that someone killed me. And that same someone is watching Emma as closely as I am.

Does this scare me? Yes. But through Emma, I've been given a chance to uncover what happened in those final moments before I took my last breath. And the more I discover about who I was and the secrets I kept, the more I realize how much danger surrounds my long-lost twin.

My enemies are everywhere. And sometimes, those we least suspect turn out to be our biggest threats.

1

A CHARMED LIFE

"This way to the terrace." A tanned, button-nosed hostess grabbed four leather-bound menus and marched through the dining room of La Paloma Country Club in Tucson, Arizona. Emma Paxton, Madeline Vega, Laurel Mercer, and Charlotte Chamberlain followed her, snaking around tables full of men in tan blazers and cowboy hats, women in tennis whites, and children munching on organic turkey sausage.

Emma dropped into a booth on the stucco veranda, staring at the tattoo on the back of the hostess's neck as she glided away—a Chinese character that probably meant something lame, like *faith* or *harmony*. The terrace had a view of the

Catalina Mountains, and every cactus and boulder was in sharp relief in the late-morning sun. A few feet away, golfers stood around a tee, contemplating their drives or checking their BlackBerrys. Before Emma had arrived in Tucson and assumed her twin sister's life, the closest she'd gotten to setting foot in a country club was working as an attendant at a mini-golf course outside Las Vegas.

I, however, knew this place like the back of my hand. As I sat, invisible, next to my twin, tethered to her always like a balloon tied to a little kid's wrist, I felt a tingle of memory. The last time I ate at this restaurant, my parents had brought me to celebrate getting straight Bs on my report card—a rarity for me. A whiff of peppers and eggs brought back my favorite meal—huevos rancheros, made with the best chorizo in all of Tucson. What I wouldn't give for just one bite.

"Four tomato juices with lime wedges," Madeline chirped to the waitress who'd appeared. When the waitress sauntered off, Madeline straightened her spine into her signature ballet-diva posture, whipped her obsidian black hair over her shoulder, and produced a silver flask from her fringed purse. Liquid sloshed as she shook the container back and forth. "We can make Bloody Marys," she said with a wink.

Charlotte tucked a piece of red-gold hair behind her freckled ear and grinned.

"A Bloody Mary might knock me out." Laurel pinched her thumb and forefinger on the bridge of her sun-kissed nose. "I'm still exhausted from last night."

"The party was definitely a success." Charlotte inspected her reflection in the back of a spoon. "What do you think, Sutton? Did we properly usher you into adulthood?"

"Like she'd know." Madeline nudged Emma. "You weren't even *there* half the time."

Emma swallowed. She still wasn't used to the taunting banter between Sutton's friends, the kind that grew out of years of friendship. Just sixteen and a half days ago, she'd been living as a foster child in Las Vegas, suffering silently with Travis, her vile foster brother, and Clarice, her celeb-obsessed foster mom. But then she discovered an online strangulation video of a girl who looked exactly like her, down to the oval shape of her face, high cheekbones, and blue-green eyes that changed colors depending on the light. After contacting Sutton, the mystery doppelganger, and discovering that they were long-lost identical twins, Emma took a road trip to Tucson, giddy and excited to meet her.

Fast-forward to the very next day when Emma learned that Sutton had been murdered—and that Emma would be next unless she took Sutton's place. Even though she felt anxious about living a lie, even though her skin prickled every time someone called her "Sutton," Emma didn't see any other option. But it didn't mean she was going to sit silently by and let her sister's body languish somewhere. She had to find out who killed Sutton—no matter what. Not only was it justice for her twin, but it was the only way for Emma to get her own life back and stand a chance of keeping her new family.

The waitress returned with four glasses of tomato juice, and as soon as her back was turned, Madeline unscrewed the cap of the stainless-steel flask and dumped clear liquid into each cup. Emma ran her tongue over her teeth, her journalism-obsessed mind producing a headline: *Underage Girls Caught Boozing at Local Country Club.* Sutton's friends . . . well, they lived on the edge. In more ways than one.

"Well, Sutton?" Madeline slid a glass of spiked tomato juice toward Emma. "Are you going to explain why you bailed on your own birthday party?"

Charlotte leaned in. "Or if you told us, would you have to kill us?"

Emma flinched at the word *kill.* Madeline, Charlotte, and Laurel were her number-one suspects in Sutton's murder. Someone had tried to strangle Emma with Sutton's locket during a sleepover at Charlotte's house last week, and whoever had done it was either capable of hacking the house's many alarms . . . or already inside. And last night, at Sutton's birthday party, Emma had discovered that her friends were behind Sutton's strangulation video. It was only a prank; Sutton's friends were part of a secret club called the Lying Game that prided itself on scaring the crap out of its members and the other kids at school. But what if Sutton's friends had meant to take things much, much further? They'd been interrupted by Ethan Landry, Emma's only real friend in Tucson, but maybe they'd finished Sutton off later.

To calm her nerves, Emma took a long sip of spiked tomato juice and summoned her inner Sutton, a girl she'd learned was snarky and sassy and didn't take shit from anyone. "Aww. Did you miss me? Or were you nervous that someone dragged me away and left me for dead in the desert?" She glanced at the three faces staring back at her, trying to detect anything that looked like an admission of guilt. Madeline picked at her chipped peach nail polish. Charlotte coolly sipped her Bloody Mary. Laurel gazed out at the golf course as if she'd just spotted someone she recognized.

Then Sutton's iPhone chimed. Emma pulled it out of her bag and checked the screen. She had a text from Ethan. HOW ARE YOU AFTER LAST NIGHT? LET ME KNOW IF YOU NEED ANYTHING.

Emma shut her eyes and pictured Ethan's face, his raven hair and lake-blue eyes, and the way he'd looked at her, a way no boy had ever looked at her before. Her body flooded with desire and relief.

"Who's that from?" Charlotte leaned over the table, nearly impaling her boobs on the cactus arrangement. Emma covered the screen with her hand.

"You're blushing!" Laurel pointed a finger at Emma. "Is it a new boyfriend? Is that why you ran out on Garrett last night?"

"It's just Mom." Emma quickly deleted the text. Sutton's friends wouldn't understand why she'd left her birthday bash with Ethan, a mysterious boy who was more interested in stargazing than popularity. But Ethan was the sanest person Emma had met in Tucson so far—and the only person who knew who she really was and why she was here.

"So what exactly happened with Garrett?" Charlotte pursed her glossy, blackberry-tinted lips. From what Emma had gleaned in the past two weeks, Charlotte was the bossiest of their four-girl clique—and also the most insecure about her looks. She wore way too much makeup and talked too loudly, as though no one would listen to what she had to say otherwise.

Emma jabbed the ice at the bottom of her Bloody Mary with her straw. Garrett. *Right*. Garrett Austin was Sutton's boyfriend—or, more accurately, *ex*-boyfriend. Last night, his birthday gift to Sutton had been his naked, willing body and a pack of Trojans.

It had been painful to see the shattered look on my boyfriend's face when Emma rejected him. I could only guess at what our time together had been like, but I knew our relationship hadn't been a joke. Although now he probably thought that's what it had been to me.

Laurel's crystal-clear blue eyes narrowed as she took a sip of her drink. "Why did you run out on him? Does he look freaky naked? Does he have a third nipple?"

Emma shook her head. "None of that. It's my deal, not his."

Madeline pulled the wrapper off her straw and blew it in Emma's direction. "Well, you'd better find a rebound. Homecoming's in two weeks, and you need to snag a date before all the decent guys are spoken for."

Charlotte snorted. "As if *that's* ever stopped her?"

Emma flinched. Sutton had stolen Garrett from Charlotte last year.

It didn't make me the nicest friend, I admit. And from the doodles of Garrett's name on Charlotte's notebook and the pictures of him hidden under her bed, she was clearly still pining for him—which gave her a pretty solid reason to want me dead.

A shadow fell over the round table. A man with slicked-back hair and hazel eyes stood above Emma and the others. His blue polo was starched to a crisp and his khakis were perfectly pressed.

"Daddy!" Madeline exclaimed in a shaky voice, her controlled, cool-girl disposition instantly melting away. "I-I didn't know you were going to be here today!"

Mr. Vega gazed at their half-drunk glasses on the table. His nostrils twitched, as if he could smell the alcohol. The smile remained on his face, but it had a false edge that made Emma uneasy. He reminded her of Cliff, the foster father who sold used cars in a dusty lot near the Utah border and could swing from volatile dad to smarmy, ass-kissing salesman in four seconds flat.

Mr. Vega was silent a moment longer. Then he leaned forward and squeezed the top of Madeline's bare arm. She flinched slightly.

"Order anything you want, girls," he said in a low voice. "It's on me." He turned with military precision and started toward the brick-arched doorway to the golf course.

"Thanks, Daddy!" Madeline called after him, her voice trembling just slightly.

"That's sweet," Charlotte murmured hesitantly after he left, glancing sideways at Madeline.

"Yeah." Laurel traced her pointer finger around the scalloped edge of her plate, not making eye contact with Madeline.

Everyone looked like they wanted to say more, but no one did . . . or dared. Madeline's family was rife with secrets. Her brother, Thayer, had run away before Emma arrived in Tucson. Emma kept seeing his missing-person poster everywhere.

For just a moment, she felt a pang of nostalgia for her old life, her *safe* life—a feeling she'd never thought she'd have about her foster-care days. She'd come to Tucson thinking she'd find everything she'd always wished for: a sister, a family to make her whole. Instead, she'd found a family that was broken without even realizing it, a dead twin whose life seemed more complicated by the minute, and potential murderers lurking around every corner.

A flush rose on Emma's skin, the unspoken tension suddenly too much for her. With a loud scrape, she pushed her chair away from the table. "I'll be back," she said, fumbling through the French doors toward the bathroom.

She entered an empty lounge filled with mirrors, plush, cognac-colored leather couches, and a wooden basket containing Nexxus hair spray, Tampax, and little bottles of Purell. Perfume lingered in the air, and classical music played through the stereo speakers.

Emma collapsed in a chair at one of the vanities and inspected her reflection in the mirror. Her oval face, framed by wavy sienna hair, and eyes that looked peri-winkle in some lights, ocean-blue in others, stared back at her. They were the very same features as the girl whose image smiled happily from the family portraits in the

Mercers' foyer, the same girl whose clothes felt scratchy against Emma's skin, as if her body sensed Emma didn't belong in them.

And around Emma's neck was Sutton's silver locket—the same locket the killer used to strangle Emma in Charlotte's kitchen, the one Emma was sure Sutton had been wearing when she was murdered. Every time she touched the smooth silver surface or saw it glinting in the mirror, it reminded her that all of this, no matter how uncomfortable, was necessary to find her sister's killer.

The door swished open, and the sounds of the dining room rushed in. Emma whipped around as a blonde, college-age girl in a pink polo with the country club's logo on the boob crossed the Navajo-carpeted floor. "Uh, are you Sutton Mercer?"

Emma nodded.

The girl reached into the pocket of her khakis. "Someone left this for you." She proffered a Tiffany-blue ring-sized box. A small tag on the top read FOR SUTTON.

Emma stared, a little afraid to touch it. "Who's it from?"

The girl shrugged. "A messenger dropped it off at the front desk just now. Your friends said you were in here."

Emma took it hesitantly, and the girl turned and walked out the door. The lid lifted easily, revealing a velvet jewelry box. All kinds of possibilities flashed through Emma's mind. A small, hopeful part of her wondered if it was from Ethan. Or, more awkwardly, maybe it was from Garrett, trying to win her back.

The box opened with a creak. Inside was a gleaming silver charm in the shape of a locomotive engine.

Emma ran her fingers over it. A shard of paper poked up from the velvet pouch inside the lid. She pulled out a tiny rolled-up scroll to find a note written in block letters.

THE OTHERS MIGHT NOT WANT TO REMEMBER THE TRAIN PRANK, BUT I'LL BE SEIZED BY THE MEMORY ALWAYS. THANKS!

Emma jammed the note back into the box and shut it. *Train prank.* Last night, in Laurel's bedroom, she'd frantically skimmed through at least fifty Lying Game pranks. None of them had to do with a train.

The train charm etched itself in my mind and suddenly, a faint glimmer came to me. A train's whistle shrieking in the distance. A scream, and then whirling lights. Was it . . . were we . . . ?

But as quickly as it arrived, the memory sped away.

2

CSI, TUCSON

Ethan Landry opened the chain-link gate to the public tennis court and let himself in. Emma watched him stroll toward her, his shoulders slumped and his hands in his pockets. Even though it was after ten, there was enough moonlight overhead to see his perfectly distressed jeans, scuffed Converse, and messy dark hair that curled sweetly over the collar of a navy flannel shirt. An untied shoelace dragged across the court behind him.

"Mind if I leave the lights off?" Ethan gestured to the coin-operated meter that turned on giant floodlights for night play.

Emma nodded, feeling her insides leap. Being in the dark with Ethan didn't sound so shabby.

"So what's this train prank?" he asked, referring to the text Emma had sent hours earlier when she asked him to join her at the courts. It had become a meeting place for them, somewhere that felt uniquely theirs.

Emma handed the silver charm to Ethan. "Someone left it for Sutton at the country club. There was a note attached." A chill ran down her spine as she relayed what the note had said.

A motorcycle rumbled in the distance. Ethan turned the charm over in his hands. "I don't know anything about a train, Emma."

Emma's heart tugged when Ethan called her by her real name. It was such a relief. But it also felt dangerous. The killer had told her to tell no one. And she'd broken the rule.

"But it sounds like whoever gave it to you was part of the prank," Ethan went on, "or a victim of it."

Emma nodded.

They were silent for a moment, listening to the sounds of a lone basketball bouncing on the far court. Then Emma reached in her pocket. "I have something to show you." She passed her iPhone to him, her stomach flipping over as their fingers accidentally brushed. Ethan was cute—really cute.

I had to admit Ethan was cute, too—in that disheveled, brooding, mystery-boy way. It was fun to watch my sister's crush develop. It made me feel closer to her, like it was something we would've obsessed over together if I were still alive.

Emma cleared her throat as Ethan scrolled through the page she'd loaded. "It's a list of everyone in Sutton's life," she explained, the words tumbling quickly out of her mouth. "I've gone through everything—Sutton's Facebook, her phone, her emails. And now I'm almost positive I've got the date of her death narrowed down to August thirty-first."

Ethan turned toward her. "How can you be sure?"

Emma took a quick breath. "Check this out." She tapped the Facebook icon. "I wrote to Sutton at ten-thirty the night of the thirty-first." She moved the screen over so Ethan could read her note: *This will sound crazy, but I think we're related. You're not by any chance adopted, are you?* "And then Sutton responded at twelve-fifty-six, here." Emma scrolled down the message page and showed what Sutton had written back: *OMG. I can't believe this. Yes, I was totally adopted . . .*

An unreadable expression flickered across Ethan's face. "Then how can you think she died on the thirty-first if she was writing you messages on Facebook?"

"I was the only person Sutton wrote or talked to that

night." Emma scrolled through Sutton's call log from the thirty-first. The last answered call was from Lilianna Fiorello, one of Sutton's friends, at 4:32 P.M. Then at 8:39, MISSED CALL, LAUREL. Three more missed calls at 10:32, 10:45, and 10:59 from Madeline. Emma flipped ahead to the next day's log. The missed calls began again the following morning: 9:01, Madeline; 9:20, Garrett; 10:36, Laurel.

"Maybe she was busy and didn't pick up her phone," Ethan suggested. He took back the phone and clicked to Sutton's Facebook page, scrolling through her Wall posts.

Emma grasped Sutton's locket. "I've looked through Sutton's entire call log back to December. Practically every call she gets, she answers. And if she doesn't answer it, she calls whoever it was back later."

"Then what about this post she wrote on the thirty-first?" Ethan asked, pointing to the screen. "Couldn't this mean she was avoiding everyone?" The last post Sutton had ever written was a few hours before Emma's note: *Ever think about running away? Sometimes I do.*

Emma shook her head vehemently. "Nothing fazed my sister. Not even being strangled." Just saying the words *my sister* connected her to Sutton in a deep, powerful way. At first, Emma had wondered if Sutton really *had* run away— maybe sticking her long-lost twin sister in her place had been part of an elaborate prank. But once someone nearly strangled Emma in Charlotte's house, she became convinced Sutton's death was for real.

"Ethan, think about it," she went on. "Sutton writes this random post about wanting to run away . . . and then someone kills her? It's too much of a coincidence. What if Sutton didn't write this—what if the killer did? That way, if someone noticed Sutton was missing, they'd read her Facebook and assume she ran away, not died. It was a way for the killer to cover her ass."

Ethan rolled a forgotten tennis ball on the ground with the sole of his foot. A gash along the seam marred the bright yellow fabric. "It still doesn't explain the note Sutton wrote you a few hours later telling you to come to Tucson. Who wrote that?" The tremble in his voice betrayed his nerves.

A feathery chill darted along Emma's spine. "I think the killer wrote both notes," she whispered. "Once the killer realized I existed, she wanted me here so I could slip into Sutton's life. No body, no crime."

Ethan's eyes darted across the court, like he still didn't believe Emma, but I was almost positive my sister was right. I woke up in Emma's life the night of August 31, just hours before Emma discovered the snuff film of me. I doubted I'd straddled both Alive Sutton and Ghost Sutton worlds at the same time.

Emma gazed at the dark silhouettes of trees in the distance. "So what was Sutton *doing* that night? Where was she, who was she with?"

"Have you found any hints in her room?" Ethan asked. "Any emails, notes in her calendar . . . ?"

Emma shook her head. "I've scoured her journal. But it's so cryptic and random, like she assumed it was going to fall into enemy hands one day. There's nothing anywhere about what she did the night she died."

"What about receipts in pockets?" Ethan tried. "Crumpled-up notes in her trash can?"

"Nope." Emma's eyes dropped to the space between her feet. Suddenly, she felt exhausted.

Ethan sighed. "Okay. How about her friends? Do you know where they were that night?"

"I asked Madeline," Emma said. "She told me she didn't remember."

"That's convenient." Ethan scuffed the tip of his sneaker over the court. "I could see Madeline doing it, though. The beautiful, unhinged ballerina. Like *Black Swan* for real."

Emma gave a short laugh. "That's a little bit of an exaggeration, don't you think?" She'd hung out several times with Madeline over the past week. They'd even had a heart-to-heart about Thayer and a few laughs in a spa hot tub. In those moments, Madeline had reminded Emma of her tough-but-caring friend Alexandra Stokes, who lived in Henderson, Nevada.

Emma looked at Ethan. "Maybe Madeline was telling the truth. I mean, do *you* remember what you were doing on the thirty-first?"

"Actually, I do. It was the first day of the meteor shower."

"The Perseids." Emma nodded. The first time she'd met Ethan, he'd been stargazing.

A shy smile crept onto Ethan's face like he was remembering the moment, too. "Yep, I was probably on my front porch. The shower goes on for, like, a week."

"And you were camping out there because stars are more interesting than people, huh?" Emma teased.

Pink colored Ethan's cheeks and he looked away. "*Some* people."

"Should I ask Madeline again?" Emma pressed. "Do you think she's hiding something?"

Ethan shook his head slowly. "You never know with those girls. Not that I was privy to their inner-circle secrets, but something has always seemed off about Madeline and Charlotte. Before you came to town, when Sutton was still alive, it constantly seemed like they were vying for her attention and her position at the same time." He stared off into the distance. "Like they loved her and hated her."

Gripping Sutton's phone, Emma touched the Twitter icon and called up each of Sutton's friends' pages, finding nothing remarkable on the thirty-first. But when she flipped to the tweets on September 1, something on Madeline's page caught her eye. She'd written a shout-out to @Chamberlainbabe, Charlotte's Twitter handle. *Thanks for being there for me last night, Char. True friends stick together, no matter what.*

"True friends," Ethan said sarcastically. "Aw."

"More like *Huh?*" Something wasn't right. "Madeline and Charlotte aren't touchy-feely. At all." To Emma, they seemed more like uneasy comrades in the same popular-girl army. Then Ethan pointed to *last night.* "Madeline's talking about the thirty-first."

I shivered. Maybe they'd been with me that night. Maybe they'd finished off their pseudo–best friend together. And maybe, if Emma wasn't careful, she'd be next.

Emma ran her hands down her face, then glanced at Ethan again. Guilt welled up in her chest. Whoever killed her sister was monitoring Emma's every move. How long before the murderer realized Ethan knew the truth about her and tried to silence him, too?

"You don't have to help me, you know," she whispered. "It's not safe."

Ethan turned to face her, his eyes intense. "You shouldn't have to do this alone."

"Are you sure?"

When he nodded, Emma was suddenly overwhelmed with gratitude. "Well, thank you. I was drowning by myself."

Ethan looked surprised. "You don't seem like the kind of girl who drowns in anything."

Emma wanted to reach out and touch the spot where moonlight splashed his cheek. He shifted an inch closer until their knees bumped and his face angled toward hers, like he was about to kiss her. Emma felt the heat of his body as he moved closer, very aware of his full bottom lip.

Her mind swirled, remembering the night before, when he'd told her he'd begun to fall for the girl who'd taken over Sutton's life. That he'd begun to fall for *her*. A different kind of girl would know how to seal the deal. Emma kept a list in her journal called Ways to Flirt, but she'd never actually put any of the techniques into action.

Snap.

Emma shot up, cocking her head to the right. Across the court, just behind a tree, came the faint blue glow of a cell phone, like someone was standing there, watching them.

"Do you see that?"

"What?" Ethan whispered.

Emma craned her neck. But there was only darkness, leaving her with the unsettling feeling that someone had seen—and *heard*—everything.

3

SPINNING HER WHEELS

On Monday morning, Emma sat at a potter's wheel in the ceramics room at Hollier High. She was surrounded by lumps of cement-gray clay, wood tools for carving and cutting, and lopsided bowls on wooden slats waiting for kiln firing. The air smelled earthy and wet, and there was the constant whir of wheels spinning and clunky feet clopping the treadles.

Madeline perched on the stool to Emma's right, glowering at her potter's wheel as though it were a torture device. "What's the point of making pottery? Isn't that what Pottery Barn is for?"

Charlotte snorted. "Pottery Barn doesn't sell pottery!

Do you think Crate and Barrel sells crates and barrels, too?"

"And Pier 1 sells piers?" Laurel giggled a row ahead of them.

"Less talking, more *creating*, girls," said Mrs. Gilliam, their ceramics instructor, snaking around the wheels, her bell anklet jingling as she walked. Mrs. Gilliam was one of those people who looked as though she couldn't be anything but an art teacher. She wore billowing jersey pants, jacquard vests, and statement necklaces over batik tunics that smelled like musty patchouli. Her words were emphatic, reminding Emma of an old social worker she'd known named Mrs. Thuerk, who always spoke as though she was delivering a Shakespearean monologue. *How now, Emma . . . art thou being treated well in this Nevada home for children of fosterly care?*

"Great work, Nisha," Mrs. Gilliam cooed as she passed the glazing table, where several students were painting their pottery in earth tones. Nisha Banerjee, who was Sutton's cocaptain on the tennis team, turned around and smirked triumphantly at Emma. Her eyes flashed with pure hate, which sent a ripple of fear through Emma's chest. It was clear Nisha and Sutton had some seriously bad blood between them—Nisha had been giving Emma the evil eye ever since she stepped into Sutton's life.

Looking away, Emma positioned a gray clay blob in the center of the wheel, cupped her hands around it, and slowly let the wheel turn until she had a bowl-like shape. Laurel let out a low whistle. "How do you know how to do that?"

"Uh, beginner's luck." Emma shrugged like it was no big deal, but her hands trembled slightly. A headline popped in her head: *Master Pottery Skills Expose Emma Paxton Posing as Sutton Mercer. Scandal!* Emma had taken pottery back in Henderson. She'd spent hours using the wheel after school; it was a welcome alternative to going home to Ursula and Steve, the hippie foster parents she'd lived with at the time, who didn't believe in bathing. The No-Suds rule applied to them, their clothing, and their eight mangy dogs.

Emma sliced her hand through the bowl and let out a fake sigh of disappointment when it collapsed. "So much for that."

As soon as Mrs. Gilliam disappeared into the kiln, Emma eyed Madeline and lifted her foot from the treadle. Madeline and the others still made the most sense to be Sutton's killers. But she had no proof.

Wiping her hands on a towel, she pulled out Sutton's iPhone and scrolled through the calendar feature. "Uh, guys?" she said. "Does anyone know when I had my last highlights appointment? I forgot to put it in my calendar and I want to make a note for when I need to go in next. Was it . . . August thirty-first?"

"What day was that?" Charlotte asked. She looked exhausted, like she hadn't slept at all the night before. She mashed her hands way too hard into the clay, turning the bowl she was making into a soupy pancake.

Emma tapped on the phone again. "Uh . . . the day before Nisha's party." *The day before Mads kidnapped me at Sabino Canyon, thinking I was Sutton. Or maybe* knowing *I wasn't Sutton.* "Two days before school started."

Charlotte glanced at Madeline. "Wasn't that the day we—"

"No," Madeline snapped, shooting Charlotte an icy glare. Then she turned to Emma. "Neither of us know where *you* were that day, Sutton. Someone else will have to cure your amnesia."

Fluorescent light gleamed over Madeline's porcelain skin. Her eyes narrowed at Emma, as though challenging her to drop the subject. Charlotte glanced from Emma to Madeline, looking suddenly alert. Even Laurel's back was stiff in front of them.

Emma waited, knowing she'd hit on something and hoping someone would tell her what it was. But when the tense silence persisted, she gave up. *Take two,* she thought, reaching into her pocket and wrapping her fingers around the silver train charm. "Whatever. So I was thinking it's time for a new Lying Game prank."

"Cool," Charlotte murmured, her eyes focused back

on the spinning lump of clay in front of her. "Any ideas?"

Across the room, a girl washed her hands at the sink, and a loud crash sounded from the kiln. "The prank where we stole my mom's car was awesome." She remembered seeing a video of the girls doing just that on Laurel's computer. "Maybe we should do something like that again."

Madeline nodded, thinking. "Maybe."

"Except . . . with a twist," Emma went on, saying the words she'd rehearsed the night before in Sutton's bedroom. "Like, we could leave someone's car in the middle of a car wash. Or drive it into a swimming pool. Or abandon it on the train tracks."

At the word *tracks*, Charlotte, Laurel, and Madeline tensed. A hot, sharp pain streaked through Emma's gut. *Bull's-eye.*

"Very funny." Charlotte slapped her clay down with a *thwap.*

"No repeats allowed, remember?" Laurel hissed over her shoulder.

Madeline swiped the back of her hand across her forehead and glared at Emma. "And are you hoping the cops come again, too?"

The cops. I tried my hardest to force a memory to the surface. But that flash I'd gotten about train tracks had faded into dust.

Emma looked at Sutton's friends, her mouth feeling

cottony dry. But before she could assemble her next question, feedback screeched through the PA system.

"Attention!" spoke the tinny voice of Amanda Donovan, a senior who read the daily announcements. "It's time to announce the winners of the Homecoming Halloween Dance Court, voted in by Hollier's talented boys' football, soccer, cross-country, and volleyball teams! It's in two weeks, ghosts and goblins, so get your tickets today before they sell out! My date and I already have!"

Madeline's lips pursed in disgust. "Who could Amanda possibly be going with? Uncle Wes?"

Charlotte and Laurel snickered. Amanda's uncle was Wes Donovan, a sportscaster who had his own Sirius radio show. Amanda name-dropped him so often during morning announcements that Madeline swore they were secret lovers.

"Please join me in warm congratulations to Norah Alvarez, Madison Cates, Jennifer Morrison, Zoe Mitchell, Alicia Young, Tinsley Zimmerman . . ."

Every time a name was called, Madeline, Charlotte, and Laurel pantomimed a thumbs-up or a thumbs-down.

". . . and Gabriella and Lilianna Fiorello, our first Homecoming Court twins *ever*!" Amanda concluded. "A warm congratulations, ladies!"

Madeline blinked several times as if waking up from a dream. "The Twitter Twins? On the court?"

Charlotte sniffed. "Who would vote for them?"

Emma looked back and forth between them, trying to keep up. Gabby and Lili Fiorello, the Twitter Twins, were fraternal twins in their grade. They both had big blue eyes and honey-blonde hair, but each girl also had other features all her own, like the mole by Lili's chin or Gabby's Angelina Jolie lips. Emma still was unclear whether Gabby and Lili were in or out of the clique; they'd attended Charlotte's sleepover two weekends ago, when the anonymous attacker nearly strangled Emma to death, but they weren't members of the Lying Game. With their dopey expressions, twin-brain mentality, and iPhone addictions, they struck Emma as all fluff and no substance, the girl equivalent of low-calorie Cool Whip.

I wasn't sure about that, though. If there was one thing I was learning, it was that looks could be deceiving. . . .

As if on cue, four sharp ringtones filled the room. Charlotte, Madeline, Laurel, and Emma all fumbled for their phones. On Emma's screen were two new texts, one from Gabby, one from Lili. WE KNOW WE'RE GORGEOUS! Gabby's said. CAN'T WAIT TO WEAR OUR CROWNS! Lili wrote.

"Divas," Madeline said next to her. Emma glanced at her screen. Madeline had received the same texts.

Charlotte snorted, staring at her phone, too. "They should go as twin Carries. Then we'd get to dump pig's blood on their heads."

Emma's phone chimed once more. Lili had sent her an additional missive. WHO'S THE FAIREST OF THEM ALL? TAKE THAT, QUEEN BEE-OTCH!

"Well, now they're officially not coming camping with us after the dance," Charlotte declared.

"We're doing that again?" Laurel said, wrinkling her nose.

"It's tradition," Charlotte said sharply. She looked at Emma. "Right, Sutton?"

Camping? Emma raised an eyebrow. These girls didn't seem the outdoorsy types. But she nodded along. "Right."

"Maybe we could try those awesome hot springs on Mount Lemmon," Madeline said, twisting her dark hair into a bun. "Gabby and Lili say they're filled with natural salts that make your skin feel amazing."

"Enough talk about Gabby and Lili," Charlotte groaned, adjusting the the cornflower-blue headband in her hair. "I can't believe we have to plan a party for them. They're going to be impossible."

Emma frowned. "Why would we have to plan a party?"

For a moment, everyone just stared at her. Charlotte clucked her tongue. "Remember a little organization called Homecoming Committee? The only activity you've been doing since freshman year?"

Emma felt her pulse quicken. She forced a fake *heh-heh* laugh. "I was being *ironic*. Ever heard of it?"

Charlotte rolled her eyes. "Well, unfortunately, the court party *can't* be ironic. We have to beat last year's."

Emma shut her eyes. Sutton . . . on a dance committee? Seriously? When Emma attended school at Henderson High, she and her best friend Alex used to make fun of the dorky dance committee girls. They were all Martha Stewarts–in-training, obsessed with cupcake baking, streamer hanging, and picking the most perfect slow-dance mixes.

But from what I remembered, it was an honor to be on the Homecoming Committee at Hollier. The school also had a strict policy that those planning Homecoming couldn't be members of the court, which was why Amanda hadn't called my name just now. If my spotty memory served me correctly, though, last prom I'd paraded into the ballroom with a court sash across my torso.

I wondered: Would Emma still be here to take my place at this year's prom? Could my murder really go unsolved for *that* long? Could Emma still be living a lie in the spring? The thought of all of it filled me with dread. It also filled me with the now-familiar ache of sadness: There would be no more proms for me. No more cheesy wrist corsages or stretch limos or after parties. I even missed the bad prom music, the goofy DJs who thought they were the next Girl Talk. When I was alive, I'd let it all pass by so fast, barely registering any of the moments, unaware of how good I had it.

The bell rang, and the girls rose from their wheels. Emma stood at the sink and let cool water wash over her clay-gunked hands. As she dried them on a paper towel, Sutton's cell phone chimed in her bag once more. Groaning, Emma pulled it out. Had Gabby and Lili sent *another* text?

But it was an email message from Emma's own account, which she'd loaded onto Sutton's phone. FROM ALEX, it said. THINKING OF YOU! CALL WHEN YOU CAN. CAN'T WAIT TO TALK! XX.

Emma clutched the sides of the iPhone, contemplating how to reply. It had been days since she'd written to Alex, the only person besides Ethan who knew about her trek to Arizona. But unlike with Ethan, Emma had fudged the truth: Alex still thought Sutton was alive and had taken Emma in. Sometimes, when Emma woke up in the morning, she tried to pretend like that was what really happened, and that the previous events and threats had all been a dream. She'd even started a section of her journal called Stuff Sutton and I Would Do Together if She Were Here. She would teach Sutton how to make French cream puffs, something she'd learned at an after-school catering job. Sutton would show her how to curl her eyelashes, which Emma had never been able to properly master. And maybe, at school, they'd switch places for the day, going to each other's classes and answering to each other's names.

Not because they had to. Because they *wanted* to.

Suddenly, Emma had the distinct feeling someone was watching her. She whirled around to find the ceramics room was now mostly empty. But out in the hall, two pairs of eyes stared at her. It was Gabby and Lili, the Twitter Twins. When they noticed that Emma had spotted them, they smirked, leaned their heads close, and whispered. Emma flinched.

A hand touched Emma's arm, and she jumped once more. Laurel stood behind her, leaning against the big gray trash barrel of wet clay next to the sink.

"Oh, hey." Emma's heart pounded in her ears.

"Just waiting for you." Laurel brushed a lock of high-lighted blonde hair over her shoulder and stared at the iPhone in Emma's hands. "Writing to anyone interesting?"

Emma dropped Sutton's phone into her bag. "Uh, not really." The spot where the Twitter Twins had stood was now empty.

Laurel caught her arm. "Why did you bring up the train prank?" she asked, her voice hushed and hard. "No one finds it funny."

Sweat prickled on the back of Emma's neck. She opened her mouth, but nothing came out. Laurel's words echoed the note she'd gotten: *The others might not want to remember the train prank, but I'll be seized by the memory always.* Something had happened that night. Something horrible.

Emma took a deep breath, rolled back her shoulders, and slung her arm around Laurel's waist. "Don't be so sensitive. Now let's go. It smells like ass in here." She hoped she sounded breezier than she felt.

Laurel glared at Emma for a moment, but then followed her into the crowded hall. Emma let out a sigh of relief when Laurel headed in the opposite direction. She felt like she'd dodged a huge bullet.

Or maybe, I thought, opened up a huge can of worms.

4

PAPER TRAIL

After tennis practice, Laurel steered her black VW Jetta onto the Mercers' street, a development in the Catalina foothills with sand-colored stucco houses and front yards full of flowering desert succulents. The only sound in the car was Laurel's jaw working the piece of gum she'd shoved into her mouth.

"So . . . thanks for the ride home," Emma offered, breaking the awkward silence.

Laurel shot Emma a frosty glare. "Are you ever going to get your car out of the impound lot, or am I going to have to chauffeur you forever? You can't keep lying about it being at Madeline's, you know. Mom and Dad aren't *that* stupid."

Emma slumped down in the seat. Sutton's car had been impounded since before Emma arrived in Tucson. It looked like she'd have to retrieve it if Laurel wouldn't drive her around anymore.

Then Laurel fell into silence again. She'd been frosty with Emma ever since ceramics, turning away when Emma asked to partner with her for tennis volleying and shrugging off Emma's suggestion that they hit Jamba Juice on the drive home. Emma wished she knew the magic words to get Laurel to open up, but navigating the world of sibling relationships was something with which she had no real experience. She'd had foster siblings, sure, but those relationships rarely ended well.

Not that mine and Laurel's had either. We hadn't been close for years. I saw flashes of us when we were much younger, holding hands on the Tilt-A-Whirl at the county fair and spying on our parents' dinner party when we were little, but something had happened between now and then.

After passing by three large homes—two of which had gardeners out front, watering the mesquite trees—Laurel pulled into the Mercers' driveway. "Shit," she said under her breath.

Emma followed Laurel's gaze. Sitting on the wrought-iron bench on the Mercers' front porch was Garrett. He was still in his soccer cleats and practice shirt. Two muddy pads covered his knees, and he cradled a bike helmet in his arms.

Emma exited the car and slammed the door. "H-hey," she said tentatively, her gaze on Garrett's face. The corners of his pink mouth curved into a scowl. His soft brown eyes blazed. His blond hair was sweaty from practice. He sat at the very edge of the porch seat like a cat ready to pounce.

Laurel followed her up the driveway, waved at Garrett, and headed inside.

Slowly, Emma walked up the porch steps, standing a safe distance away from Garrett. "How are you?" she asked in a small voice.

Garrett made an ugly noise at the back of his throat. "How do you think I am?"

The automatic sprinklers hissed on in the front yard, misting the plants. In the distance, a weed whacker growled to life. Emma sighed. "I'm really sorry."

"Are you?" Garrett palmed his helmet with his large hands. "So sorry you didn't return my calls? So sorry you won't even look at me right now?"

Emma took in his strong chest, toned legs, and just a hint of stubble on his chin. She understood what Sutton had seen in him, and her heart panged that he didn't know the truth.

"I'm sorry." The words lodged in Emma's throat. "It's

been a weird summer," she said. *That* was an under-statement.

"Weird as in you met someone else?" Garrett balled his fist, making the muscles in his forearms pop.

"No!" Emma took a startled step back, almost bumping into the wind chimes Mrs. Mercer had hung from the eaves.

Garrett wiped his hands on his shirt. "Jesus. Last month you were into this. Into *me*. Why do you hate me all of a sudden? Is this what everyone warned me about? Is this classic Sutton Mercer?"

Classic Sutton. The words echoed painfully in my ears, a refrain I'd heard so many times over the past few weeks. From my new vantage, I'd begun to realize how badly I used to treat people.

"I don't hate you," Emma protested. "I just . . ."

"You know what? I don't care." Garrett slapped the sides of his legs and stood. "We're done. I don't want your excuses. I'm not falling for your games anymore. This is just like what you did to Thayer. I should have known."

Emma recoiled at the harshness of Garrett's voice—and at the mention of Madeline's brother.

Thayer. Just hearing his name made his clear green eyes, high cheekbones, and mussed dark hair flicker across my mind. And then, I saw something else: an image of the two of us standing in the school courtyard. Tears streamed down my face as Thayer talked to me in urgent tones, as if he were trying to get me to understand something, but the memory flaked apart at my fingertips.

Emma struggled to regain her voice. "I'm not sure what you think I—"

"I'd like my *Grand Theft Auto* game back," Garrett interrupted, turning to face the Mercers' impeccable lawn. A black lab lifted his leg on an ash tree. "It's in your PS3."

"I'll look for it," Emma mumbled.

"And I guess I don't need this either." Garrett pulled a long, thin ticket from his gear bag. HALLOWEEN HOMECOMING DANCE, it proclaimed in melting letters. He thrust it at her almost violently, then stepped closer to her until they were almost touching. His body shivered with what seemed like coiled, pent-up energy. Emma held her breath, acutely aware that she had no idea what he might do next.

"Have a nice life, Sutton," Garrett whispered, his voice icy. His cleats made loud clacking sounds as he stalked across the driveway, mounted his bike, and cruised away.

"Goodbye," I whispered to his receding back.

That went well. Technically, this had been Emma's first breakup ever—all her previous relationships had either ended in mutual friendship or fizzled away. No wonder people said it sucked.

Shaken, Emma turned to head inside. As she walked across the porch for the front door, a white SUV on the street caught her eye. She squinted at the flash of blond hair through the windshield. But before she could make out a face, the car sped up, rocketing away in a plume of gray exhaust.

Emma found Laurel in the kitchen, slicing an apple into thin pieces. "Do we know anyone who drives a white SUV?" she asked.

Laurel stared at her. "Besides the Twitter Twins?"

Emma frowned. The twins lived all the way across town.

"So?" Laurel asked. "What happened with Garrett?" There was a smug look on her face. Now *she wants to talk*, Emma thought bitterly.

Emma walked up to the island and popped a juicy apple slice into her mouth. "It's over."

Laurel's expression softened just a bit. "Are you okay?"

Emma wiped her hands across her tennis shorts. "I'll be fine." She looked at Laurel. "Do you think he'll be okay?"

Laurel crunched an apple slice and glanced out the French doors into the backyard. "I don't know. Garrett always struck me as sort of an enigma," she finally said. "I always wondered if there was something more lurking beneath the surface."

Emma flinched, thinking of how Garrett had loomed over her on the porch. "What do you mean?"

"Oh, I don't know." Laurel waved her hand dismissively,

as if she suddenly remembered she wasn't speaking to Emma today. She slid a stack of mail across the kitchen table. "These are for you."

Then she wheeled around and sauntered down the hallway. As Emma absentmindedly sorted through the catalogs, mulling over Garrett's visit and Laurel's haunting words, an envelope with a bank logo in the upper corner caught her eye. AMEX BLUE, said the label. It was addressed to Sutton Mercer.

Emma's breath caught in her throat as she tore it open. This was Sutton's credit card statement, the one from the month leading up to her murder. With shaking fingers, she unfolded the paper and scanned the column of charges in August. BCBG . . . Sephora . . . Walgreens . . . AJ's gourmet market. Then, her gaze landed on a charge on August 31. *Eighty-eight dollars. Clique.*

Nerves snapped inside of her. *Clique.* The word suddenly seemed ominous, like the sound of a safety latch releasing from a gun.

Emma yanked Sutton's phone from her bag. Ethan answered on the second ring. "Clear your schedule for tonight," Emma whispered. "I think I've got something."

5

EXTREME TIMES CALL FOR
EXTREME MEASURES

Hours later, Emma and Ethan sat in Ethan's beat-up, dark red Honda in the back parking lot of a series of shops near the University of Arizona. The smell of brick-oven pizza filled the air, and tipsy college students walked past, singing Taylor Swift songs off-key. There was a head shop called Wonderland, a punk-rock beauty salon called Pink Pony, and a place called Wildcat Central, which sold University of Arizona sweatpants and shot glasses. On the very end was a boutique called Clique.

Ethan pulled down the brim of his red Arizona Diamondbacks ball cap. "Ready?"

Emma nodded, suppressing her nerves. She *had* to be ready.

As Ethan unlatched his seat belt, Emma felt a surge of gratitude rush through her. "Ethan?" She touched the soft spot behind his elbow, tiny pricks of heat shooting down her fingertips. "I just wanted to say thank you. Again."

"Oh." Ethan looked slightly embarrassed. "You don't have to keep thanking me. I'm not Mother Teresa." He pushed the car door open with his foot. "C'mon. It's showtime."

The mannequins in the Clique storefront wore avant-garde Halloween masks. Luxurious cashmere coats, silk dresses, and diaphanous scarves draped their bodies. Their hollow black eyes stared at Emma. Bells dinged when she and Ethan pushed through the front door.

I looked around the place, trying to get a tingle of recognition. A large table stuffed with skinny jeans, skinny chinos, skinny cargo pants, and even skinnier skinny leggings took up most of the real estate in the front of the store. Boots, flats, heels, and espadrilles were lined up on the windowsill like soldiers readying for battle. But nothing stood out; it just looked like the normal sort of boutique I used to frequent.

Emma walked to a rack and checked the price tag on a plain white cotton tee. *Eighty dollars*? Her entire junior year wardrobe cost less than that!

"Can I help you?"

Emma whirled around to see a tall brunette with a Megan Fox scowl and Heidi Montag boobs. When the girl saw Ethan, her face brightened. "Ethan? Hey!"

"Oh hey, Samantha." Ethan ran his fingers along a garment on the table, then blushed and backed away when he realized it was a pair of lacy pink panties. "I didn't know you worked here."

"Only part-time." The shopgirl glanced at Emma again. Her expression soured. "Are you two . . . *friends*?"

Ethan glanced at Emma, the corner of his mouth twitching. "Sutton, this is Samantha. She goes to St. Xavier. Samantha, this is Sutton Mercer."

Samantha snatched the cotton tee from Emma and placed it back on the rack. "Sutton and I are already acquainted."

Emma squared her shoulders, wary of Samantha's tone. "Um, right," she said. "Actually, I was wondering if you kept transaction records?" She held up her sister's Amex bill. "I'm kind of in trouble for overspending on my credit card, and I want to return some stuff I bought on August thirty-first." She let out an embarrassed giggle. "The problem is, I can't remember what I bought where."

Samantha pressed her hand to her chest, feigning surprise. "You don't remember what you purchased?"

"Uh, no." Emma wanted to roll her eyes. If she knew the answer, why would she be asking? But she needed

Samantha's help, so she'd have to bite her tongue and save her retort for her Comebacks I Should Have Said folder, a collection of nasty responses she'd thought of but hadn't dared to say.

"Do you remember what you *stole*?" Samantha challenged.

"Excuse me?"

"The last time you were in," Samantha said slowly, like she was speaking to a kindergartener, "you and your friends stole a pair of hammered gold earrings. Or have you conveniently forgotten that, too?"

Looks like I spent my last day on Earth as a shoplifter.

Emma clung to Samantha's words. "My friends? Which ones?"

"Seriously, what are you on?" Samantha's eyes were on fire. "Trust me, if I knew who they were or had solid proof of what you guys did, I'd press charges in a heartbeat." With that, she whipped around, strode to the back of the store on her spike-heel booties, and began feverishly reorganizing a display of argyle sweaters.

For a moment, the only sounds in the store were the pounding beats of a Chemical Brothers dance mix. Then Emma ran her fingers over an itchy wool sweater dress and glanced at Ethan. "Which friends could Sutton have been with? Why wouldn't they have just told me?"

Ethan picked up a ballet flat, turning it over in his

hands before setting it next to its twin. "Maybe the shop-lifting had them freaked out."

"Freaked out about shoplifting? Are you serious?" Emma moved closer to Ethan and lowered her voice to a whisper. "These are the same girls who strangled Sutton for *fun*. And when the police escorted me to Hollier in a cop car on the first day of school, they were thrilled."

Emma's mind drifted back to her brief encounter at the police station. The cops had written her off so fast when she tried to explain who she was, not believing for a second she could've been anyone other than Sutton. Then again, Sutton had a long track record—the cop on duty, Detective Quinlan, had brought out an enormous manila file packed with Sutton's past misdeeds. It probably contained countless Lying Game pranks.

Emma straightened up, a thought striking her hard. What if the file contained something about the train prank? Madeline had said something about the cops showing up. At the back of the store, Samantha glanced at Emma out of the corner of her eye.

Ethan touched Emma's shoulder. "I don't like that look on your face," he said. "What are you thinking?"

"You'll see." Emma casually picked up a teal Tori Burch clutch from the table. When she was sure Samantha was watching, she shoved it up her shirt. The leather was soft on her bare skin.

"What the hell?" Ethan made a frantic slashing motion across his throat. "Are you nuts?"

Emma ignored him.

Her pulse quickened. This felt so foreign, so *wrong*. Becky used to steal from convenience stores all the time— swiping a candy bar here, slipping a pack of gum into Emma's pocket there, once even walking out with several two-liter bottles of Coke stuffed up her shirt like two freaky boobs. Emma had lived in fear that the cops would haul both of them off to jail—or, worse, take her mother away from her. But in the end, it hadn't been the police who'd taken Becky away. Becky abandoned her daughter of her own volition.

"Stop right there!"

Emma froze, her hand on the doorknob. Samantha spun her around. Her eyebrows made a perfect *V.* "Nice try. Give it back."

Sighing, she removed her hand from her midriff and shook out her shirt. The clutch clunked to the ground, the gold chain clanging on the tiled floor. A half-dressed girl poked her head out of the fitting room and gasped.

Samantha scooped up the clutch with a smug grin and pulled a BlackBerry from the pocket of her skintight jeans. She placed the call on speaker.

"Wait." Ethan scuttled around a wine-colored velvet sofa. "This was a misunderstanding. I can explain."

"Nine-one-one, what's your emergency?" a voice squawked on the other line.

Samantha's eyes narrowed on Emma. "I'd like to report a robbery in progress."

Emma shoved her shaking hands in her pockets and tried to keep the saucy, entitled, I'm-Sutton-Mercer-and-I'm-thrilled-to-be-hauled-off-to-jail smirk glued to her lips.

In a way, it wasn't hard—going to the police station was exactly what she'd wanted.

6

A CRIMINAL HISTORY

Emma sat on a plastic yellow chair in a cinder-block room inside the police station. The room was no bigger than a chicken coop, smelled like rotting vegetables, and, inexplicably, had two pictures of serene-looking Japanese geishas hanging on the far wall. It would be a great setting for a news story . . . if she were the writer, not the subject.

The door creaked open, and Detective Quinlan stepped inside, the same cop who had refused to believe Emma when she said she was Emma Paxton and her long-lost twin, Sutton, was missing. There, hooked under his arm, was a file bearing the name SUTTON MERCER. Emma bit back a grin.

Quinlan plunked himself down across from her and

laced his fingers atop the folder. Boots thundered down the hall, shaking the whole shoddily built complex. "Shoplifting, Sutton? Honestly?"

"I didn't mean to," Emma squeaked, shrinking down in her seat.

Long ago, Emma had sat in a police station with Becky in the middle of the night after the cops had brought her in for reckless driving. At one point, a cop lifted the big black telephone and handed it to Becky, but Becky pushed it away, imploring, "Please don't call them. *Please*," she said. At dawn, after Becky was released with a warning, Emma asked whom the policewoman had tried to call. But Becky just lit a cigarette and pretended she had no idea what Emma was talking about.

"You didn't mean to get *caught*?" Quinlan held up Sutton's file. "Have you forgotten you already got busted for shoplifting?" He pulled a sheet of paper from the folder. "A pair of boots from Banana Republic, January sixth. So you're a repeat offender. That's serious, Sutton."

Emma scuffed her feet over the linoleum, her sweaty bare legs sticking to the plastic seat.

The handcuffs on Quinlan's belt jingled as he sat back in the chair. "What are you trying to do, go to juvie? Or are you going to pretend you're someone else this time, too, Sutton's secret twin? What did you say your real name was? Emily . . . something?"

But Emma wasn't listening. With a jerk, she grabbed her throat. She gasped, buckled over at the waist and began to cough. She hacked until it hurt her lungs.

Quinlan frowned. "Are you okay?"

Emma shook her head, dredging up another series of hacks. "Water," she croaked between breaths. "Please."

Quinlan rose from the table and pushed out into the hall. "Don't move," he growled.

Emma let out a few more coughs after he shut the door and then sprang into action, sliding the manila folder over to her seat. Her fingers trembled as she opened it and shuffled through the pages. On the top was the most recent write-up, when Emma had visited the station on the first day of school. *Returned Miss Mercer to school in squad car,* someone had typed. Four more forms had been filled out saying exactly the same thing.

"Come *on,*" Emma muttered under her breath, flipping through more pages. There were reports for disturbing the peace and a claim for Sutton's impounded car, a 1960s Volvo, for unpaid parking tickets. Next on the stack was a statement Sutton had made about Thayer Vega's disappearance. Emma's eyes scanned the transcript. *We hung out sometimes,* Sutton said to the interviewer. *I guess he had a little crush on me. No, of course I haven't seen him since he vanished.* Further down the page were the interviewer's notes: *Miss Mercer was very fidgety. Evaded several questions, mostly about Mr. Vega's . . .*

Emma flipped the page and rooted through the files until two words caught her eye. *Train tracks.* Emma yanked the paper out of the stack. It was a police report, dated July 12. Under LOCATION OF INCIDENT, it said *Train tracks, corner of Orange Grove and Route 10.* Under the description of the incident it said *S. Mercer . . . vehicle endangerment . . . oncoming train.* Sutton had been interviewed along with Charlotte, Laurel, and Madeline. Gabriella and Lilianna Fiorello were listed as witnesses, too.

Gabby and Lili? Emma frowned. Why had they been there?

I saw a flash and felt a strange tingling sensation. A far-off train whistle roared in my head. I heard screams, desperate pleas, and sirens.

Just like that, the memory of that night whooshed back to me.

7

THE ULTIMATE PRANK

I'm behind the wheel of my British racing-green 1965 Volvo 122. My hands squeeze the leather-wrapped steering wheel, and my foot shifts easily on and off the clutch. Madeline sits next to me, twisting the dial on the souped-up radio. Charlotte, Laurel, and the Twitter Twins squish in the back, giggling whenever the car careens around a corner and flattens all of them to one side. Gabby waves around a tube of red lipstick like a magic wand.

"Don't you dare get lipstick on Floyd's leather seats," I warn.

Charlotte giggles. "I can't believe you call your car Floyd."

I ignore her. Saying I adore my car is putting it mildly. My dad bought it on eBay a couple of years ago, and I helped him restore it to its former glory—hammering out the dents in the body panels, replacing the rusty grille with a bright new chrome one, reupholstering the front and back seats with soft leather, and installing a new engine that purrs like a contented puma. I don't care that it doesn't have modern amenities like an iPod adapter or parallel-parking assist—this car is unique, classy, and ahead of its time—just like I am.

We sweep past Starbucks, the strip mall of art galleries all the retirees love, and the clay courts where I took my first tennis lesson when I was four. The moon is the exact same amber as the eyes of the coyote that nosed under our backyard fence last year. We're on our way to a frat party at U of A, which promises to be a rager. Just because I'm with Garrett doesn't mean I can't ogle the hot college-boy merchandise now and then.

Madeline stops on a station playing Katy Perry's "California Gurls." Gabby squeals and starts to sing along. "Uch, I'm so sick of this song," I moan, reaching over and twisting the volume knob down again. I usually don't mind singing, but something irks me tonight. Or, more accurately, two someones.

Lili pouts. "But last week you said Katy was awesome, Sutton!"

I shrug. "Katy's so five minutes ago."

"She writes the best songs!" Gabby whines, twirling her honey-blonde highlights and pursing her extra-plump lips into a pout.

I take my eyes off the road for a moment and glare at them. "It's not as if Katy writes the songs herself, guys. Some fat, middle-aged producer guy does."

Lili looks horrified. "Really?"

If only I could pull over and let them out. I'm so sick of Twitter Dee and Twitter Dum's faux-ditziness. I shared a trig class with them last year, and they're not as stupid as they look. Guys find the dumb act cute, but I'm not buying it.

The light changes to green, and Floyd makes a satisfying roar as he guns off the line, kicking up dust and flying past the desert broom. "Well, I think it's a good song," Mads breaks the silence, slowly turning up the volume again.

I shoot her a look. "What would your dad say if he knew slutty Katy was your role model, Mads?"

"He wouldn't care," Madeline says, trying to sound tough. She picks at the SWAN LAKE MAFIA ballerina sticker on the back of her cell phone. I don't know what the sticker means—none of us do. I think Mads likes it that way.

"He wouldn't?" I repeat. "Let's call Daddy and ask. Actually, let's call him and tell him you're hoping to score with a college guy tonight, too."

"Sutton, don't!" Madeline growls, catching my hands before I can reach for my phone. Mads is notorious for lying to her dad; she probably told him she was at a study group.

"Relax," I say, slipping my phone back into the center console again. Madeline slumps down in the seat, making her I'm-not-speaking-to-you face. Charlotte catches my eye in the mirror and gives me a look that says Cut it out. *Teasing Madeline about her*

dad is a low blow, but that's what she gets for inviting the Twitter Twins tonight. It was supposed to be just us, the real Lying Game members, but somehow Gabby and Lili found out about our plans, and Madeline was too nicey-nice to tell them they couldn't come. I've felt their imploring stares the whole drive, their hopes and dreams written in thought bubbles over their heads: When are you going to let us into the Lying Game? When can we be one of you? *It's bad enough my little sister weaseled her way into our club. There's no room for anyone else, especially not them.*

And more than that, I have a plan for tonight—a plan that doesn't involve Gabby or Lili. But who says Sutton Mercer can't be flexible?

The northern part of Tucson goes dead after ten o'clock, and there are barely any other cars on Orange Grove. Before we can merge onto the highway, we must cross the train tracks. The X-shaped RAILROAD CROSSING *sign glows in the dark. Once the light turns green I edge Floyd over the bumpy rails. Just as I'm about to accelerate toward the highway entrance, the car dies.*

"Uh . . ." I mumble. "California Gurls" falls silent. Cool air-conditioned vapors stop flowing from the vents, and the lights on the dash darken. I twist the key in the ignition, but nothing happens. "Okay, bitches. Who filled Floyd's gas tank with sand?"

Charlotte fakes a yawn. "This prank is so two years ago."

"It wasn't us," Gabby chirps, probably thrilled that I've

58

quasi-included her in a conversation that involves the Lying Game. "We have way better prank ideas, if you'd ever let us share them with you."

"Not interested," I say, dismissing her with a wave.

"Um, does anyone care that we're stopped on train tracks?" Madeline peers out the window, her fingertips clutching the door. Suddenly, the red lights on the RAILROAD CROSSING sign begin to flash. The warning bell clangs, and the striped gate lowers across the road behind us, preventing all other cars at the light—not that there are any—from passing over the tracks. A hazy beam of the Amtrak train blinks in the distance.

I try the ignition again, but Floyd just coughs. "What's the deal, Sutton?" Charlotte sounds annoyed.

"Everything's under control," I mutter. The Volvo-symbol keychain swings back and forth as I twist the key again and again.

"Yeah, right." The leather squeaks under Charlotte's butt. "I told you guys we shouldn't have gotten into this death trap."

The train blows its whistle. "Maybe you're starting it wrong." Madeline reaches over and tries the ignition herself, but the car only makes the same wheezing sound. The lights don't even flicker on the dash.

The train is getting closer. "Maybe it'll see us and hit the brakes?" I say, my voice shaking as adrenaline courses through my veins.

"The train can't stop!" Charlotte unbuckles her seat belt. "That's why those warning gates go down!" She pulls at the door handle in the back, but it doesn't budge. "Jesus! Unlock it, Sutton!"

I press the UNLOCK button—my dad and I had installed an electronic power feature on all four doors and windows—but there isn't the familiar heavy click sound of the barrel releasing. "Uh . . ." I jab the button again and again.

"What about the manual unlock?" Lili tries to lift the button on her door. But something jams that button, too.

The train whistles once more, a low harmonica chord. Laurel tries to unroll the windows, but nothing happens. "Jesus, Sutton!" Laurel screams. "What are we going to do?"

"Is this a prank?" Charlotte shouts, yanking hard on the door handle, which doesn't give. "Are you messing with us?"

"Of course not!" I pull at my door handle, too.

"Seriously?" Madeline yells.

"Seriously! Cross my heart, hope to die!" It's our fail-safe code, the thing we're supposed to yell out to show something is dead serious.

Madeline reaches over and stabs the center of the steering wheel. The horn bleats feebly, like a dying goat. Laurel dials a number on her cell phone.

"What are you doing?" I scream at her.

"What's your emergency?" a voice squawks on speakerphone.

"We're stuck on the train tracks of Orange Grove and I-ten!" Laurel screams. "We're trapped in the car! The train's about to run us down!"

The next few seconds are mayhem. Charlotte leans forward and pounds on the windshield. Gabby and Lili blubber uselessly. Laurel gives our details to the 911 operator. The train rockets toward us. I jiggle the keys in the ignition back and forth. The train barrels closer . . . closer . . . until I swear I can see the conductor's panicked face.

Everyone screams. Our death is mere seconds away.

And that's when I calmly reach to the dashboard and release the choke.

Gunning the engine, I roll us off the train tracks and spin out in a small, dusty area in the underpass. A moment later, I unlock the doors, and everyone falls to the dusty gravel, watching as the train thunders by just feet from their bodies.

"Gotcha, suckas!" I yell. My body is on fire. "Was that not the best prank ever?"

My friends stare at me, momentarily stunned. Tears streak their faces. Then their eyes blaze with anger. Madeline rises unsteadily to her feet. "What the fuck, Sutton? You used the fail-safe! You broke the rules!"

"Rules are meant to be broken, bitches. Wanna hear how I did it?" I can't wait to explain. I've been planning this prank for weeks. It's my pièce de résistance.

"I don't care how you did it!" Charlotte screams. Her face is a knot of fury. Her hands twist at her sides. "No one thinks it's funny!"

I look at my sister. But she just licks her lips and darts her eyes back and forth, like the prank has turned her into a mute.

Madeline is shaking with rage. "You know what, Sutton? I'm sick of this club. I'm sick of you."

"Me, too," Charlotte echoes. Lili looks back and forth, eating this up.

I tilt my chin. "Is that a threat? Do you want to quit?"

Madeline straightens up to her full five-foot-ten height. "Maybe."

"Fine, then! Quit!" I say to Madeline and Charlotte. "There are plenty of girls who can replace you! Right?" I whirl around to glare at Lili and Gabby, but only Lili stares back. "Where's Gabby?" I ask.

Charlotte, Madeline, Laurel, Lili, and I squint in the darkness.

But Gabby is gone.

8

TRUTH OR CONSEQUENCES

Emma scanned the rest of the police report.

Stalled mid-1960s Volvo 122 escaped collision with the Sunset Limited Amtrak train from San Antonio, Texas. Miss Mercer claims her car malfunctioned and failed to either accelerate over the tracks or unlock to allow passengers to safely exit. In speaking with passengers M. Vega, C. Chamberlain, and L. Mercer, all three backed up Miss Mercer's claims that the car's faulty electrical system was to blame. No charges filed at present. Hospitalization of one victim, G. Fiorello. Ambulance arrived at 10:01 P.M. and took her to the Oro Valley Hospital.

Emma's spine turned to ice. Gabriella? *Hospital?*

Footsteps sounded in the hallway. Emma quickly shoved the papers back into the folder and pushed it away from her seat seconds before Quinlan swung the door open. He slammed a paper cup of water on the desk, little drops cascading over the side and splashing the table.

"Here you go. I hope you're pleased."

Emma hid a satisfied smile—she *was* pleased . . . but also puzzled. Her mind raced with what she'd found. Surely Sutton had stalled the car on purpose but the report listed the incident as an accident. How in the world did Sutton get the others to lie about something that had landed Gabby in the hospital? She wasn't sure she'd met *anyone* as all-powerful as Sutton in her life—a girl who could silence her friends even in tragedy.

But I didn't know the answer of how I got them to shut up either. Sure, I'd been powerful—but not *that* powerful. Madeline and Charlotte had been so furious in my memory, after all. Their white-hot rage scared me even now.

Emma took a sip of water. It was lukewarm and tasted like metal. The details of the prank still swirled in her head. How could Sutton put them all at risk like that in the first place? Stalling a car on the train tracks—was she insane?

I bristled at Emma's thoughts. There were tons of risky things in life: riding your bike on the shoulder of the highway, diving into a canyon pool without knowing how deep the water was, touching a germy doorknob in a public bathroom. I must have known my car was going to come back to life as soon as I pulled the choke. I would never put my friends in that kind of danger . . . would I?

"So." Quinlan pointed his fingers into a steeple. "Have you come up with a good explanation of why you decided to steal today, Miss Mercer?"

Emma took a deep breath, then suddenly felt drained. "Look, it was a really, really stupid mistake. I'll pay for the purse, I promise. And I'll change. No more pranks. No more shoplifting. I swear. I just want to go home."

Quinlan let out a low whistle. "Well, sure, Sutton! Go on home! You're totally absolved! No consequences at all! Hell, I won't even tell your parents!" He didn't even try to hide his sarcasm.

As if on cue, a knock sounded on the door. "Come in," Quinlan barked.

The door opened, and Mr. and Mrs. Mercer entered. Mr. Mercer was in surgical scrubs and New Balance sneakers. Mrs. Mercer wore a black business suit and grape-tinted lipstick and carried a snakeskin briefcase. It was clear both of them had been yanked from work, probably from meetings or procedures. Neither looked happy.

One of the worst things about being dead was watching my parents' reaction to me from a distance. Surely this wasn't the first time they'd had to deal with a call from the police station. From my new vantage point, it looked like it broke their hearts. How many times had I hurt them like this? How many times hadn't I cared?

Emma shrank down in her chair. She barely knew the Mercers yet, only that they were in their fifties, worked high-powered jobs, and stuck to the organic aisles in the grocery store. But if the scattered family photos in the foyer were any indication—the snapshots of them with Minnie Mouse at Disneyland, in scuba gear on the Florida Keys, and grinning next to the pyramid in front of the Louvre in Paris—it was clear Mr. and Mrs. Mercer tried to be good parents to their daughters and gave them everything they wanted. Certainly they hadn't expected their adopted older child to become a criminal.

"Sit down." Quinlan gestured to two seats across the table.

Neither of the Mercers took him up on the offer. Mrs. Mercer's white knuckles clutched her briefcase. "Jesus, Sutton," Mrs. Mercer hissed, turning her tired eyes to Emma. "What on earth is wrong with you?"

"I'm sorry," Emma mumbled into her chest, pinching Sutton's silver locket between her thumb and forefinger.

Mrs. Mercer shook her head, making her pearl teardrop earrings wobble back and forth. "Didn't you learn your lesson the first time you got caught?"

"It was stupid." Emma hung her head. She'd gotten what she wanted, but when she looked up, she saw worry etched across the Mercers' faces. Most of her foster parents wouldn't have cared if she'd stolen unless it meant they had to fork over money for bail. In fact, most of them would've let her rot in jail for the night. She felt a knot of envy for the involved parenting Sutton got— something her sister didn't seem to have appreciated while alive.

Mr. Mercer turned to Quinlan, speaking for the first time. "I am so sorry to trouble you like this."

"I'm sorry, too." Quinlan balled his fingers at his sternum. "Perhaps if you kept a better eye on Sutton—"

"We're keeping a very careful eye on our daughter, thank you very much." Mrs. Mercer's voice was shrill. Her defensiveness reminded Emma of visits with social workers when, without fail, no matter whether or not it was true, foster parents defended what a good job they were doing with the kids in their care. Mrs. Mercer reached into her Gucci handbag for her wallet. "Is there a fine involved?"

Quinlan made an awkward sound in his throat like he'd swallowed a bug. "I don't think a fine will cut it this time, Mrs. Mercer. If the boutique wants to press charges, it will go on Sutton's permanent record. And there might be other consequences."

Mrs. Mercer looked like she was about to faint. "What *kind* of consequences?"

"We'll just have to wait and see what the boutique wants to do," Quinlan answered. "They could issue a fine, or they could pursue a harsher punishment, especially because Sutton has shoplifted before. She might get community service. Or jail time."

"Jail?" Emma's head whipped up.

Quinlan shrugged. "You're eighteen now, Sutton. It's a whole new world."

Emma shut her eyes. She'd forgotten that she'd just passed that milestone birthday. "B-but what about school?" she muttered, a bit stupidly. "What about tennis?" What she really wanted to ask was *What about the investigation? What about finding Sutton's killer?*

The door squeaked as Quinlan pulled it open. "You should have thought about that before you stuffed that purse under your shirt."

Quinlan held the door for Emma and the Mercers, and they exited into the parking lot. No one spoke. Emma was afraid to even breathe. Mrs. Mercer guided Emma by the elbow toward her waiting Mercedes with a PROUD HOLLIER TENNIS MOM sticker on the bumper.

"You'd better pray that boutique drops the charges," Mrs. Mercer growled through her teeth as she slid into the driver's seat. "I hope you've learned something valuable from all this."

"I did," Emma answered quietly, her mind spinning with everything she'd read in the file. She'd found a new motive, new leads, and a dangerous situation that would make even the most loyal friends furious.

9

DADDY'S LITTLE GIRL

The ride home from the police station was filled with a stony, implacable silence. The radio remained off. Mrs. Mercer didn't even complain about the aggressive driver who merged in front of her. She stared straight ahead like a wax figure in Madame Tussauds, not looking at the girl she thought was her daughter slumped in the seat next to her. Emma kept her eyes on her lap, picking at the skin around her thumbs until a tiny red drop of blood slipped across her skin.

Mrs. Mercer pulled the Mercedes into the driveway behind her husband's Acura, and everyone trudged into the house like prisoners on a chain gang. Laurel leapt up from the leather couch in the living room as soon as the door swung open. "What's going on?"

"We need a minute with Sutton. Alone." Mrs. Mercer flung her handbag onto the coat and umbrella stand that stood guard at the front door. Drake, the family's Great Dane, bounded up to greet Mrs. Mercer, but she swished him away. Drake was more lovable doofus than guard dog, but he never failed to put Emma on edge. She'd been afraid of dogs her whole life after a foster parent's chow chow used her arm as a chew toy when she was nine.

"What happened?" Laurel's eyes were wide. No one answered. Laurel tried to meet Emma's gaze, but Emma just studied the massive spider plant in the corner.

"Sit down, Sutton." Mr. Mercer pointed to the couch. A glass of sparkling water sat on a wood coaster on the mesquite coffee table, and an upended copy of *Teen Vogue* lay on the floor. "Laurel, please. Give us some privacy."

Laurel sighed, then tromped down the hall. Emma heard the soft sucking sound of the refrigerator door opening in the kitchen. She perched on the suede wing chair and stared helplessly around the room at the southwest chic design—lots of desert-y tans and reds, a zigzag Navajo blanket thrown over the leather couch, a white fluffy shag rug that was amazingly clean, despite Drake's big and often-muddy paws, and a wood-beamed ceiling with several slowly rotating fans. A Steinway baby grand piano stood by the window. Emma wondered if Sutton and Laurel had taken lessons on something so exquisite. She felt another twinge of envy that her identical twin had been cared for so lovingly, given everything she wanted. If fate had dealt her a different hand, if Becky had abandoned Emma as a baby instead of Sutton, maybe Emma would've had this life instead. She definitely would've appreciated it more.

I felt the same flare of annoyance I always got whenever Emma passed judgment on me. How could any of us truly appreciate our lives if we had nothing else to compare them to? It was only after we lost something, after a mother abandoned us, after we *died*, that we realized what we were missing. Although that raised an interesting question: If Emma had lived my life, would she have died my death, too? Would she have been the one who'd been murdered instead of me? But as I bitterly mulled this over, a sinking feeling told me that my death had somehow been my fault—something *I* had done, the result of a choice Emma might not have made. It had nothing to do with fate.

Mrs. Mercer paced back and forth, her high heels clicking on the stone floor. Her face was drawn and her gray streak looked more prominent than ever. "First of all, you're going to work off this punishment, Sutton. Chores. Errands. Whatever I ask you to do, you're going to do it."

"Okay," Emma said softly.

"And second of all," Mrs. Mercer went on, "don't think you're leaving the house for two weeks. Unless it's for school, tennis, or community service, if that's what they decide to give you. Let's *hope* that's what they give you." She paused by the piano and placed a hand to her forehead, as though the thought made her woozy. "What do you think colleges are going to say about this? Did you even *think* about the consequences, or did you just grab whatever it was from that store and run?"

Laurel, who'd clearly been lurking, appeared in the doorway, an unopened bag of Smartfood popcorn in her hands. "But Homecoming is next week! You have to let Sutton go. She's on the planning committee! And then there's the camping trip after."

Mrs. Mercer shook her head, then turned back to Emma. "Don't try to sneak out either. I'm having someone put outside locks on your windows. I know you've been sneaking out that way. Yours, too, Laurel."

"I haven't been sneaking out!" Laurel protested.

"I noticed footprints all around the flower beds this morning," Mrs. Mercer snapped.

Emma pressed her lips together. The footprints outside Laurel's room were hers. She'd fled through Laurel's window during her birthday party, right after she'd found the unedited version of the snuff film that showed Laurel,

Madeline, and Charlotte pranking Sutton. But Sutton wouldn't have admitted to trampling the flowers, and now, neither would she. Maybe she was becoming more like her twin than she realized.

Mrs. Mercer fumbled through her bag to answer her buzzing phone. She pressed the tiny device to her ear and disappeared down the hall. Mr. Mercer checked his beeper, too, then turned wearily to Sutton. "I have a chore for you right now, actually. Get changed and meet me in the garage."

Emma nodded obediently. Let the punishment begin.

Ten minutes later, Emma had changed into a T-shirt and a worn pair of jeans—well, as worn as a pair of Citizens of Humanity jeans could be—and was standing in the Mercers' three-car garage. It was lined with shelves full of rakes, shovels, cans of paint, and extra bags of dog food. In the middle of the big concrete room stood an old motorcycle with the word NORTON written in script on the side. Mr. Mercer squatted by the bike's front wheel, inspecting the tire. He wore white protection pads on his knees.

When he saw Emma, he stood up halfway and gave her a nod.

"I'm here," Emma said, feeling a little sheepish.

Mr. Mercer stared at her for a long few beats. Emma braced for a lecture, but instead, he just looked sad.

Emma wasn't sure what to say. Disappointment was something she was used to feeling herself, but she'd never been on the receiving end of it. She'd always tried to be whatever her foster parents required of her—a nanny, a cleaning lady, and once, even a massage therapist. Never had she intentionally made trouble.

Mr. Mercer turned back to the bike. "This place is a mess," he finally said. "Maybe you can help me toss stuff out and put everything back where it's supposed to be."

"Okay." Emma pulled a large black trash bag from a box on a nearby shelf.

She looked around the garage, surprised to see that she and Mr. Mercer might have a bit in common. On the wall was a tattered poster of a flame-burst Gibson Les Paul, one of Emma's favorite guitars from when she'd gone through her I-want-to-be-in-a-band phase. There was also a framed reprint of Emma's favorite incorrect newspaper headline, DEWEY BEATS TRUMAN. And to the left of the racks of car-detailing equipment and weed killer was a small shelf that held ragged, well-loved crime-fiction paperbacks, many of which Emma had devoured, too. She wondered why they weren't on the built-in bookshelves in the main house. Was Mrs. Mercer ashamed that her husband wasn't into literary fiction? Or was it a dad thing to keep his favorite possessions in his own space?

Emma had never met her own father. When she was

in kindergarten, a bunch of kids' dads came into class and talked about what they did for a living; there was a doctor, a guy who owned a musical instrument shop, and a chef. Emma went home that day and asked Becky what *her* dad did. Becky's face drooped, and she blew cigarette smoke through her nose. "It doesn't matter."

"Can you tell me his name?" Emma tried, but Becky wouldn't answer. Shortly after that conversation, Emma went through a phase pretending that various men they met on their endless travels—Becky could never hold down a job for long—might secretly be her father. Raymond, the gas station cashier who slipped Emma a few free Tootsie Rolls with her purchase. Dr. Norris, the ER doctor who stitched up her knee when she fell on the playground. Al, a neighbor in their apartment complex who waved to Emma every morning. Emma pictured one of these men scooping her up, swinging her around, and taking her to the local Dairy Queen. But it never happened.

A barrage of moments came to me: my dad and me sitting at a table at a blues club, listening to a band play. My dad and me on a mountain trail, binoculars to our faces, watching birds. Me falling off my bike and running inside, searching for my dad to comfort me. I had a feeling my dad and I had had a special bond at one point in our lives. Suddenly, in light of what Emma went through, I felt lucky to have all those memories. But now my dad didn't even know I was gone.

Emma leaned over the motorcycle, inspecting it carefully. "Why is the shifter on the wrong side?"

Mr. Mercer blinked at her, as if Emma had suddenly started speaking Swahili. "Actually, it's not. This is a British bike. Before 1975, the gearshift was on the right side." He laughed uncomfortably. "I thought your interest in cars stopped with 1960s Volvos."

"Oh, well, I just read something about it," Emma covered. One of her foster families, the Stuckeys, had a car that constantly gave them trouble, and the responsibility had somehow fallen to Emma to figure out how to fix it. She'd befriended the mechanics at the local gas station, and they'd taught her how to change a tire, check for oil, and replace various fluids and parts. The owner of the place, Lou, had a Harley, and Emma hung around him while he fixed it up, helping out now and then. Lou took a shine to her and started to call her Little Grease Monkey. If she ever wanted an apprenticeship as a mechanic, he said, his door was wide open.

I smiled. Now *there* was a career path. But it impressed me how resourceful she was. It was like Ethan said the other night: Nothing seemed to overwhelm her.

"Thayer had a Honda bike, right?" Mr. Mercer said. "You didn't ride on it with him, did you?"

Emma shrugged, her skin prickling at Thayer's name. Emma had found out last week that Laurel and Thayer had been best friends, and that Laurel had a not-so-secret crush on him. But she'd also discovered that, at the very least, Thayer had liked Sutton.

I tried desperately to remember what Thayer meant to me. I kept seeing flashes of the two of us standing in the school courtyard, Thayer grabbing my hands and saying something in an apologetic voice, me wrenching my hands away and spitting something back at him, my words flinty and abrasive. But then the memory dissolved.

Mr. Mercer sank down on an overturned milk crate. "Sutton . . . why did you steal today?"

Emma ran her fingers over the shifter. *Because I'm trying to solve your daughter's murder.* But all she said was "I'm really sorry."

"Was it because of . . . everything at home?" Mr. Mercer asked gruffly.

Emma blinked, turning to face Mr. Mercer. "Meaning . . . ?" Suddenly, a new list began to form in her mind: Things That Are Awkward About a New Family You Don't Know but Are Supposed To. Heart-to-heart conversations with a dad she'd only met two weeks ago would be first on the list.

Mr. Mercer's face folded into an exasperated, please-don't-make-me-explain expression. "I know it's a lot to take in. I know you've gone through a lot of . . . changes."

More than you know, Emma thought wryly.

Mr. Mercer gave Emma a meaningful look. "I want to know what you're feeling. I want you to know you can talk to me. About anything."

The AC unit shuddered off and an earsplitting silence settled over the garage. Emma tried to keep her composure. She had no idea how to answer his question, and for a moment, she considered telling him the bald truth. But then she remembered Sutton's killer's threat: *If you tell anyone, if you say anything, you're next.*

"Okay . . . thanks," Emma said awkwardly.

Mr. Mercer fiddled with the wrench. "And are you sure you didn't steal because, well, you *wanted* to get caught?"

I studied my dad's clear blue eyes and a sudden flash came to me of voices and accusations flying through the air. I saw myself sprinting down a desert trail, heard my father's angry voice calling out for me, and felt tears running down my face.

When Emma didn't respond, Mr. Mercer broke his stare, shook his head, and threw a balled-up yellow rag on the grease-stained floor. "Never mind," he mumbled, now seeming annoyed. "Just throw the trash bag in the bin when you're done, okay?"

He closed the door with a muffled *thud*. Behind it was a cork bulletin board that contained a calendar several years out of date, a business card for a local HVAC service, and a snapshot of Laurel and Sutton standing in the middle of the backyard, smiling into the camera. Emma stared at the photo long and hard. She wished the photo could talk back, wished Sutton could tell her something, *anything*, about who'd she'd been, what kinds of secrets she'd kept, and what had really happened to her.

A snicker sounded behind her. Then a warm tickle, like someone's breath on the back of her neck. Emma swung around, her heart in her throat, but found herself staring into the empty garage. Then, out the narrow square windows, she caught sight of an SUV slowly passing by the Mercers' house. She ran to the windows and looked out, recognizing the white Lincoln SUV immediately. And this time she also recognized the two faces behind the windshield.

It was the Twitter Twins.

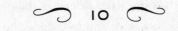

10

FISH OUT OF WATER

Plink. Plink.

Emma shot up in Sutton's bed. The moon cast a silver slant of light across the carpet. The screen saver on Sutton's computer was playing a slideshow of photographs of happy Lying Game sleepovers. Sutton's flat-screen TV was tuned to an episode of *The Daily Show*. *The Bell Jar*, which Emma was rereading after she and Ethan had discussed it last week, sat overturned on the nightstand. The door to the hall was closed tight. Everything was exactly where Emma had left it when she'd gone to bed.

Plink.

The sound was coming from the window. Emma

threw back the covers. Just last week, she'd had a dream that had begun exactly like this. When she'd looked out the window in the dream, Becky stood in the driveway. Warning her. Telling her to be careful. And then she'd vanished.

Emma hesitantly padded to the window and peered out. The streetlight made a soft golden circle on the prickly pear cactus beside the sidewalk. Laurel's Jetta was parked directly below. Sure enough, someone stood in the driveway beneath the basketball court. She half expected it to be Becky, but then the figure stepped into the light, arm aimed to pitch another rock at the window.

It was Ethan.

She inhaled sharply and moved away from the window. She pulled on a heather-gray bra under Sutton's see-through camisole and kicked her bare legs into a pair of striped pajama pants. Then she reappeared at the glass, waved, and hefted open the window. Mrs. Mercer hadn't locked it yet, and it gave easily. The night air was stiflingly hot without the faintest trace of wind.

"Have you heard of using your phone instead of a rock?" she called softly.

Ethan squinted up at her. "Can you come out?"

Emma listened for sounds in the hallway—a toilet flushing, Drake's jingling tags, anything. The Mercers would kill her for sneaking out the very day she'd been caught stealing. But there was only silence. She lifted the window higher and shimmied out.

A thick tree branch extended toward the roof; Emma grabbed it easily and swung to the ground. No wonder Sutton used this as an escape route. She dropped to the gravel and headed toward Ethan, a smile on her face.

But Ethan wasn't smiling back. "What on earth got into you? Have you lost your mind?"

"*Shhh.*" Emma glanced around. The neighborhood was eerily still, all lights off, cars silent in driveways. "It was the only way I could get into the police station."

"Why did you want to do *that*?"

Emma sat down on the big boulder in front of the Mercers' house. "I had to see Sutton's police file."

As Emma told Ethan about the police report and the incident at the train tracks, his eyes bulged wider and wider. "Sutton put everyone's lives at risk," Emma finished. "And something happened to Gabby that night. She went to the hospital."

"Whoa." Ethan sank down on the boulder next to her. "And *no one* told on Sutton?"

"According to the report, no." Their legs were just barely touching; Emma could feel the tough fabric of his jeans through her thin pajama pants.

Ethan turned his phone over in his hands. "Why do you think they kept quiet?"

"I don't know. The train prank was serious. They all could have died," she said, watching a shadow pass across the window of a neighboring house. "Maybe they wanted to give Sutton a taste of her own medicine?"

"Through a prank . . . or something else?"

A chill coursed through Emma's veins. "You said yourself that Sutton's friends looked like they wanted to kill her the night of the snuff film, right?"

Ethan gazed down the street, his top teeth sinking into his bottom lip. "That's what it looked like to me," he finally said. "Even though they said it was a prank, Sutton seemed really scared."

"Sounds like payback," Emma said.

Ethan had a better memory of that night than I did. When I'd seen Ethan standing over me, I'd felt woozy and vulnerable. If only I could remember the hours and days after the strangling incident . . . had I really resumed normal activities with my friends as if it hadn't mattered? Had I been able to shake off my fear that easily?

"But I'm not sure we should write off the Twitter Twins either," Emma said. "Gabby went to the hospital, after all—maybe she was really hurt. They were at Charlotte's sleepover, too. And I've seen them driving up and down this street, watching me. Plus they've been giving me really weird looks in school." She shut her eyes, thinking about Garrett. "Then again, a *lot* of people have been giving me weird looks."

Ethan nodded. "You can't write off any of them until they have a clear alibi."

Emma arched her neck up to the sky and let out a groan. Everything felt so . . . *difficult.* "Sutton's parents would kill me if they knew I was out here," she said, eyeing the dark windows in the house. "I'm already grounded for life."

Ethan shifted in the gravel. "So this is your only night of freedom?"

"You could say that. Tomorrow there will probably be a big bolt on my window."

Ethan smiled. "We'd better do something more fun than talk about Sutton's murderer, then."

Slowly, Emma raised her eyes to his. "Like what?"

"There's a pool in your neighbor's yard." Ethan gestured over the block wall that separated the Mercers' house from the neighbors'. "Wanna go for a swim?"

"They'll see us!" Emma cried. The Mercers' next-door neighbors, the Paulsons, had waved to Emma a few times from their driveway. They wore matching J.Crew outfits, drove matching champagne-colored Lexuses, and plastered their last name over everything—a big PAULSON on the mailbox, PAULSON, ESTABLISHED 1968 on a stone plaque in the front garden, even their vanity plates read PAULSON1 and PAULSON2. They seemed friendly enough, but Emma doubted they took kindly to pool crashers.

Ethan pointed to their driveway. Several blue

plastic-wrapped newspapers lay near the mailbox. The lights in the house were dark, and there wasn't a car in the driveway. "I think they're out of town."

Emma paused. She knew she should march back inside and get into bed, but a devilish little voice in her head pointed out Ethan's deep-set eyes and hopeful smile, egging her on.

Maybe the devil was me. Emma deserved to have a little fun.

"I'm in," Emma said with a grin.

Within seconds, they'd scaled the Paulsons' wall and reached the oval-shaped pool in the middle of the patio. Inner tubes and rafts were stacked neatly on the deck. A black Weber gas grill stood under the pergola, and a beehive-shaped fire pit loomed farther out in the yard. Two towels, both with purple monogrammed *P*s in the center, hung over the chaises. Emma glanced cautiously once more at the Paulsons' dark house. No lights snapped on.

It took Ethan less than five seconds to strip off his T-shirt and jeans, kick off his New Balance running sneakers, and dive into the pool. When he surfaced, he grinned at Emma. "The water's awesome! Come in!"

Emma kicked out a pajama leg. "Uh, I'm not exactly dressed for swimming."

Ethan waggled his brows. "Take 'em off. I don't mind."

Emma mock-glared at him, but shed her pajama

bottoms, grateful she was wearing opaque, black cotton boy shorts underneath. Tiptoeing to the edge, she lowered her body into the pool, the cool water slipping over her skin inch by inch. She pushed off from the wall and did a couple of breaststroke pulls underwater. Her camisole billowed out beneath her like an inflated parachute. When she came up for air, Ethan had stopped in the center of the pool. The golden lights reflected off his cheekbones, showing off his slicked-back hair, angular face, and broad, golden shoulders. Ethan caught her eye and smiled back, but Emma quickly looked away. She didn't want him to think she was staring.

"This was a good idea," Emma said, twisting around to float on her back.

"Told you." Ethan paddled toward the diving board. "I have a confession to make," he said a moment later, his strong arms cutting the water. "I'm a serial pool crasher. When I was younger, I used to sneak into my neighbor's pool all the time."

"Well, I'm a pool-crashing virgin," Emma said, hoping the night was dark enough that Ethan couldn't see her blushing at the word *virgin*.

"I always wanted my own pool." Ethan reached up and grabbed both sides of the diving board. "My parents never went for it. My mom thought I'd be one of those kids on the news who drowned."

It occurred to Emma how little she knew about Ethan's life. "What are your parents like?"

Ethan shrugged. "They're . . . well, my mom's a chronic worrier. And my dad's . . . absent."

"He's gone?" Maybe the two of them had something in common.

Air slowly escaped Ethan's lips. "Not exactly. He just travels a lot. His work means everything to him. He got an apartment in San Diego that's close to his company's main office, and he's there more than he's home. He probably likes being away from us."

"You shouldn't joke about that."

One of Ethan's shoulders rose. It looked like he was going to say something more, but then he shook his head forcefully as if to erase the thoughts and dropped from the diving board. "Did you have a pool when you were grow-ing up, Emma?"

Emma laughed, kicking her legs faster as she tread water. "A foster kid with a pool? I was lucky if I had a clean bathtub. But I hung out at public pools a lot. When I was younger, a social worker got me into free swimming lessons."

"That's nice."

"I guess." It would've been nicer if Becky had taught her to swim. Or if one of her foster moms had bothered to come and watch her lessons. Emma used to look to the bleachers when she was in the water, thinking she might see someone for her there, but she was always disappointed. Eventually, she stopped looking altogether.

"Do you have a favorite pool game from when you were growing up?" Ethan asked.

Emma thought for a moment. "I guess Marco Polo." They used to play it at the end of swimming lessons.

"Wanna play?" Ethan asked.

Emma giggled, but Ethan's face was serious. "Uh, sure," she said. "*Quietly.*" She shut her eyes, spun around in the water a few times, and whispered, "Marco!"

"Polo!" Ethan answered back, his voice low. Emma drifted toward his voice, sticking her arms straight in front of her.

Ethan snickered. "You look like the undead."

Emma laughed, but it felt wrong somehow. What if Sutton's body was floating somewhere just like hers was right now?

An image of cold, dark water raced through my mind. Waves lapped a body wrapped in soaked clothing. I couldn't get close enough to make out the figure lying facedown on the riverbed. Could it have been me lying there, left for dead?

Emma halfheartedly swam toward Ethan's voice, trying to shake off the feeling of dread that had bloomed in her stomach. Her hands swiped air.

"I'm the Marco Polo master," Ethan teased. It sounded like he was now in the shallow end. "So did being a foster kid suck?"

Emma cleared her throat. "Pretty much," she said, squeezing her eyes tighter. "But since I'm eighteen, I guess it's over. Marco!"

"Polo," Ethan answered, now sounding on Emma's left. "It's also over because you're *here*, living Sutton's life. And once we figure this out, you can go back to being Emma again."

Emma swished her fingers through the cool water, considering this. It was hard not to think about what might happen to her after Sutton's murder was solved—*if* it was solved. She wanted more than anything to stay here, to get to know the Mercers as *herself*, but what if they kicked her out once they discovered she'd been impersonating their dead daughter?

Ethan broke the silence. "I don't know how you got through years of foster care and turned out so . . . normal. I'm not sure I would."

"Well, I kind of disappeared into my own head." Emma skimmed through the water, focused on the sound of Ethan's low voice. "Made up a world of my own."

"Meaning . . . ?"

"I kept journals and wrote stories. And I created a newspaper."

"Really?"

Emma nodded, her eyes still closed. "It was sort of . . . the *Daily Emma*. I would take pictures and write down stuff that happened to me as if it were a top story on the front page. You know, 'Girl Cooks Yet Another Lentil Loaf for Hippie Foster Parents.' Or 'Foster Sister Breaks Emma Paxton's Prized Possession Just 'Cause She Feels Like It.' It helped me cope. I still compose headlines in my head, sometimes."

"How come?"

Emma wiped water from her face. "I guess it makes me feel . . . significant. Like I'm good enough to be a headline on a front page—even if it's my own made-up newspaper."

"I went into my own little world, too," Ethan confessed. "I used to get picked on all the time when I was younger."

"*You* were picked on?" Emma wanted to open her eyes and stare at him. "Why?"

"Why does anyone ever get picked on?" Ethan's voice cracked. "It was just something that happened. Except instead of writing newspapers, I drew mazes. First, they were pretty basic, but eventually I made them more and more complicated until even I couldn't solve them. I would get lost in those mazes. I imagined that they were a garden labyrinth I could disappear into forever."

Suddenly, she felt fluttering kicks underwater. She thrust her hand out, touched skin, and opened her eyes. Ethan was wedged in the corner near the built-in hot tub.

Before Emma knew what she was doing, she touched a little shaving cut on Ethan's chin. "Does it hurt?"

Ethan blushed. "Nah." Then he grabbed her waist and pulled her closer. Their legs collided and Emma felt the friction between their skin. She stared at Ethan's dewy lips, the droplets of water on his eyelashes, the smattering of freckles scattered across his shoulders.

Crickets chirped. The mesquite trees sighed in the wind. Just as Ethan leaned closer, Sutton's necklace caught the moonlight and sent a glimmer across the surface of the pool.

The water suddenly felt like ice on Emma's skin. This was all happening too fast. "Um . . ." she muttered, turning and swimming away.

Ethan twisted awkwardly, too, wiping water from his face.

"*Ugh!*" I screamed at them. Talk about frustrating!

Emma moved to the ladder. "We should probably get out."

"Yeah." Ethan pushed out of the pool. He looked at the flower beds and the cone-shaped bird feeder that hung from a birch tree—anywhere but at Emma.

They stood wet and shivering and almost naked on the

deck. Emma wished she could think of something to dispel the tension, but her mind felt blank and waterlogged.

A deep groan made her turn. Lights shone through the slats in the fence. A car idled on the street. Emma grabbed Ethan's arm. "Someone's here!"

"Shit." Ethan tucked his shoes and clothes under his arm and ran barefoot to the back of the block fence. Emma shimmied into her pajama pants, wrung out her camisole, and ran after him. He gave Emma a boost, then climbed over himself. On the other side of the Paulsons' backyard was a dried-out creek bed filled with random sticks and rocks, tumbleweeds, and overgrown cacti. The Mercer house was to the left, but Ethan veered right.

"I should get home," he said.

"You walked here?" Emma asked, surprised.

"Jogged, actually. I like jogging at night."

The car's engine idled on the street. Emma squinted in the darkness. The desert went on forever. "Are you sure you'll be all right?"

"I'll be fine. Catch you later."

Emma watched Ethan until she could no longer see the reflective patches on the back of his sneakers. Then she followed the path to Sutton's backyard, crept close to the edge of the fence, and emerged onto the driveway next to Laurel's Jetta. When she looked over, she fully expected to see a car in the Paulsons' driveway, maybe even Mr.

Paulson prowling around the property with a baseball bat. But the driveway was empty. The newspapers lay in the exact same spots they'd been an hour before. No lights were on inside the house either.

A cold, slimy realization washed over Emma's skin. The car didn't belong to the Paulsons at all. Whoever had been idling there, watching them, had been someone else entirely.

11

NOTHING LIKE A THREAT AT 2 A.M.

A few minutes later, Emma scampered up the front walk of the Mercers' house. The tree outside Sutton's bedroom window didn't have a low enough branch to climb back up, so the only way she could get back inside was through the front door.

The key was under a large rock beneath a desert hackberry tree, just as it had been the first night Emma had entered the Mercer home. She slid it into the lock, praying that the Mercers hadn't set an alarm tonight. The lock turned. Silence. *Score*.

The door swung open easily, and Emma scuttled inside. The AC was on full blast, and goose bumps warped her damp skin. The glass panes over the family portraits glimmered in the pale streetlight. Detective Quinlan's card sat on the console table by the door, just where Sutton's mother had left it that afternoon. Emma cupped her palm over her wrist and remembered what it had felt like when Ethan rested his fingers there. She shut her eyes and leaned her head against the wall.

What was *wrong* with her? I wanted to ask. Why hadn't she kissed him?

Creak. Emma froze. Was that a footstep?

Creak. Creeaaaak. A shadow appeared at the end of the hall. Feet tapped the floor, getting louder and louder, until Laurel stepped into the light. Emma jumped back and suppressed a scream.

"Whoa!" Laurel held up her hands. "Someone's jumpy!" She stared closer at Emma. "Why are you all wet?"

Emma glanced down at the soggy camisole clinging to her skin. "I just took a shower," she said.

"In your *clothes*?"

Emma walked into the powder room and dried her face with a sea-green hand towel. When she glanced at her reflection, she saw Laurel watching her in the mirror. Had Laurel seen her and Ethan in the pool? Had she heard their conversation? Was *she* the one who'd turned the headlights on them?

It seemed possible. From the flashes I'd seen of my past,

Laurel was a hanger-on, a snoop, a spy. I didn't know why we'd let her into the Lying Game, but I knew I hadn't supported it. I think, deep down, I was jealous. Laurel was my parents' real daughter, clearly loved more than me. I didn't want my friends to love her more, too.

Laurel padded into the powder room and sat down on the closed toilet seat. "So when were you going to tell me?"

"About what?" Emma pretended to be fascinated with the mini soaps lined up on the edge of the sink.

"About who you've been seeing. About who you were talking to outside just now."

Nerves snapped under Emma's skin. So Laurel *had* seen. And if Laurel had killed Sutton, if Laurel knew Emma was with Ethan, Emma might have just risked Ethan's life, too. "I don't know what you're talking about." Her voice trembled slightly.

"Come on," Laurel snapped. "You were with someone named Alex, weren't you?"

Alex? Emma let the towel go slack in her hands, racking her brain for someone named Alex at Hollier. The only Alex she knew was her friend from Henderson. . . .

"I saw that text on your phone in Ceramics," Laurel said, crossing her arms and staring at Emma's face in the mirror. "Someone named Alex wrote to you. He said he was *thinking of you*." Her eyes sparkled. "Was this the guy you vanished with at your party, too?"

Emma's head spun. "Alex is a girl," she blurted.

"Uh-huh." Laurel rolled her eyes. "When are you ever going to trust me again?" she asked in a low voice. Something painful passed between the two of them, something Emma couldn't quite get a grip on. Sutton had hurt Laurel in the past—of that Emma was sure—and it seemed that maybe Laurel had hurt Sutton, too.

"She *is* a girl." Emma wheeled around, banging her hip against the edge of the sink. "And . . . and that's not cool that you looked at my phone."

Laurel lowered her chin and gave her a knowing smirk. "Like you don't look at mine all the time? So who is this Alex guy? Someone from Valencia Prep? U of A? Were you guys skinny-dipping? Good thing the Paulsons are in Hawaii!"

"I wasn't in the pool," Emma repeated, but then she looked down at herself. Droplets of water from the ends of her hair cascaded down her shoulders. She reeked of chlorine. "Okay. Fine. I was in the pool. But I was alone."

Laurel traced her fingers on top of a wrought-iron sculpture of the words LIVE, LAUGH, LOVE that sat on the back of the toilet. "Why won't you tell me the truth?" she said, sounding injured. "I won't tell anyone. I promise. I can keep a secret."

Emma lowered her eyes. The only person she could

trust in Tucson was Ethan. "I was alone in the pool, I swear. I was hot, I was awake . . . end of story. And Alex is a girl I met at tennis camp." Hopefully, Sutton had gone to tennis camp . . . and hopefully Laurel hadn't gone with her. Then, trying to act annoyed and aloof, she pushed around Laurel and into the hall.

"Sutton, wait."

Emma turned around. Laurel stood behind her, a dangerous smile on her lips. "I'm onto you. You're going to tell me what you're up to. Or else . . ."

The words hung in the air, almost palpable. "Or else *what*?"

Laurel was so close Emma could smell her lemony shampoo. Her shoulders were square and strong. Her broad hands curled at her sides. All at once, Emma was transported back to that awful night in Charlotte's house when someone had grabbed her from behind and nearly killed her. Laurel was taller than Emma, about the right height of the person who'd assaulted her. And there was a solid strength about her, a sureness that made Emma think she could be capable of such a thing. After all, Emma had watched Laurel violently choke Sutton in the fake snuff film.

Laurel stepped even closer, and Emma flinched and looked away. "You'd better tell me what you're up to soon, or I'll really give you something to be scared about.

You think the train prank is something to laugh about now? What if I tell Mom and Dad all about it? What if I tell them what *really* happened?"

Emma stepped back in surprise. *Please tell* me *what really happened*, she silently willed. But Laurel just spun around and marched up the stairs, leaving Emma alone in the darkness.

12

A SECRET OF A DIFFERENT KIND

"*Ich war in Arizona geboren*," Emma whispered to herself, the German IV textbook in her lap and a series of note cards in her hands. She frowned at how the guttural syllables sounded. German reminded her of an old man hacking up phlegm.

It was Tuesday, and Emma was sitting at a round outdoor lunch table in the courtyard, which was reserved for seniors and a few cool juniors; everyone else had to sit inside the stuffy cafeteria, which had the unfortunate tang of fish tacos. Charlotte, Madeline, and Laurel were due to meet her any minute, and Emma passed the time by reviewing German notes for a big chapter test tomorrow.

Even though Sutton had probably never studied a day in her life, Emma couldn't blow off even the littlest quiz. She'd been a straight-A student since first grade, and she wasn't going to stop now.

I chafed under my twin's judgment. Maybe I was distracted with other things, too busy to study. Or maybe I was secretly smart but just didn't see the point.

The German chapter test covered the stages of life: being born, living, dying. "*Ich war in Arizona geboren,*" Emma mouthed again. *I was born in Arizona.* That would be Sutton's answer—but was it really true? Becky had always told Emma she was born in New Mexico— meaning Sutton had been, too.

"*Sutton starb in Arizona,*" Emma mouthed quietly, reading the next vocabulary word. *Sutton died in Arizona.* Just saying it, even in another language, made Emma's stomach clench. She leafed through the glossary in the back of the book, but the German IV text didn't offer a more accurate verb like *murdered*, *killed*, *slaughtered*, or *strangled*.

"Have you bought your tickets to the Homecoming dance?"

Emma jumped at the chirpy voice above her. A girl with green face paint, a fake nose, an Elvira beehive wig, and a long black dress that looked like it was infested with bedbugs pushed a flyer that said HALLOWEEN HOMECOMING DANCE! BE THERE OR BE SCARED! into Emma's lap. When she saw who Emma was, her manic smile drooped and she stepped away. "Oh! Um, I mean, I'm sure *you* have, Sutton. Have an awesome time!"

Before Emma could say a word, Elvira skittered across the courtyard. This wasn't the first time a dork had shied away from Emma, giving her a wide berth in the hallways or scurrying out of the girls' bathroom just as Emma walked in. *Just another part of being Sutton Mercer,* Emma realized, suddenly wondering if the way people reacted to her had ever made her twin feel lonely. Did Sutton ever truly let anyone in?

I didn't know how to answer Emma's question. But considering it looked like someone close to me took my life, maybe I was right not to trust anyone.

Emma shut the German text. As she stared at the fake-happy, lederhosen-wearing German couple on the cover, she felt the distinct and prickly sensation that someone was watching her. She slowly turned around. A table of football players laughed boisterously at a guy pantomiming some joke across the patio. At the next table sat a boy and a girl. Their mouths were angry red slashes, and their gazes were squarely fixed on Emma.

Garrett and Nisha.

Today, Nisha wore a fitted kelly-green tennis sweater and Lacoste sneakers and a glare that made Emma's blood run cold. Even though Emma hadn't realized they were friends, Garrett sat hip-to-hip with Nisha, his needling gaze on Emma, too. His disgusted expression seemed to say *I know about you. I know about Ethan.*

Could Garrett know? Had he been the one idling outside the Paulsons' pool last night? Maybe he and Nisha had been there together. Emma gave Garrett a small, hopeful wave, but Garrett just shook his head ever so slightly and whispered something into Nisha's ear. Nisha giggled at whatever Garrett said and smirked at Emma.

Suddenly, Emma couldn't take their little secrets anymore. Balling her fist, she glared at the petite, dark-haired girl. "Can I help you with something, Nisha?" she asked, not bothering to hide her sarcasm.

Nisha flashed a saccharine smile and inched closer to Garrett, resting her bloodred fingernails possessively on his arm. "I was just about to remind you that the mandatory team dinner is at my house on Friday. I mean, I would've involved you in the planning, but who knows if you'll even show?"

Emma bristled. "Well, maybe I'd show if you ever threw something worth attending."

Good for you, Em, I thought. Emma was getting better at standing her ground and summoning her inner me. Maybe there was some truth to that nature versus nurture debate after all.

Then Nisha's gaze brightened at someone behind

Emma. "You're coming, aren't you, Laurel? Or will Sutton not allow it?"

Emma turned to see Laurel plopping her lunch tray down on the table. Laurel shot daggers in Nisha's direction, saying nothing. "Since when are team dinners mandatory?" she muttered under her breath. "Someone needs to tell her that just because she's cocaptain doesn't make her queen."

"She's just pissed because Sutton didn't show up last time." Charlotte dropped into a seat, too, slapping a striped canvas lunch bag on the table. She looked at Emma. "If you don't want us to go to this one, Sutton, we won't."

Laurel turned to Emma and nodded, too. Emma had noticed that, as the de facto Lying Game leader, Sutton's friends always deferred to her.

But I wasn't sure they were thrilled about that. Charlotte stared at Emma wearily, as though she was tired of Sutton Mercer's mercurial rules and regulations.

"So where *were* you today?" Madeline interrupted, sliding into the bench next to Emma. "Why weren't you at The Hub?"

Emma squinted. "We were supposed to meet at The Hub?" That was the name of the school store and coffee bar next to the cafeteria. The place mostly sold Hollier sweatshirts, dance raffle tickets, and Number 2 pencils.

"For Court planning, yes! Hello, tradition?" Madeline

handed Emma a coffee from a cardboard carrier. "Whatever. I got a latte for you. I guess someone's a little distracted today, huh? Perhaps from her time in the slammer last night?"

Laurel opened her Sprite Zero with a sharp *thwock*. "I told them about it this morning." She held Emma's gaze, innocently batting her eyelashes as if to say, *And guess what else I'll tell?*

"Apparently *you* weren't going to." Charlotte rested her hands on a Tupperware container full of spinach salad. "What happened?"

Madeline fidgeted with a plastic knife, running her fingers along the jagged edge. "Since when do you shoplift without us?" She looked annoyed, like Emma had slighted her.

"And getting caught at Clique?" Charlotte clucked her tongue. "We had that place mastered by eighth grade!"

"Laurel told me you took a Tori Burch clutch." Madeline wrinkled her nose. "Sutton, Tori is *not* worth stealing."

Emma removed the top from her coffee cup, and steam billowed into her face. "You know how it is when you've just *got* to have something," she said vaguely. "I would've totally gotten away with it, too, if the bitch working the register had been actually doing her job instead of obsessing over me. I think she has a little crush."

"Someone's losing her touch," Charlotte sing-songed, biting into a carrot with a decisive crunch. She seemed almost happy Emma had gotten caught.

Emma took a dainty sip of the latte and winced— it was piping hot. "I've blown my chances for going to Homecoming. I'm grounded for the next millennium."

"Oh please. You're going." Madeline popped a yogurt-covered raisin into her mouth. "We'll find a way. And you're going camping with us afterward, too."

Then, Madeline snickered at something behind her. "CourtZillas at twelve o'clock."

Even though the twins traditionally dressed like opposites—Gabby had a Stepford Wife thing going, with preppy headbands and grosgrain-piped everything, and Lili went for the Taylor Momsen look, with plaid flannels, über-short skirts, and lots of raccoonish eye makeup— today they both wore tight-fitting pink dresses with frothy tulle skirts and mile-high platform heels that laced up their thin ankles. As usual, they clutched their iPhones. Everyone—from the band kids in the corner to the sullen, arty types by the stucco wall—stared at them.

"Hi, girls!" Gabby trilled as she reached their table.

"*Ciao!*" Lili said. "Did someone say camping? Where are we going this year?"

"*We* are camping at Mount Lemmon," Charlotte said pointedly. "I don't know where *you* are camping."

"That's too bad," Lili said just as pointedly back. "Because we're the only ones who know where the best hot springs are."

"And we've got an adorable little hibachi grill. We could make s'mores," Gabby added.

"I don't know if starting a fire in the desert is the best idea." Laurel smirked.

Emma ran her tongue over her teeth as she stared at the girls, thinking of their car slowly passing Sutton's house. Had *they* been the ones lurking outside Sutton's house last night, watching her and Ethan swim?

Madeline appraised their outfits. "Voting for court already *happened*, ladies. You don't have to dress like Homecoming Barbies anymore."

"Maybe we like it." Lili put her hands on her bony hips. "So, girls. Have you figured out the plans for our ceremony yet?"

"It'd better be good," Gabby jumped in, chomping hard on a piece of gum. The scent of watermelon wafted through the air. "Servants . . . awesome food and music . . . and per-haps a Lying Game initiation ceremony as the cherry on top?" Gabby ticked off each request on her fingers.

"We have some killer prank ideas," Lili said, a glint dancing in her light eyes.

"We'd be an asset to the group," Gabby said in a low voice, staring directly at Emma. Emma drew back slightly, her heart speeding up just a tick. Gabby pulled a tiny bottle from the pocket of her dress, flicked open the pink lid, and placed a round pill on her tongue. Her throat rose as she swallowed. Her gaze never left Emma's, as though passing an unspoken message between them.

"No can do on the Lying Game invite, ladies," Emma said, trying to sound confident and poised. Sutton hadn't allowed Gabby and Lili into the club before—maybe for a good reason.

Gabby's eyes flickered over Emma's body, as if sizing her up for a fight. "We'll see about that, won't we?" she said, her words suddenly hard.

Lili lightly touched Gabby's wrist. "Chill, Gabs," she said in a hushed voice. Then she yanked Gabby across the patio. "No autographs!" she called to their gaping classmates, shielding her face as though she was being chased by the paparazzi. As soon as Lili let go of her, Gabby spun around and made her finger into a gun, pointing at Emma and pretending to shoot. Emma's mouth fell open.

A flash instantly swarmed my vision of me ushering the twins out of my room at a sleepover, simpering, "Sorry, girls. We have private Lying Game stuff to discuss. Stay out in the den with the other nobodies." Gabby's knuckles had gone white as she clutched her iPhone tighter. Then Lili had risen to full height. "Mark my words, Sutton, *it won't always be this way*," she'd spat.

But now, Madeline just rolled her eyes at the Twitter Twins. "Something's gotten into those two lately. They're crazier than ever."

"That's for sure," Charlotte said, sipping her coffee and staring at the double doors the twins had disappeared through. "But they do have a point—we have to plan their ceremony."

"Let's do it Saturday." Madeline stuffed her empty Tupperware container into her purse. "My house?"

"I can't," Emma said. "I'm grounded, remember?"

Charlotte let out a snort. "When has that ever stopped you?"

The bell rang, and everyone rose en masse, tossed their leftovers into the trash, and headed back into the school. Laurel and Charlotte split off in opposite directions, but Madeline hung back and waited for Emma to pack her bag so they could walk together.

They turned a corner into the music wing. Off-key notes blared from open doorways. At the end of the hall, Elvira handed out more flyers for the Homecoming dance. Her fake nose threatened to fall off her face, and a couple of kids snickered as they passed. Madeline glanced at Emma out of the corner of her eye.

"What's with you lately?" Madeline asked, slowing their pace.

"What do you mean?" Emma replied, startled.

Madeline skirted around a girl struggling with a tuba case. "You've been . . . weird. Cautious, disappearing and not explaining why, shoplifting by yourself . . . Char and I think an alien life-form has come down and taken over your body."

Emma felt a flush creep over her face and chest. *Calm down*, she said silently. She tugged on Sutton's necklace, fighting for composure. And then she had an idea. "I guess I'm upset because you and Char seem to be really close lately," she said in a pinched voice, trying to sound petulant and jealous. "Am I being replaced as your BFF?" She eyed Madeline's tall ballet-dancer frame, clad in skinny cargo pants and a gray dolman-sleeve sweater, hoping she'd take the bait.

Madeline's finely drawn features tightened. "Char and I have always been friends."

"Yeah, but something has changed between you two," Emma goaded. "You seem tight now. Does this have to do with the night before Nisha's party? I *know* you were together, Mads."

Madeline stopped short in the hall, letting students stream around them. A vein at her temple pulsed. "Would you lay off about that night?"

Emma blinked. A fire raging in her belly fueled her forward. "Why?"

"Because I don't want to talk about it, okay?"

"But . . ."

"Just leave it, Sutton!" Madeline turned and blindly pushed through the nearest door, which led to the school library.

Emma shoved her shoulder against the library door and followed Madeline inside. Kids hunched over homework at long, wide desks. Computer screens glowed behind a wall of glass. The big room smelled like old books and the disinfectant spray-cleaner Travis used to huff.

Madeline disappeared down one of the back aisles.

"Mads!" Emma called, sweeping past a low shelf of atlases and encyclopedias. "Mads, come on!"

The librarian put her finger to her lips. "*Quiet!*" she ordered from behind the checkout desk.

Emma hurried past posters of the Twilight and Harry Potter series, which gave her a tiny twinge of longing. Becky used to read Harry Potter to her, making up the voices for each of the characters and wearing a dingy black velvet cape she'd picked up at a garage sale after Halloween. Emma had loved being read to; she didn't care that the cape kind of smelled like mildew.

Emma turned down the aisle Madeline had veered into. Madeline had stopped at the very end of the row, next to a bunch of copies of *The Riverside Shakespeare*. Her long, dark hair cascaded down her back, her posture ramrod-straight.

All of a sudden I had a sharp, distinct memory of Madeline standing in that same taut but wounded pose. We were in her bedroom, and there was a commotion coming from down the hall, muffled voices gaining in volume. I'd heard tiny gasps, as though she was trying to stifle tears.

"Mads?" Emma whispered. Madeline didn't answer. "Come on, Mads. Whatever I said, I'm sorry."

Madeline whipped around and stared at Emma with red-rimmed eyes. "Look, I called you first, okay?" Her voice caught, and she pressed her lips together. "You didn't answer. I guess you had more important things to do."

She sniffed and took a choked breath. "The world doesn't revolve around you, you know. I always jump when you tell me to jump, but it would be nice if you reciprocated sometimes. I called Charlotte next, and she stayed with me all night. So *yeah*, of course we've been tight lately. Satisfied?"

Steeling her jaw, Madeline swept past Emma as though she were a faceless student clogging up the library aisles.

"Mads!" Emma protested. But Madeline didn't stop. She stormed through the doors and out into the hall.

Everyone in the library turned and stared at Emma. She ducked back into an aisle and leaned against a stack of books. Madeline was hiding something big, but it wasn't what Emma thought. There was no faking the reaction

Madeline just had. Whatever she'd dealt with the night Sutton went missing was her own issue, something completely divorced from what had happened to Sutton. Madeline was busy that night. *Innocent.* And now, because they were together, Charlotte likely was, too.

Relief washed over me, hard and fast. I wanted to cheer aloud. My two best friends were actually my best friends—not my murderers.

A series of shrill *beeps* sounded as the librarian scanned books for a scrawny red head. Emma turned to leave, but her knee caught the corner of a copy of *The Riverside Shakespeare* and knocked it to the floor. The book splayed open, its paper-thin pages full of highlights and notes from kids who didn't seem to care that it was a library book. A line from *Hamlet* caught Emma's eye, sending a chill up her spine.

One may smile, and smile, and be a villain.

It made me shiver, too. Charlotte and Mads were in the clear, but my killer was still out there—smiling, watching, lurking, waiting.

13

NEVER UNDERESTIMATE
THE POWER OF SNOOPING

"She'll be good, Mom," Laurel begged. "I *promise*. Please let her go?"

It was Friday evening, and Emma and Laurel stood in the foyer of the Mercer house. Mrs. Mercer peered at the girls from the doorway of her office. Drake panted beside her, his long tongue looking like a thick slab of ham. Emma edged away from him slightly.

"It's just a stupid tennis dinner." Laurel went on in a sweet voice. "It's going to be totally boring—*Nisha's* throwing it. And anyway, didn't Coach Maggie tell you she was practically going to put an ankle monitor on Sutton once she gets there? You have nothing to worry about."

"Please?" Emma gave Mrs. Mercer puppy-dog eyes that matched Laurel's. A week ago she wouldn't have believed she'd *want* to go to something at Nisha's house. But the truth was, being grounded kind of . . . sucked. It wasn't that she was simply stuck in the house; Mrs. Mercer had taken away Emma's Internet privileges, disconnected the cable box from Sutton's room, and confiscated Sutton's iPhone. After becoming accustomed to Sutton's shiny, high-tech gear, the outdated, banged-up BlackBerry Emma had brought from Vegas wasn't exactly cutting it. She had spent the evenings scouring Sutton's room once more, searching for anything relevant to her murder, but there was nothing. The only thing left to do was home-work. Sutton was probably rolling over in her grave.

If I was somewhere as boring as a grave. Which I highly doubted.

Emma wasn't supposed to be allowed out for Nisha's ten-nis team dinner, but Coach Maggie had apparently called Mrs. Mercer at work this afternoon and urged her to let Sutton attend. It would be good for team morale, Maggie had said, assuring Mrs. Mercer she would be there and would keep an eye on Sutton. But now Mrs. Mercer was hesitating.

"You'll watch her like a hawk, Laurel?" Mrs. Mercer asked.

"Yeh-*hes*," Laurel groaned, fidgeting with the strap of her flowered camisole.

"And you two will come straight home after the dinner is over?"

"Absolutely," the two girls said in unison.

Mrs. Mercer put a finger to her lips. "Well, it *is* Nisha." She uttered Nisha's name in the same reverent way she might talk about the Dalai Lama. Mrs. Mercer was convinced Nisha was a model girl with straight As and iron-tight morals who could do no wrong.

"Okay, fine." With a sigh, Mrs. Mercer lowered her shoulders and shooed them out the door.

Emma climbed into Laurel's car, and Laurel swung into the driver's seat and whooped. "How does freedom taste?"

"Amazing!" Emma cried.

Laurel drove one-handed through the neighborhood, using her other hand to run a paddle brush through her long blond hair. Despite her messy room, Sutton's sister was permanently polished: constantly reapplying lip gloss, checking her teeth in mirrors to make sure nothing was caught between them, and dragging out the ironing board from the hall closet and smoothing her skirts and shirts. Emma liked that Laurel took care of her own clothes instead of asking Mrs. Mercer or a dry cleaner to do it. She was resourceful, like Emma was. She could take care of herself.

But that didn't mean Emma trusted her.

Emma shifted in the passenger seat and mentally assumed her sleuth mode. "So apparently, Madeline has a secret," she began, turning to Laurel and catching sight of the canine day care, Doggie Dude Ranch, that zoomed past her window. A turquoise and crystal shop was next, followed by a big outdoor pottery shop.

Laurel's eyebrows shot up, but she didn't take her eyes off the road. "Oh yeah? What?"

"She won't tell me. It has something to do with the night before Nisha's back-to-school party."

Laurel's face clouded. "You mean the night before you *ditched* me?"

Emma bit down hard on the inside of her cheek. *Oops.* Sutton was supposed to pick up Laurel for that party . . . but since she was dead, it didn't happen. "Yeah. Well, anyway, Mads called Charlotte that night and told her what it was. I guess it was kind of a big deal."

"Why weren't you with them?"

The AC in the car suddenly felt ice-cold. *You tell me,* Emma wanted to say. "I guess that means you weren't with them either?"

Laurel's mouth formed a straight line. The Jetta veered over the line on the highway, and the driver next to them blew his horn, making both girls jump. "Uh, *no,*" she answered tightly after she'd steered the car back into its rightful lane. "I wasn't."

"So where were you?" Emma tried to sound like she was making casual conversation, even though her heart was rocketing inside her chest.

Laurel's fingers clutched the steering wheel. She paused for a long moment, her eyes fixed on the horizon. "Sutton, are we seriously going to have this conversation right now?" she said finally in a steely voice. Emma stared at her, waiting, but she didn't offer anything more.

Laurel pulled the car up to a familiar low-slung ranch house with a big front yard full of desert succulents. It looked exactly the same as it had the last time Emma had come here, her very first day in Tucson, before she knew her twin was dead. Back before all of this craziness started. Several cars were parked in the driveway and at the curb, many of them pasted with bumper stickers that said TENNIS IS THE GOOD LIFE or LOVE with a yellow tennis ball as the O. All the lights were on in the house, and a giggle exploded from somewhere inside.

"Come on." Laurel hit the key fob to lock the Jetta and started up the driveway, but Emma hung back for a moment. She stared across the street at Ethan's house. The front porch was dark. The telescope Ethan had peered through the first night Emma had met him had disappeared. She wondered what Ethan was doing tonight. Had he thought about their near kiss in the pool the other night? They'd seen each other in the halls, but they hadn't really spoken since.

Nisha's front door flung open, and the tennis team greeted them with hugs and squeals. Emma poked her head into the room and nudged Laurel. "Where's Maggie?"

Laurel started to laugh. "Maggie's not actually *here*."

Charlotte emerged through the crowd wearing an off-the-shoulder striped top and wide-leg jeans. She linked her elbow through Emma's. "I see my little plan worked!" The freckles on her nose scrunched together as she grinned.

Emma frowned. *Little plan?*

Charlotte extended her thumb and pinkie to make the shape of a phone. "'Hello, Mrs. Mercer?'" she said in an adult voice. "'This is Coach Maggie. I'd really, really like Sutton to attend the tennis team dinner tonight. It's such a show of solidarity! Oh, I understand she's grounded, but I'll watch her carefully, I promise. You can count on me!'"

Not even I saw that one coming. My friends were *good*. With a rush of relief, I tried to wrap my arms around Charlotte, thrilled once more that she wasn't my killer. But, as usual, my fingers just passed through her skin.

Charlotte put her arm around Emma's shoulders and squeezed. "No need to thank me. Now all we have to do is figure out how to spring you for Homecoming."

She pulled Emma into the dining room, where platters of roast chicken and panini sandwiches lay on a checkered tablecloth next to big bowls of pasta salad, crispy, foil-wrapped garlic bread, and a tier of chocolate-iced cupcakes for dessert. Red plastic cups sat next to bottles of Gatorade, Smartwater, and Diet Coke. Everyone else on the team had already dug in, scooping food onto their plates with long-handled plastic spoons.

As Emma stepped toward the table, an icy hand circled her wrist. "Glad you could make it, Sutton," Nisha said with a saccharine smile.

Emma flinched, jittery at the sight of Nisha. Something about the girl was *too* glossy, starting with the way she was styled to anal-retentive perfection: her cream-colored silk blouse perfectly tucked into a pair of dark-wash trouser jeans. The gold bangle bracelets on her wrist looked as though they'd been spit-polished. Her hair was a smooth, glassy sheet that hung down her back, and her makeup looked as though it had been professionally applied.

"I'm glad you're *enjoying* it," Nisha went on. "It was kind of hard work to put all this food together. Especially because I had to do it alone."

"*Liar!*" I wanted to call out. In the kitchen, past all the girls, I spotted a bunch of AJ's market grocery bags on the kitchen island. No doubt Nisha had bought all this stuff ready-made and just arranged it artfully on plates.

"So," Nisha's voice oozed with faux sweetness. "What's

it like for Sutton Mercer not to have a boyfriend? It must be the first time since, oh, I don't know, kindergarten!"

Emma straightened. "I'm actually really enjoying myself," she said, reaching forward to pop a cracker into her mouth. "It feels good to be free."

The corners of Nisha's mouth curled up into a sickly pink grin. "I heard you wouldn't have sex with him," she added, loudly enough to turn the heads of two sophomores lining up for pasta-salad seconds.

Emma's hand froze over the crackers. "Where did you hear that?"

A tiny giggle escaped from Nisha's mouth. The answer was obvious. Other than her friends, Garrett was the only person who knew what happened in Sutton's bedroom.

Ew. I suddenly was glad that Emma broke up with him.

"I had no idea you were such a prude!" Nisha trilled, exposing her pearly teeth. Then, without allowing Emma to get another word in, she whipped around and sashayed into the den.

Emma stabbed at a piece of chicken on the platter, hating Nisha more with every second. Had Sutton hated her this much, too? But it was more than that. There was something about Nisha that unnerved her. The strange looks she gave Emma, the whispers. It was like she was toying with Emma. Like she *knew* something— something big.

Emma peered out of the dining room. A large, state-of-the-art kitchen was to her right; on the other side of the foyer was a long, dark hallway, which most likely led to Nisha's bedroom. Did she dare?

"Be careful," I warned, even though Emma couldn't hear me. There was no way Nisha would take kindly to snooping.

Emma stared at the chicken leg she'd selected from the platter, the thin, yellowish flesh suddenly turning her stomach. Discarding her plate, she mumbled something about the bathroom to no one in particular and tiptoed down the hall.

Tiny night-lights illuminated the baseboards. The air smelled like Febreze and Indian spices. Emma pressed open the first door with the very tips of her fingers and stared into a walk-in closet full of towels and sheets. She moved to the next door. It was a hall bathroom, adorned with a paisley shower curtain and a mosaic-tiled mirror. The next door, which led to the master bedroom, stood ajar. The king-sized bed hadn't been made, and men's dress shirts, black socks, and shiny black shoes were strewn messily all over the carpet. *I guess someone's cleaning lady didn't come this week*, Emma thought, surprised at how accustomed to an immaculate home she'd become after just a few weeks. A twinge of guilt pinched her when she remembered that Mrs. Banerjee had died this summer.

Emma pushed inside the final door to the right. A light glowed from a meticulous desk. A Compaq laptop sat closed, and a white iPod waited in a charging dock next to it. The rest of the surface was empty and sterile, like a hotel room. Nisha had smoothed the bedspread of all creases, organized eight fluffy pillows just so, and lined up her stuffed animals—one of which was a large tennis racket with two googly eyes—along the headboard. She'd alphabetized all the books on her shelf—which seemed mostly of the stuffy, Victorian, Brontë-sisters variety. Even the slats of the venetian blinds tilted precisely at the same angle.

A peal of laughter sounded from the den, and Emma froze. She peeked through the gap between the door and the wall and counted to three. No one appeared at the end of the hall.

She tiptoed farther into the room to take a closer look at the collage of photos housed under a glass pane near Nisha's bed. Most of the photos showed Nisha in action: hitting a backhand shot, a drop shot, serving, raising her hands above her head when she'd won a match. In the center of the collage, Nisha stood in the first-place spot on a podium, a shiny gold medal around her neck. Sutton stood in the third-place spot, scowling. There was a tan-colored brace on her knee.

Tacked along the border were several group shots of

the tennis team: the girls holding a team tournament cup, Sutton standing as far away from Nisha as she could. Charlotte had darker hair in the photo, and Laurel's hair was cut in a sleek blonde bob. Another photo showed the girls standing at an airport gate. Sutton posed off to the side, jutting her leg up on one of the benches and giving the camera a sexy pout. Emma noticed blinking slot machines in the background. Was that Vegas? Had she and Sutton been in the same city at the same time? For a fleeting moment, she pictured the two of them running into each other at the New York–New York casino where she had worked. Would Sutton have noticed her? Would they have smiled at each other?

A final team shot was pinned in the corner of the bulletin board, overlapping other photos as if it had been hastily stuck there. The tennis team gathered around Nisha's dining table. Sutton and Charlotte were missing, but Laurel smiled broadly, her hair as long as it was today. BACK TO SCHOOL TEAM SLEEPOVER was scrawled at the bottom of the photo. Emma's finger traced over the date written in Nisha's calligraphic handwriting: 8/31. She had to stare at it for a few long beats before she believed it was real.

"What are you *doing*?"

Emma flinched. Nisha stood in the doorway, her arms crossed over her chest. She stalked over and pushed Emma's shoulder. "I didn't say you could come in here!"

"Wait!" Emma pointed at the photo. "When was this taken?"

Nisha inspected the photo and rolled her eyes. "Can't you read?" she asked in a smart-ass tone. "It says August thirty-first."

Nisha placed her palm between Emma's shoulder blades and shoved her out the door. She slammed it before turning to face Emma. "Attending team activities is what being on a team *means*. At least for those of us who care about supporting one another."

"Even Laurel was there," Emma said slowly, lifting her eyes to meet Nisha's.

A haughty grin widened on Nisha's face as she glanced over Emma's shoulder. "Speak of the devil! We were just talking about you."

Emma whipped around. Laurel stood at the end of the hall, a red plastic cup in her hand. "You were?" she asked, her gaze bouncing between the two of them.

"I was just telling Sutton about the ah-*mazing* time we all had at my back-to-school tennis sleepover a few weeks ago," Nisha chirped.

Laurel's cheeks flushed and her plastic cup made a crinkling sound as she squeezed it tighter. "Oh," she said quietly. Her eyes flickered to Emma and then to the mauve carpet lining Nisha's hallway. "Oh, Sutton, I'm sorry, I . . ."

"Is it really *that* embarrassing?" Nisha slapped her arms to her sides. "You came, Laurel. I'd say you even had *fun*."

Laurel's mouth morphed from a smile to a frown to a wiggly line. "It was okay," she whispered.

Nisha's eyes gleamed triumphantly. She pulled on her bedroom doorknob one more time for good measure and pushed past Emma and Laurel. She glanced at her father's room, color draining from her face, and pulled that door shut, too.

After Nisha disappeared down the hall, Laurel peeked at Emma sheepishly. "I'm sorry, Sutton. I know you and Nisha hate each other. But I thought the sleepover was mandatory. I didn't know you and Charlotte weren't going to come. Please don't be mad at me."

More giggles erupted from the den. The wind gusted outside, pressing up against the windows. Maybe the real Sutton would have been pissed to find out what Nisha had just told her—clearly Laurel hadn't admitted she'd gone to Nisha's tennis party because Sutton's friends were supposed to be united in Nisha-hate. Sutton might've interpreted this as betrayal.

But Emma was delighted—*relieved*. Laurel attending Nisha's tennis team sleepover meant she had an airtight alibi for the thirty-first. Neither she—nor Nisha—could have killed Sutton.

"It's fine," Emma said to Laurel, throwing her arms

around Sutton's sister's neck so hard she knocked her off balance.

"Sutton?" Laurel said, her voice muffled in the sleeve of Emma's flowy lavender top.

I twirled in an invisible circle next to the two of them. This was even better than clearing Charlotte and Madeline. My own sister was *innocent*.

14

DOUBLE THE TROUBLE

"What's all *that*?" Madeline asked as she flung open the door to her house and stared at Laurel, Emma, and Charlotte on the porch. It was Saturday afternoon, and all three carried paint-spattered jeans, grubby T-shirts, and old sneakers.

"Our costumes for when we go home." Laurel set the dirty clothes on the porch swing. "I told my mom that Char and I were volunteering with the Habitat for Humanity house-painting crew today. I said Sutton should come, too—I promised it would be a *rewarding experience* for her."

"The lengths we go to free you, Sutton," Madeline said

dramatically, batting a long black braid over her shoulder.

Charlotte winked at Emma, and Emma giggled. She didn't have to hold her breath around them anymore; they were Sutton's friends, not her killers. She was so grateful she'd let Laurel have the last low-fat muffin this morning, and she'd given Charlotte a huge hug as soon as they'd gotten in her car. "*Someone's* cheerful this morning," Charlotte had commented. "Are you in love?"

Now Emma glanced around. This was the first time she'd been in Madeline's house, a bungalow with authentic adobe walls, an old-school, pueblo-style fireplace, and a Mexican-tiled kitchen with cheerful red pendant lights. Outside the window was a stunning view of the Catalina Mountains; Emma could just make out a line of people hiking on one of the upper trails.

"C'mon." Madeline grabbed a big bowl of popcorn from the kitchen island and padded into the den. Corduroy couches surrounded a large flat-screen TV in the corner. Scattered between wooden wall placards that said things like BLESS OUR HAPPY HOME and WE ARE FAMILY were framed photographs of Madeline and her brother, Thayer.

Emma moved closer to the photos and tried to inspect them without Madeline noticing. There were pictures of Thayer in soccer gear. Thayer standing in front of a local Italian restaurant, pretending to take a big bite out of a large

cardboard pizza sign. Thayer standing on top of a moun-
tainous desert rock, dressed in a red T-shirt and khaki cargo
shorts. The wind blew his black hair into his warm, hazel
eyes, and there was a whisper of a smile on his clear-skinned,
strong-jawed face. Every shot showed him grinning at the
camera except one: a photo taken of the group, going to a
prom. Sutton and Garrett stood together, dressed in formal
wear. Madeline was with Ryan Jeffries, who Emma recognized from school, and Charlotte was with a dark-haired
guy Emma didn't know. Thayer stood a little off to the
side, his arms crossed over his well-fitted tux. His eyes were
narrowed and his face was hard, like he was trying to look
debonair. *Mysterious Boy Disappears Without a Trace*, Emma
thought, giving the photo a caption.

But something in Thayer's expression stirred an emotion deep inside of me. Thayer wasn't trying to look
debonair—he was pissed. But what was he pissed *about*?

Who are you? Emma wished she could ask the boy in
the photos. *Why did you leave? And why, every time I see a
picture you, do I get the chills?*

That made two of us.

Madeline aimed the remote at the TV, and *Jersey Shore*
appeared on the screen. She opened a big white binder
labeled HALLOWEEN HOMECOMING in bright orange letters.
"Okay. Char, are we all set with the decorator?"

"Check." Charlotte nodded, pulling her light yellow

shorts down over her thighs as she sat on the shaggy cream carpet. "Her name's Calista—my mom's used her for lots of parties. We're doing cauldrons, skeletons, werewolves, and a haunted house. The rest of the gym is going to look like MI6 in L.A. Dark and sexy."

"A perfect place to sneak booze," Madeline piped up.

"*Or* a perfect place to hook up with someone who isn't your date," Charlotte added. Then she turned to Emma. "Don't get any ideas, Sutton."

Emma didn't bother protesting. Let Charlotte make her jabs; she knew now that they didn't mean anything.

"Now we need a theme for this court fete," Laurel said.

Charlotte rolled her eyes. "It's so stupid the court fete has to have a different theme than the dance. Sometimes I want to kill the seniors who came up with that tradition."

Madeline walked to the window and heaved it open with her long, slender arms. "Oh, let's just plan it and get it over with. I say it should be something spooky yet glam, but not so glam that the faculty will be pissed and not let us do it."

Laurel propped her legs up on the coffee table. "What about vampires?"

"Ugh." Madeline made a face. "I'm tired of vampires."

"What about a gala event for the dead?" Emma said. "You know, a really fancy party, except everyone invited is a corpse?"

Charlotte narrowed her eyes, thinking.

"Wish you'd thought of it yourself, don't you, Char?" Emma teased. She knew it was something Sutton would say.

Charlotte just shrugged. "It's interesting," she admitted. "But it should be rooted in something real. Not just a party full of dead people."

A thought popped into Emma's mind. "What about a fancy ball on the *Titanic*? Except it can be *after* the ship sank. So it can be at the bottom of the ocean, and everyone can be a corpse, but they're still partying in high style. Something Kate Winslet's character in the movie would've approved of."

Laurel widened her eyes. "I like that!"

"Agreed." Charlotte clapped her hands. "I bet Calista could rustle up some really good *Titanic* décor."

Madeline reached into her pocket and extracted a pack of Parliaments and a pink lighter. A blue spark shot into the air, followed by the heady smell of cigarette smoke. "Anyone want one?" she asked, exhaling out the window.

Everyone shook their heads. "You should stop that, Mads." Charlotte hugged a throw pillow. "What's Davin going to say when he goes to kiss you and you smell like an ashtray?"

"I'm not a hundred percent sure I'm into him yet." Smoke poured out of Madeline's nose. "Maybe ashtray breath will keep him at bay."

"Well, don't breathe on me." Charlotte formed her arms into an *X* and held them out in Madeline's direction. "I don't want anything ruining my chances of hooking up with Noah."

"Who are you taking, Laurel?" Madeline asked.

Laurel ran a hand over a snag in the carpet. "Caleb Rosen."

"Don't know him," Charlotte announced in a loud voice.

Madeline gave Laurel a tepid smile. "I have math with him," she said. Her monotone made it unclear whether she approved or disapproved.

Emma blinked. "You guys have dates?"

Madeline ashed out the window. "You mean you *don't?*"

"Well, I was going with Garrett," Emma said, remembering the ticket Garrett had given her when they broke up. He and Sutton must have planned it before she vanished. "But then I got grounded. So I didn't ask anyone else."

Madeline blew a plume of smoke out the window. "Just ask someone, Sutton. Tons of guys would be thrilled to go with you."

Emma stared at the back issues of *National Geographic* and *Motor Trend* that lined the bookshelf. She wondered if school dances were Ethan's thing. "I can't think of anyone," she said after a moment.

I wanted to elbow her. Sutton Mercer did *not* go stag to dances. Madeline gestured a wide arc with her cigarette like she was doing the top half of a ballet move. "Really, Sutton? You don't even have a little crush on someone?"

"Nope."

Charlotte smacked Emma with a pillow. "Stop lying. Laurel told us."

Emma stared at Laurel, but Laurel just raised her shoulders unapologetically. "I know you snuck into that pool with someone. I *heard* you guys."

"Spill it!" Madeline's eyes twinkled.

Heat flooded Emma's cheeks. "It's no one, I swear."

"Come on, Sutton!" Laurel pressed her palms together. "You can tell us!"

Emma ran her tongue over her teeth. Did she dare tell them about Ethan? They were Sutton's friends, after all, not her murderers. And now that Emma had cleared them, they'd begun to feel like *her* friends, too.

Tell them, I wished I could say. My friends would probably encourage Emma to get over her oh-so-*un*-Sutton-Mercer shyness and ask Ethan out. Sure Ethan was a loner, but he was a hot loner.

Suddenly, the front door slammed. "Hello?" a man's voice called out.

Madeline leapt up, stabbed out the cigarette on the

windowsill, and fanned the fumes outside. There were footsteps, and then Mr. Vega peered into the den. "Oh. Hello, girls. Madeline didn't tell me you were coming over today."

"They're just here to plan the Homecoming dance, Daddy," Madeline said, jumping from the window seat to the La-Z-Boy chair. Her face was even paler than usual.

Mr. Vega turned and gave her a long, discerning stare. He tilted his nostrils up and sniffed the air. "Was someone smoking?" The transformation of Mr. Vega's stony face into a fiery scowl now reminded Emma of Mr. Smythe, another one of her foster dads. He was like Dr. Jekyll/Mr. Hyde: sweet one moment and volatile the next. The only way Emma could tell he was going to freak out was when he started feverishly licking his lips.

Madeline shook her head. "Of course not!"

"It's from outside," Charlotte said at the same time. "A bunch of kids walked by, and they were all smoking."

A neutral look settled over Mr. Vega's face again, but his eyes still burned. "Well, if you girls need anything, I'll be in my office." Then he eyed the episode of *Jersey Shore* on TV. "You shouldn't watch that trash, Madeline."

Madeline clicked the remote. A chase scene of a male lion taking down a frantic zebra filled the screen. After he left, Charlotte walked over and touched Madeline's arm.

A tinny *bleep* issued from Madeline's iPhone, which sat facedown on the coffee table. Everyone started. She grabbed it and studied the screen. "Surprise, surprise. *Another* text from Lili and Gabby. They've been begging to come to Mount Lemmon with us all day."

"That's not going to happen," Charlotte said.

Sutton's phone, which Mrs. Mercer had let Emma have back in case of an emergency, rang, too. Emma pulled it from her bag. HELLO, SWEETS! Gabby wrote. YOU TOTALLY WANT TO BE US, DON'T YOU? THAT MAKES THREE OF US—WE LOVE US, TOO! MWAH!

Charlotte groaned as she read her BlackBerry. "If they were any more full of themselves, they'd have to have ego liposuction."

Their phones lit up once more. GUESS THE *L* IN LYING GAME STANDS FOR *LOSER*!

"*That's* not cool." Laurel jabbed at her phone to delete the message. "If they keep this up no one will ever vote for them again."

"I don't know how they got voted in at *all*," Charlotte mused, fiddling with a ceramic donkey statue on the coffee table. "I took a look at the ballots online—Isabel Girard and Kaitlin Pierce were also on it, and guys are much more into them than Gabby and Lili."

"I vote we stop hanging out with them." Madeline reached for a handful of popcorn.

"I second that," Emma said quickly, remembering Gabby's eerie gun-trigger gesture at lunch the other day.

I third that, I thought.

The phones beeped once more, and everyone diverted their attention to their screens. TWO PRETTY COURT GIRLS DESERVE A SMOKIN' PARTY! STEP IT UP, BITCHES!

"You know what I think we should do?" Madeline leaned back on the couch and curled her knees to her chest. "We should knock those princesses down to size. Hit 'em where it hurts."

"A prank?" Laurel's eyebrows shot up.

Emma shifted her weight. "I don't think so. . . ." She thought about the file at the police station—Gabby going to the hospital, all of it being Sutton's fault. She still hadn't figured out how Gabby had gotten hurt, but a trip to the ER couldn't have been good. "It might be going too far. Especially after what happened . . ." She let her voice trail off and gazed out the window, figuring Sutton's friends knew far more about the train incident than she did.

Sutton's friends were silent. Laurel stared at her hands and picked at a cuticle. Madeline flipped through her binder. "Oh please," Charlotte finally said. "Now that you're all buddy-buddy with them, they're off-limits?"

Emma raised an eyebrow. *Buddy-buddy?* Not from what she'd noticed of the Twins.

Charlotte draped her arms over the top of the couch. "They said they shoplifted with you at Clique," she said, rolling her eyes. "Gabby and Lili bragged about it like it was the *coolest* thing, like we all hadn't done it a million times before."

Madeline's mouth dropped open. "Were they with you the other day when you got arrested?"

"No, not that time," Emma said quickly, her mind racing.

"It was before that," Charlotte butted in.

Emma turned away, needing a moment to process all of this. According to Sutton's credit card statement, the last time Sutton was at Clique was on the thirty-first. And Samantha at Clique had said Sutton stole something from the store while she'd been with someone else—or, more specifically, a posse of someones. *And* the very last phone call Sutton picked up on the thirty-first was from Lili.

"Yeah, I went to Clique with them right before school started," Emma said slowly.

All of a sudden, a memory ignited in my mind: Gabby and Lili, flanking me behind a rack of silky camisoles and lingerie at Clique. "Do it, Sutton," Gabby had whispered, her warm, mint-scented breath on my neck.

"C'mon, Sutton," Laurel urged. "Those bitches deserve to be pranked."

The room still smelled slightly of smoke. On the television, a lion sunned itself in the grass, blood from a fresh kill on its lips. Emma ran her fingers through her hair, her chest feeling hot and tight. Puzzle pieces began to slot into place. The Twitter Twins had been in all the right places at all the right times—with Sutton the night she died, in Madeline's car the night Emma was kidnapped and mistaken for Sutton, at Charlotte's sleepover when Emma had been strangled.

"I still don't know, guys," Emma said, her vocal cords taut. "After last time . . ." She trailed off.

Charlotte sniffed. "That was ages ago."

"It's just . . ." Emma swallowed hard. "I just don't . . ."

"Stop being such a wuss." Madeline reached over and shoved Sutton's iPhone at Emma. "We're doing this. You're calling them."

Emma stared at the phone's black screen. "A-and telling them what?"

Madeline, Charlotte, and Laurel looked at one another. A plan unfolded in minutes, the events rocketing forward out of Emma's control. They turned to Emma and nudged their chins toward Sutton's phone. Emma pulled her dark hair into a ponytail, scrolled to find Gabby's number, and pressed CALL. When the line began to ring, she put the call on speaker.

Gabby answered. "Sutton! Have you been getting our tweets?"

Charlotte rolled her eyes. Madeline snickered softly. "Of course," Emma said brightly, tucking her trembling hands under her butt. "They're awesome!" This made Sutton's friends shake even harder with silent laughter. "So, listen, Gabs. Can you put Lili on, too?"

Gabby rustled up her sister, and soon both Twitter Twins were on the line "So, I have some information about the Court Ceremony," Emma said, glancing at Sutton's friends around her. They nodded encouragingly.

"It's *about time!*" Lili trilled. "This had better be good!"

"It's *awesome!* Sort of a ghoulish *Titanic* meets *Baywatch*. Everyone will wear bikinis."

"*Baywatch*," Laurel mouthed, bending over in silent laughter.

"Bikinis?" Gabby sounded skeptical. "Is the school going to allow that?"

"Of course they're going to allow it," Emma cooed. "We've already had it approved."

Charlotte swallowed a loud, snorting giggle.

"This ceremony is going to be fabulous, girls," Emma went on. "*Super* glamorous in an old-school kind of way." For a split second, she wondered if Sutton would be proud of her. If Sutton were here, would she be laughing, too, squeezing Emma's hand and egging her on?

I would . . . and I wouldn't. Not with what I now knew about the Twitter Twins. Emma was skating on thin ice.

"*Nice*," Gabby and Lili said in unison.

"We're going to tell the other nominees soon, but I wanted to let you guys know first so you could get a jump on them and be the most fabulous court girls up there," Emma said. "Go out and buy amazing suits this weekend. The skimpier, the better!"

"We're on it." Lili's voice sang through the receiver. "Wow, Sutton. You're *so* good at this. Keep up the good work."

As soon as they hung up, the girls collapsed into laughter. Laurel rolled off the couch onto the floor. Charlotte giggled into a throw pillow. Madeline kicked her legs in front of the TV screen, which now showed two hyenas perched on a rock. "They are *so* stupid!" she crowed. "They're going to look like the biggest idiots!"

Emma tried to laugh along, too, but Lili's words clanged in her mind. *You're so good at this. Keep up the good work.* She was almost positive Lili's voice had a sinister edge, an unspoken subtext: Keep up the good work . . . *of being Sutton.*

Emma looked around at the laughing, smiling faces of Sutton's friends. No matter how safe she finally felt with them, there was an entire world outside—a world where someone watched her every move and waited for her to slip up.

I couldn't agree more. Trust no one, sister.

15

AN OPENING . . . AND A CLOSING

CAN YOU SNEAK OUT?

Emma rolled onto her back to read the text Ethan had just sent. Pulling one of Sutton's soft blue throw blankets over her bare legs, she texted back: MERCERS ARE OUT TO DINNER. I'D HAVE TO BE BACK BEFORE TEN.

I'LL PICK YOU UP IN FIFTEEN, Ethan responded. WEAR A DRESS.

A dress? Emma frowned. UM . . . OKAY, she wrote. CAN I ASK WHAT WE'RE DOING?

NOPE. IT'S A SURPRISE.

Emma sprang from Sutton's bed and padded to her closet. She pushed aside a row of soft cotton tops and skinny jeans and examined Sutton's dress selection, which was plentiful and expensive. She touched a long black dress with gold straps. Too fancy, it seemed, for a Tuesday. Her fingers traced the feathered collar of a short silver cocktail dress. Maybe it was *too* short. She ran her hands along the hem of a fire engine-red minidress. Too sex goddess.

I couldn't help but groan. Was there even such a thing as being too much of a sex goddess? As far as I was concerned, Emma needed to get down with her sexy self. This had to be the night they were finally going to kiss, right?

Then Emma's palms rested on a light gray one-shouldered dress. The gauzy silk felt soft beneath her fingertips. She slid it over her head and glanced at herself in the gold-framed full-length mirror on the back of the door. It was perfect.

After mascara, lip gloss, black patent heels, and chandelier earrings that matched Sutton's silver locket, she was ready. The phone beeped once more, and Emma ran to the bed, thinking it was Ethan. But it was from her friend Alex instead. YOU SHOULD DEFINITELY CHECK THIS PLACE OUT! Attached was a website for a vintage store near the University of Arizona. I KNOW HOW YOU LOVE YOUR THRIFT SHOPS, Alex added, with an emoticon smiley. Emma wrote back a quick thank-you followed by a series of *X*s and *O*s. Then she glanced at herself in the mirror, dolled up in Sutton's designer dress, jewelry, and expensive shoes. Would Alex even *know* her right now?

She sat on the bottom step of the Mercers' staircase, the house quiet around her. Laurel was out with a friend at *Les Misérables*—since Emma was grounded, she couldn't use the ticket Laurel had given her for her birthday. Only Drake watched her from his sprawled-out post on the living room floor, and he was too lazy to get up.

Bright headlights shone in the driveway. Emma rose, carefully opened the front door, and looked both ways as she stepped off the porch. Some of the windows in the houses next door were lit; she hoped no nosy neighbors would mention this to the Mercers. *Your daughter looked lovely all dressed up! And who was that dashing young man escorting her?*

Ethan had gotten out of the car to open the passenger door for her. He wore a dark suit jacket, khaki pants, and shiny black shoes, a huge change from his usual disheveled shorts and tees.

"Wow." Emma paused for a moment before getting into the car. "You look so . . . *handsome*."

"Handsome, huh?" Ethan grinned.

Emma blushed. "Yeah, handsome like a Ken doll."

Ethan's eyes traveled along her body. "And you look really pretty," he said, his words spilling out awkwardly. "But *not* like a Barbie."

Emma pressed her lips together in a bashful smile. After a moment, she swung into the passenger seat. Ethan jogged to the driver's door and revved the engine. Emma rested her hand on the console between them, wondering for just a moment whether Ethan would try to link his fingers through hers. Instead, he took out a plaid handkerchief from the inside of his coat and turned to face her.

"You're going to have to wear this," he said, a mischievous grin crawling across his face. "Our destination is a secret."

She burst out laughing. "You can't be serious."

"Serious as a heart attack." He motioned for her to twist and tied the scarf around her head. In moments, Emma was enveloped in darkness. She felt the car lurch into reverse and then pivot to the right, onto the street. With anyone else, she probably would've been freaked out by such a gesture—Madeline and the Twitter Twins had kidnapped her at Sabino Canyon in a similar fashion, after all. But with Ethan, she felt safe. Excited.

"It won't be too long," he assured her. Emma heard the soft *tick-tick-tick* of the turn signal. "No peeking!"

A new song by the Strokes played softly on the stereo. Emma sat back and shut her eyes, wondering where they were going. Yesterday in school, she'd told him about Madeline's, Charlotte's, and Laurel's alibis, and Ethan had nodded, businesslike—he'd been cordial but distant since the almost-kiss. The bell had rung before she could tell him about her new suspects, the Twitter Twins. There had been no mention of anything personal. There had been no mention of what had happened at the pool. Maybe Ethan just wanted to forget it had happened. But then again, this seemed a lot like a date.

She felt a slight jerk as the car stopped for a light. Close by, a car stereo thudded.

I tried to look at where they were going, but ran up against one of the weird side effects about my dead life with Emma—whenever her eyes were closed or covered, mine were, too. It made me wonder who or what was behind all this—not my murder, but *me*, here, trailing Emma from beyond the grave. Believe me, I hadn't been a what-does-it-all-mean kind of girl when I was alive, reading philosophy and praying to Buddha or whatever. But this opportunity with Emma, as scary as it was, made me feel kind of . . . blessed. Undeserving, too. I'd clearly been a bitch in life; why was I given this special gift? Or was this what happened to *everyone* after they died, or at least those with unfinished business?

Finally, Emma sensed the car easing to a stop and heard Ethan shift it into PARK. "Okay," he said softly. "You can look now."

Emma lowered the scarf and blinked. They were downtown, near the college. A large, sand-colored building stretched across the horizon. Sweet-smelling lemon trees lined a stone walkway. Golden lights illuminated the grand front steps. Across the front of the building was a black banner that read TUCSON PHOTOGRAPHY INSTITUTE.

"Oh!" Emma cried, feeling more confused than ever.

"There's an exhibit for three London-based photographers starting tonight," Ethan explained. "I know you like photography, so . . ."

"This is great!" Emma breathed. Then she looked down at her dress. "But why are we dressed up?"

"Because tonight's the opening party."

"And we're . . . invited?"

Ethan shot her a devious smile. "Nope. We're going to crash."

Emma's hands went slack in her lap. "Ethan—I can't get in trouble again. The Mercers will kill me if they know I'm out. I'm supposed to be in Sutton's bedroom right now, repenting my life as a criminal."

Ethan gestured to two party guests climbing the grand stairs. A tuxedoed man at the top smiled at them and politely opened the doors without checking for credentials. "Live a little. I promise you we won't get caught."

"But what does this have to do with Sutton?"

Ethan sat back against his seat, looking a little surprised by the question. "Well, nothing. I just thought it would be fun."

Emma gazed from the photo institute's elegant columns back to Ethan's face. A fancy party with Ethan? That *would* be fun. Maybe she deserved some time to relax and just be herself.

"Okay." She pushed open the door, casting a grin over her shoulder. "But at the first sign of trouble, we're leaving."

Good girl, I thought. For a second, I had been sure Emma was going to demand that Ethan take her home. The problem with Emma being grounded was that I'd been cooped up for days, watching her pace in my bedroom. Crashing a party is just what the boredom doctor ordered.

They ascended the stone staircase. The punishing heat of the day had broken, and a cool breeze tickled their cheeks. The scent of lemon trees and a musky mix of women's and men's colognes hung in the air. The tuxedoed man eyed them as they approached, and Emma sucked in her stomach. Was he ticking off his mental list of invitees? Could he tell they were high school students?

"Act naturally," Ethan murmured to Emma, apparently noticing how stiff she'd become. "The opposite of how you acted when you stole that handbag."

"Very funny." When Emma reached Mr. Tuxedo, she shot him the most carefree smile she could muster. "Good evening," the man said, opening the door for them.

"See?" she whispered when they were safely in the

lobby. "I totally played it cool. I'm not as big a loser as you think I am."

Ethan looked at her sideways. "I most definitely don't think you're a loser." Then he touched the back of Emma's arm to guide her inside the exhibit. For a moment, all sounds and sights dulled, and Emma felt like she and Ethan were the only ones in the universe. When he let go at the end of the lobby, she adjusted the strap of Sutton's silky dress and tried to breathe normally.

The museum was dark and smelled like fresh flowers. Guests mingled around the wide, terra-cotta-tiled space, some gazing at the black-and-white photos on the walls, some chatting with one another, others scoping out the crowd. Everyone wore sleek gowns, chic party dresses, and dapper suits. There were clusters of people surrounding three awestruck guys who looked like they were in their twenties, probably the artists. A jazz band played an Ella Fitzgerald song, and waitresses in simple black sheaths swirled around with trays of canapés and drinks. A couple of guests glanced at Emma and Ethan curiously, but Emma tried to stand as straight and confidently as she could.

"Stuffed shrimp?" a waitress asked as she floated past. Emma and Ethan each took a treat.

A second waitress materialized, offering them flutes of champagne. "Of course," Ethan said, taking two glasses and handing one to Emma. The crystal sparkled, and the bubbles rose to the top of the glass.

Champagne. How I wished I could have one tiny, beyond-the-grave sip.

"Cheers," Ethan said, offering his glass in a toast.

Emma clinked her champagne flute to his. "How did you know about this?"

A slight flush crawled up Ethan's neck. "Oh, I just came across it online."

Warmth spread through Emma's chest as she imagined Ethan sitting at his computer, scrolling through events they could attend together.

They walked toward the artwork. Around each photograph was a large black square frame. Small beams of light from the ceiling illuminated each image. The first photo was of a long, straight road as seen from the inside of a car. It was printed in black archival pigment ink on cotton paper, and there was something haunting about the dark trees and eerily lit sky. Emma glanced at the small placard off to the side. Besides listing the artist's name, it also showed the price. Three thousand dollars. *Whoa.*

"So I haven't told you the latest," Emma whispered as they moved to the next photo, a triptych of desert vistas. The champagne tickled her throat, and she felt increasingly aware of how close Ethan stood to her as he examined each photo. To outsiders, they probably looked like boyfriend and girlfriend. She took another sip of champagne. "I'm almost positive Sutton was with the Twitter Twins at Clique on the night she died."

Ethan lowered his glass from his lips. "What makes you say that?"

Emma explained the conversation she'd had at Madeline's house on Saturday. "It's too much of a coincidence. They had to be the friends Sutton was with when she shoplifted. And what if they . . ." She looked away, fixating on a fire extinguisher mounted to the wall across the room.

"Gabby and Lili, killers?" Ethan tilted his head and squinted as if trying to picture it. "Those two are definitely off-kilter, that's for sure. They have been for years."

Emma skirted around an enormous potted plant with spidery leaves to get to the next photo. "Part of me thinks they're too vapid to pull it off."

"They're the poster girls for vapid," Ethan agreed. "But whatever happened to Gabby on the night of the train prank gives them motive."

"And maybe that ditzy-girl act is just that—an act," Emma said. She'd certainly known fake ditzes before, like her foster sister, Sela, who acted like the quintessential dumb blonde in front of their foster parents but sold pot out of an abandoned split-level at the back of the neighborhood.

"They're good actresses, then." Ethan walked to another photograph. "Did anyone tell you that Gabby ran over Lili's foot last year with their dad's Beemer?"

"No . . ."

"And then when Lili came home with a cast on, apparently Gabby was like, 'Oh my *God*! What happened to you?'"

Emma giggled. "She did not!"

"There's another story about Gabby somehow locking herself inside her gym locker in ninth grade." Ethan paused to take another canapé from the tray. "I didn't even know someone could *fit* inside one of those. And when we were in junior high? Someone caught Lili and Gabby talking in British voices on the playground, calling each other 'Miss Lili Tallywacker' and 'Gabby Pony Baloney.' They had no idea the terms were slang for penis; they just thought they sounded funny. They didn't live that down for a long time."

Emma almost coughed up a mouthful of champagne. "Oh my God."

"But despite all that, something tells me you shouldn't write them off so easily," Ethan said. "You should be careful around them, figure out what they know."

Emma nodded. "Madeline and the others want to prank them. But I think it's a terrible idea."

"I'd stay away from that plan. If they are the killers, the

last thing you want to do is piss them off more."

The AC clicked on, and the air suddenly felt chilly. The band played something more appropriate for a 1920s speakeasy, and a couple of the drunker attendees started to dance. Ethan waved his hands around his face to dispel a cloud of cigar smoke.

They were quiet as they moved to the next set of photographs. It was a collage of Polaroids, each depicting different body parts: eyes, noses, feet, ears. "I love Polaroids," Ethan said.

"Me, too," Emma answered, relieved at the change in subject. "My mom gave me a Polaroid camera when I was little, before she took off."

"Do you miss her?" Ethan asked.

Emma fingered the stem of her champagne glass. "It's been so long," she said vaguely. "I hardly remember what there is to miss."

"What do you think happened to her?"

"Oh, I don't know." Emma sighed and moved past a clump of patrons talking loudly about how they'd all been friends with Andy Warhol back in the glory days of the art scene. "A long time ago, I used to think she was still nearby, watching me. Following me from home to home, staying close to make sure I was okay. But I know now how stupid that was."

"It's not stupid."

Emma stared intently at the price list on the wall as though she were thinking of making a purchase. "No, it is. Becky left me. She made a choice; I can't change that."

"Hey." Ethan turned Emma to face him. For a moment, he just stared at her, which sent a thousand butterflies flapping through Emma's stomach. Then, he reached out and tucked a stray lock of hair behind her ear. "She made the wrong choice. You know that, right?"

A swell of emotions washed over Emma. "Thank you," she said quietly, staring into his round blue eyes.

"*Kiss him,*" I whispered, feeling like the singing hermit crab in *The Little Mermaid*. I was all out of my own first kisses, so I had to root for Emma now.

A woman in a magenta dress bumped into Emma. "Sorry," she slurred, her eyes glazed and her cheeks a boozy red. And Emma pulled away, giggling.

"So how do you know so much about crashing art openings?" Emma said, smoothing the front of Sutton's dress. "I thought you were anti-party."

Ethan strolled to a bank of windows at the back of the gallery that overlooked a stone terrace festooned with Christmas lights. "I'm not. I'm just against the kind of party with spiked punch and body shots. It's so . . ."

"Juvenile?" Emma filled in for him. "But sometimes that's a part of having a social life. Sometimes you just have to grin and bear it to have friends."

Ethan drained his glass of champagne and set it on a side table. "If that's the price I have to pay, then I'd rather be alone."

"What about girlfriends?" she asked nervously. She'd wracked her brain for days, thinking of how to ask him this.

A tiny smile danced across Ethan's lips. "Yeah, I've had a few of those."

"Anyone I know?"

Ethan just shrugged and sank into one of the angular leather chairs that could've been an art exhibit themselves.

"Were any of them serious?" Emma pressed as she settled next to him and cradled a soft, overstuffed pillow.

"One was. But it's over now. What about you?" His gaze canvassed her face. "Did you leave anyone behind in Vegas?"

"Not exactly." Emma stared at her lap. "I had some boyfriends, but nothing was too serious. And then there was this one guy, but . . ."

"But what?"

Emma's throat tightened. "It ended up being nothing."

She hated lying, but she didn't want to get into her embarrassing fiasco with Russ Brewer, whom she'd made the mistake of liking. After he'd asked her out, she'd prepared for the date, borrowing a dress from Alex, wearing the last-season Kate Spade shoes she'd scored at Goodwill, rewashing and restyling her hair three times to get it right. But when she'd gone to the mall entrance, Russ wasn't there. Instead it was his ex-girlfriend, Addison Westerberg, and her posse, their laughs high, horrible cackles. *As if Russ would date the foster girl?* they'd teased. It had been a setup. Not, in fact, unlike a Lying Game prank.

Ethan opened his mouth, perhaps to say more, but suddenly his eyes widened at something behind them. "Shit." He leaned forward and clamped down on Emma's arm.

Emma swung around and stared. Nisha Banerjee, dressed in a high-neck black dress and snakeskin heels, stood by a huge photograph of a mostly naked man. Her father was next to her, glancing around with a blank look on his face.

"Oh my God," Emma whispered. Just then, Nisha turned and stared right at her and Ethan. A chicken satay skewer dangled from her fingers, forgotten.

"Come on." Before she could think, Emma grabbed Ethan's hand and pulled him through the crowd. She ditched her champagne flute in a big trash barrel and wound around the guests, nearly upending a waitress's tray of cheese puffs. A man in a blue ruffled suit and a teal cowboy hat sneered at them over his martini, as though they were two children escaping the scene of a school-yard scuffle. But Mr. Tuxedo opened the double doors for them placidly, as though he saw people fleeing from art openings all the time. They scurried down the stairs into the twinkling Tucson night.

Only when Emma had safely reached the street did she turn around to see if Nisha had followed them. There was no one at the entrance.

Ethan straightened his jacket and wiped a bead of sweat off his brow. All of a sudden, Emma burst into giggles. Ethan chuckled, too.

After a moment, she grew serious. "Nisha definitely saw us." Emma flopped on a green city bench and heaved a sigh.

"Who cares?" Ethan asked. He sat down, too.

"*I* care," Emma answered. "She'll tell my parents I snuck out."

"Are you sure that's all that's bothering you?" Ethan glanced at her out of the corner of his eye. "You wouldn't mind if she saw us . . . together?"

Emma's stomach flipped over. "No, of course not. Would you?"

Ethan stared at her without blinking. "What do you think?"

Jazz music drifted out from the party. Across the street, a stray cat darted between the tires of a parked car. Ethan moved a little closer so that their legs touched. Emma wanted so badly to kiss him, but her body trembled with nerves.

"Ethan . . ." She turned away.

Ethan laid his hands in his lap. "Okay, am I misinterpreting things?" He sounded both sheepish and annoyed. "Because sometimes it seems like you really want to . . . you know. But then you always pull back."

"It's . . . complicated," Emma said, trying to keep her voice steady.

"How?"

Emma bit her fingernail. She'd always wanted a serious boyfriend. Back in Vegas, she'd even named a star in the sky the Boyfriend Star, hoping it was a sign that she'd finally meet the person with whom she was meant to be. But now she was torn.

"It's this life I'm living right now," Emma started hesitantly, a lump hardening in her throat. "I love being with you. You make me laugh, and you're the only person I can be myself with—my *real* self. I'm Sutton to everyone else."

Ethan glanced up to meet Emma's gaze. His eyes were huge and imploring, but he waited for her to go on. "I'm pretending to be a dead girl, Ethan," she said. "And I'm being threatened, and you're the only person who knows about it. I don't have my own life right now, which makes this . . . bad timing." She'd always thought excuses like "bad timing" were made up, occupying the same file as "It's not you, it's me." But this was real. She did have feelings for Ethan, strong ones, but she didn't know how to be with him when her life was in such upheaval. "And what if we start something and it ends badly? What if we get in a fight? Then I'll have no one again." She wrung her hands in her lap. "Maybe, when I'm finally free of all this we can . . ." She trailed off.

Finally, Ethan exhaled loudly. A frown marred his lips. "Are you saying that if we got into a fight, if we broke up, I'd abandon you? Do you really think I'd do that?"

Emma raised her palms to the air. "Breakups can be ugly." Then she sighed. "I like you so much. But there are so few people I can trust—and you're the only one I can rely on. I can't jeopardize that. Not now."

Ethan turned away, saying nothing. Emma stared at the parked cars across the street. A cleaning service called Clean Machine had stuck flyers under each of the windshields. A convertible cruised by with its radio blasting hip-hop.

"I think we need to keep it as friends," Emma whispered into the darkness, afraid to look at Ethan head-on. "At least until I can figure out this mess and live my own life again."

Next to her, Emma felt Ethan's body slump from the weight of her words. "If you think that's best," he said slowly.

"I do," Emma insisted in the strongest voice she could manage.

Without answering, Ethan rose and reached into his pocket for his car keys. Emma followed behind him to the Honda, feeling like someone had scooped out her insides with a big ladle. Had she just ruined everything?

As she swung into the passenger seat, a crackling sound made her turn. Her eyes scanned the dark road. Then, she spied something moving in the bushes across the street near the bench where they'd been sitting. The cherry-red tip of a lit cigarette glowed in the darkness. It dangled, disembodied, as though held by a ghost.

"Ethan," she whispered, grabbing his arm. But as soon as Ethan twisted around to look, the spooky burning cigarette vanished.

16

AN A FOR EFFORT

After tennis practice the following day, Emma threw her gear into the hatchback of Laurel's VW. *"Ahem,"* Laurel whispered, nudging Emma's side. "Looks like you have an anti–fan club."

Emma swung around, and her stomach dropped. Two figures stared from the gym doorway, their mouths angry red slashes. It was Nisha . . . and *Garrett*.

"Do you think she's still pissed about you sneaking into her room?" Laurel asked.

"I doubt it," Emma said slowly. It more likely had to do with Nisha seeing Emma and Ethan at the art opening last night. Thankfully, Nisha hadn't called up the Mercer parents to rat her out, but it seemed she'd just spilled the beans to Garrett. Why else would he look at Emma with such fury?

"Let's get out of here," Emma mumbled, slamming the car door.

As Laurel plopped into the driver's seat, her phone screen flashed. "It's Mads," she said, checking the message. "Looks like Operation *Titanic* is good to go. I told the other girls on the court about the *real* outfits. I also told them not to discuss their outfits with anyone—that we were planning to prank two of the court members."

Emma's stomach turned, thinking about her discussion with Ethan last night. "Are you *sure* this is a good idea? Maybe we should lay off the Twitter Twins for a while."

Laurel's eyebrows made a *V.* "Of course it's a good idea. We can't back out now. Besides," Laurel went on, "I can guarantee you no one's gonna talk. They're all eager to see someone else go down. Everyone loves a big embarrassing social disaster."

Way to go, court girls, banding together in solidarity, Emma thought. An itchy feeling reminded her that she was once the girl on the receiving end of the prank. When this was all over, she would extricate herself from the Lying Game as fast as she could.

The car jostled over the hump of the curb into the

Mercers' driveway. "Is that . . . Dad?" Laurel asked, frowning at the open garage door.

Sure enough, Mr. Mercer stood next to the motorcycle. He waved as they pulled in.

"What's *he* doing home?" Emma murmured. Typically, Mr. Mercer didn't return from the hospital until early evening—unless he was on call, and then sometimes he didn't get home until the middle of the night.

Laurel cut the engine, and the girls got out of the car. "Sutton, I have to talk to you," Mr. Mercer said, wiping his hands on a dingy green towel.

Immediately, Emma tensed. Maybe Nisha *had* told the Mercers after all. "I'm sorry," she said preemptively.

"You don't even know what I'm going to say yet." Mr. Mercer chuckled. "Your mom got a call from Josephine Fenstermacher. She said you got a ninety-nine on your German test last week. The highest grade in the class."

Heat rose to Emma's cheeks. Laurel swung around and stared at her in disbelief. "*You?*"

Mr. Mercer grinned. "She said you've improved dramatically since last year. I know German is a tough subject for you. Mom and I are so proud."

Emma ran a hand over her hair. Truthfully, the chapter test had been fairly easy, but she forced a humble look on her face. "Thank you."

Mr. Mercer leaned against the back bumper of Laurel's

VW. "I convinced your mom to make you a deal: As a reward for doing so well, we're going to break your grounding for Homecoming night and let you go to the dance. And we're giving you phone privileges back," he said, handing over Sutton's iPhone.

"Seriously?" Laurel's eyes lit up. "Dad, that's amazing!"

Emma squeezed Laurel's arm and let out a squeal, too, knowing it was the right reaction for Sutton. But Homecoming was the last thing that mattered to her right now.

Mr. Mercer raised an eyebrow. "You can go, but the very next day it's back to being grounded. Got it?"

"What about the post-dance camping trip?" Laurel chirped. "Can Sutton come to that, too?"

A conflicted look passed over Mr. Mercer's face. "Well, I suppose so."

"Yes!" Laurel cried. She looked at Emma. "Maybe you'll let me borrow your Miu Miu heels for the dance as a thank-you." Then she turned and skipped toward the house.

Emma moved to follow her inside, but Mr. Mercer cleared his throat. "Sutton, will you help me for a moment?" He turned toward the motorcycle. "Can you hold this steady while I look at the tires?"

"Of course." Emma followed him into the garage and gripped the handlebars.

Mr. Mercer leaned down and examined the fine tread on the front wheel. "So. Happy about Homecoming?"

"Uh, definitely," Emma answered, trying to sound enthused. "Thank you so much. But . . . I don't really deserve it." She mentally ticked off the number of times she'd snuck out while she was grounded.

"You earned it, Sutton. Thank yourself for your test score—and thank your sister, for begging us to let you go." Mr. Mercer stood from the tire and crossed his arms over his chest. "You should call Garrett and tell him the good news."

Emma let out a short, sarcastic laugh, staring at her warped reflection in the bike's shiny frame. "I don't think Garrett will care."

Mr. Mercer frowned. "Why not?"

Emma turned toward the shelves of rags, T-shirts, and bottles of motor oil and brake fluid. "We broke up," she admitted softly. "And I sort of like someone else," she added, surprised by her own words. She thought this would be another thing to add to the Things That Are Awkward list, but she actually felt almost relieved to admit the truth aloud. Opening up to adults wasn't something she'd ever done before, and by the cautious look on Mr. Mercer's face, it wasn't usual for Sutton either.

"Does this someone else know?" Mr. Mercer sounded intrigued.

"Sort of." Emma's voice cracked, wincing at the memory of the art museum date. It had been so . . . *perfect*. But then she remembered the look on Ethan's face when he told her how he felt about her, and the utter disappointment in his eyes when she said they should just be friends. The tight feeling that had formed in her chest the moment those words had spilled out of her mouth still hadn't gone away.

"Are you and this new guy . . . going out?" Mr. Mercer used the term tentatively, as though he wasn't sure if it was the right lingo.

Emma reached for a clean rag from the metal garage shelves and twisted it into a knot. When she untied it and spread it out, she saw a faded silkscreened image of a crab and a clam dancing the tango. It advertised either a restaurant or a fish market; the lettering was too worn away to tell which.

"No," Emma answered in a tired voice. "Things are . . . complicated."

"Why is that?"

She shut her eyes. "I'm having a hard time trusting people, I guess."

A pained look Emma couldn't quite gauge crossed Mr. Mercer's face. "You should trust people, Sutton. You shouldn't let . . ."

Emma waited for him to finish, but Mr. Mercer just

twisted his mouth and looked away. "Let what?" she finally asked.

"I just mean . . ." He fumbled through his tools. They made loud clanging noises as they banged together. "I only want what's best for you. If it's meant to be, honey, it's meant to be."

"Maybe," Emma said thoughtfully. His wording made her think of the Boyfriend Star, burning brightly in the sky. *Fate.*

Then, placing the rag back on the shelf, she padded over to Mr. Mercer and wrapped her arms around his shoulders. Mr. Mercer held her tentatively for a moment, as if he wasn't sure the gesture was genuine. But then, slowly, he squeezed her hard. He smelled like cologne, black pepper, and motor oil.

It was a smell I knew so, so well. A wave of grief pounded my body until I felt like I would wash away. What I wouldn't give to hug my dad one more time. As I watched their embrace, a dark image surfaced in my mind. My dad's eyes widening when he turned and spotted me. Betrayal surging through me like he'd driven a stake through my heart. But before I could delve deeper into the memory, it submerged once more.

17

X MARKS THE SPOT

Thursday afternoon, during the last period of the school day, Emma, Charlotte, and Madeline stood backstage in the auditorium, dressed in black cocktail dresses and high heels. Old play props and sets, abandoned scripts from last year's production of *Oklahoma!,* and several full-length mirrors were littered in the otherwise barren space, but the situation on the other side of the curtain was another story. That morning, with the help of the committee's party planners, the girls had transformed the stage into an elegant, ghostly replica of the *Titanic,* complete with chandeliers, a sweeping faux-staircase, gilded fixtures, and tables set with fine china.

Emma shook her head in awe. "This is really beauti-ful." It was too bad *this* couldn't be the décor for the dance Friday night. But that would be held in the gym, not the auditorium.

Charlotte paced back and forth, tapping a clipboard. Her type-A personality made her the perfect detail-organizer. "Okay," she said. "So after everyone files into the audito-rium, we'll announce the court nominees' names. They'll walk in and waltz with their escorts. The party will last until the late bus is called."

Madeline gestured to the caterers in white uniforms scurrying around backstage and setting chrome tureens, platters, pitchers, and glasses on a long folding table. "We've got sparkling cider, hors d'oeuvres, cheeses. Non-dairy stuff for Norah, gluten-free stuff for Madison."

"And don't forget about Alicia Young," Laurel said, smoothing a nonexistent wrinkle on her cocktail dress. "She's on that grapefruit-and-cayenne-pepper cleanse."

Charlotte looked like she was going to explode. "That diet is nasty. She's just going to have to suffer."

A pang overcame me as I watched the preparations. I vaguely remembered planning last year's Homecoming Court party. The theme and decorations were no more than wisps, but I remembered the moment I'd stepped out to announce the winners, knowing I looked more glam-orous than all of them combined. And I remembered a faceless guy—my date—catching my arm afterward and telling me that I was the most gorgeous girl on the stage. "I know," I'd replied, shooting him one of my signature Sutton Mercer smiles.

Sharp, staccato, high-heeled *clack*s filled the room as court girls filed in, each with a black garment bag slung over her arm and perfectly styled hair piled atop her head or cascading down her back in soft ringlets. They oohed and ahhed over the set design, letting out little gasps and appreciative squeals. Gabby and Lili entered last, noses in the air, hairdos bigger and bouncier than anyone else's. Emma turned away fast and pretended to fix a frayed ribbon on one of the tables, but she could still feel their eyes burning on her.

"Gabby! Lili!" Laurel shot across the room and linked her elbows through the Twins'. "Let me show you your dressing rooms! We ran out of room down here, so you guys get to change upstairs in the lighting booth."

Gabby extracted herself from Laurel's grip. "Lemme just finish my tweet, 'kay?"

Laurel rolled her eyes and waited while Gabby's thumbs flew across her phone at warp speed. When Gabby finished, she let out a satisfied sigh. "We're ready to be taken to our chambers now," she said in a queen-like voice. As Laurel steered them up a staircase, both twins leveled stares at Emma. Laurel twisted around, too, signaling a covert thumbs-up to Madeline and Charlotte.

"Okay, girls!" Charlotte clapped her hands and drew the rest of the court members into a circle. "You all need to get changed for your big entrance! People are filing in here in ten minutes. Don't forget heels and a fresh coat of gloss! And remember, the makeup artist is going to come and put blood in your hair and paint blue circles under your eyes."

The girls pouted. "Do we really have to do that?" Tinsley Zimmerman whined.

"Yes," Charlotte answered sharply, her slight smirk revealing just how much she loved being the boss.

Tinsley eyed Charlotte's party dress. "*You're* not wearing corpse makeup. We'll look uglier than you!"

That's the point, I thought.

"It'll make you look avant-garde and chic," Madeline said, sounding like a fashion editor. "You're dead beauties of the *Titanic*. You drowned in the ocean. How do you *think* you should look? Like a Bobbi Brown spring campaign?" She gestured to a bunch of dressing rooms at the back. "Now go change!"

The court girls turned, giving one another cryptic, I-know-something-you-don't smiles, reminding Emma that none of them knew exactly who was getting pranked today. Tinsley slammed a dressing room door shut before anyone could join her. Alicia Young—she of the nasty cleanse diet—ducked into a tiny, curtained-off alcove to change. Madison Cates looked around furtively, then slipped into the shadows and pulled a black sequined gown over her stiff hair. The other girls disappeared as well. When they emerged from their respective dressing rooms in their black gowns, their faces registered notes of surprise.

"I was hoping the joke was on you," Tinsley, who wore a strapless gown, said to Norah Alvarez.

"Well, I hoped it was on *you*," Norah snapped back, smoothing the feather collar on her flapper dress.

Makeup artists whirled around, swiping each girl's mouth with corpse-blue lipstick. Emma leaned toward Charlotte. "So we're sure Gabby and Lili don't suspect anything?"

Charlotte glanced at the dressing room on the second floor. The door was shut tight. "Last I checked, they had no clue." Pulling a walkie-talkie from her hip, she pressed TALK. "How's everything going, Laurel?"

"Great!" Laurel's voice blared fuzzily through the speaker. "I'm just helping Gabby and Lili get dressed. They look fabulous!"

A crafty smile appeared on Charlotte's lips. "Perfect. We need them down here in five minutes, okay? Stay up there until then. We'll send the makeup artists up."

"Aye aye!"

When Laurel radioed off, Charlotte rubbed her hands together. "We need to keep them up there until the very second they have to go on stage. They'll have no time to change."

Madeline joined them, giggling. "This is going to be *so* good."

"I hope so." Charlotte stared at the velvet curtain that separated the back stage from the front, a serious look suddenly crossing her face. "Just as long as we don't land Gabby in the hospital again."

Madeline stiffened. "*We* didn't land Gabby in the hospital. *Sutton* did."

Both of them turned and glanced at Emma. Emma felt a sharp punch to her stomach. They had to be talking about the train prank. She waited for either of them to elaborate, but Madeline started fiddling with her clipboard and Charlotte strode away.

The final bell rang, and the doors to the lobby flung open. Emma peeked out from behind the curtains. Students poured down the center aisle and filled the plush red seats. Freshman girls gaped at the *Titanic* set, squealing about how they couldn't wait until *they* were old enough to be on the court. A group of girls Madeline and the others called the Vegan Virgins—for reasons Emma wasn't entirely sure of, though she had a pretty good guess—plopped down next to a couple of the corpses and screamed. The entire football team sat together, shoving one another and jockeying for attention. Nearly everyone in the audience pulled their phones from their bags and sneakily checked the screens.

Charlotte's words swirled in Emma's mind. *Just as long as we don't land Gabby in the hospital again.* What exactly happened that night? Had Sutton hurt Gabby? The message in the box with the train charm flooded back: *I will always be seized with the memory.*

"Showtime!" Charlotte scurried to the court nominees, who were all inspecting their drowning-victim makeup in the full-length mirrors. Emma let the curtain close and stared at the ceiling, as though she could see straight up to the Twitter Twins' dressing room. "Everyone line up! I'm going to announce you to the school in a couple of minutes!" The six non-prank court girls found their dates, six cute guys who looked absolutely mortified to be in tuxedos.

Charlotte glanced over her shoulder, waving her hands around like an air traffic controller. "Mads, you're going to welcome the crowd. Sutton, you'll enter from stage left—your mark is a big *X* on the floor—with all the Homecoming Court sashes for the girls and guys. I'll come in from stage right. Sutton, can you open the box of sashes? They're by the mirrors. *Sutton?*"

Emma blinked, breaking out of her trance. "Uh-huh."

She walked toward the box of sashes to the left of the stage.

Laurel's voice crackled over the walkie-talkie. "Uh, Mads? Can we come down now?"

Madeline checked her watch. "No! I need you to stay up there for a little while longer."

"Uh . . ." Feedback screeched through the walkie-talkie speaker. "Actually? I'm not sure that's possible."

The door to the lighting booth flung open, and the Twitter Twins appeared on the landing. They were dressed in skimpy string bikinis and tall silver stilettos. Their tanned skin gleamed. Their legs stretched for miles. But they also looked naked compared to the glamorous court girls in their gowns. Laurel stood behind them, shooting a helpless look to Charlotte, Madeline, and Emma on the ground. "I tried!" she mouthed.

As Gabby and Lili pranced down the stairs with proud, pageant-queen smiles on their faces, Emma was able to pinpoint the exact moment they noticed the other court nominees in their gowns. Their mouths dropped. They halted in their place. Norah nudged Madison. Alicia began to giggle. Everyone was suddenly in on the joke.

"Priceless," Charlotte murmured excitedly.

"Sweet," Madeline whispered, arching onto her toes in anticipation of the reveal to the crowd.

Emma tensed, waiting for their reaction. But the

scantily clad Twitter Twins simply shared a private look, then Lili marched to a dark alcove at the back of the room. "Fear not, Gabs!"

She unearthed a wrinkled Saks shopping bag from the nook, a bag that had clearly been planted hours—if not days—before. Tissue paper crinkled as she reached her hand inside and pulled out two slinky black dresses.

Charlotte and Madeline gaped at each other, while Laurel looked sheepishly on.

"Where did these Yigal Azrouël wrinkle-free jersey dresses come from?" Gabby said in exaggerated wonder. "And, wow! They're even in our size!"

The Twitter Twins slipped the dresses over their heads, whipped around, and glowered at Charlotte, Madeline, Laurel, and Emma. "Nice try," Lili said icily as one of the makeup artists rushed to her and swiped blue shadow under her eyes. "We could see your lame trick from a mile away."

Gabby turned to Emma. "We're not as stupid as we look, *Sutton*. You of all people should know that."

Emma pressed a hand to her chest. "I never said you were stupid."

A sarcastic snort escaped from Gabby's mouth. "*Right.*" Without averting her gaze, she marched up to Emma, reached into the Saks bag, and pulled out a pill bottle with the same pink top Emma had noticed the other day. The prescription name, written in bold black letters, flashed before Emma's eyes. TOPAMAX. Emma flinched. She'd been sure Gabby was popping Ritalin or Valium or some other party drug. But Topamax sounded serious.

Gabby removed the top and shook two capsules into her hands. She belted them down without water. After she swallowed, she shook the medicine bottle like a casta-net, her eyes on Emma once more. "Don't you think you should get our sashes and take your place now, Sutton?" she said in a taunting voice. "You're at stage left, right?"

For a moment, Emma couldn't move. It was like Gabby had cast a spell on her, paralyzing all her limbs. Charlotte nudged her side. "This blows, but she's right. It's time to go. Places, girls!"

"One sec!" Lili shouted, heading for the stairs to the lighting booth once more. "I forgot my iPhone!"

"You don't *need* your iPhone!" Madeline growled. "You're going to be busy onstage!"

But Lili didn't slow down, her heels clacking on the metal stairs. "It'll just take a second."

The door to the lighting booth slammed. Emma turned, grabbed sixteen orange silk Homecoming Court sashes, and found the X on the side of the stage where she was supposed to stand, behind a side curtain and com-pletely isolated from the rest of the court and planners. "Pull the curtain!" Charlotte commanded.

The crowd's murmurings grew louder. The court nominees, save for Lili, who was still upstairs, did a few last minute hair-fluffs and blush-brush sweeps. But when Emma looked past the blinding floodlights to the stage, Gabby was staring at her with a whisper of a smile on her face. In her corpse makeup, blue circles under her eyes, stitches across her cheeks, bloody gashes on her neck, she looked menacing. Evil.

Emma took a step back. And then she noticed something else, something she hadn't seen before: a silver charm brace-let hung from Gabby's wrist. Tiny objects dangled from the chain—a little iPhone, a tube of lipstick, a mini Scottie dog. They were made out of the same silver as the miniature locomotive engine that rested snugly in Emma's purse.

A chill came over me and Emma. The Twitter Twins had killed me. I could *feel* it.

"Greetings, Hollier High!" Madeline boomed into the microphone, so loudly it made Emma jump. "Everyone ready for Homecoming?"

A cheer rose up, and Lady Gaga's "Paparazzi" blasted out of the speakers. The noise was so thunderous that Emma barely heard the snaps of cords breaking above her head. By the time she looked up, the heavy light fixture in the rafters was hurtling swiftly toward her. She screamed and jumped away just as it crashed to the ground with an earsplitting crack.

Amber glass spewed everywhere. Someone yelled—
maybe Emma herself. She felt her body go limp and fall to
the ground, the court sashes slipping from her grasp and
landing on the hard floor. Just before her eyes fluttered
closed, she saw Lili join Gabby in the wings. Emma tried
to call out, to maintain consciousness, but she felt herself
slipping away. Gabby shook the pill bottle up and down,
up and down. It sounded like chattering teeth.

The noise reminded me of something else entirely. A
tiny pinhole opened in my mind, slowly widening. The
world began to whirl like I was on an out-of-control car-
ousel. I didn't hear pills shaking in a bottle anymore. I
heard, distinctly and most definitely, a commuter train
clacking noisily over the tracks. . . .

18

TREMORS AND TREACHERY
AND THREATS, OH MY!

"Where is Gabby?" Lili shrieks as the train whooshes past.

I whirl around, frantically checking the tracks. I planned it all so carefully. There's no way Gabby could have rolled under the train . . . right?

Then Laurel steps a few feet away and points a trembling finger at a crumpled figure by the curved walls of the underpass. It's Gabby. Her blonde hair covers most of her face. Her pale hand splays open, her crystal-studded iPhone turned over on a patch of gravel.

"What the hell?" Madeline cries.

"Gabby!" Lili screams, running to her.

"Gabby?" I stand over her limp body. *"Gabs?"*

A sudden tremor travels from Gabby's fingertips to her shoulders. Tiny pricks of spit dot her lips, and then her entire body starts convulsing. The train barrels on, rattling my teeth and blowing my hair. Gabby shakes harder and faster. Her arms and legs have minds of their own, jolting in random directions. Her eyes roll to the back of her head like she's some kind of zombie.

"Gabby?" I scream. "Gabs? Come on! This isn't funny!"

Suddenly, a black man with a carefully trimmed goatee and an earring in one ear nudges me out of the way. I catch sight of a blue jumpsuit with a glow-in-the-dark badge. PIMA COUNTY EMT. I hadn't even realized the ambulance had roared up, but there it is, a big white vehicle with whirling red lights on the top.

"What happened?" the medic asks, crouching next to Gabby.

"I have no idea!" Lili pushes in front of me. Her mouth is a triangle, her eyes wide and desperate. "What's wrong with her?"

"She's having a seizure." The medic shines a light into Gabby's eyes, but there's no color there, only two orbs that look like shiny white marbles. "Has this ever happened before?"

"No!" Lili looks around frantically, as if she doesn't believe this is real.

The EMT rolls Gabby onto one side and puts his ear next to her mouth to see if she's breathing, but he just lets her lie there, flailing. She moves like one of those cartoon characters who touch a live wire and light up like Christmas trees, white skeletons showing through skin. I want to look away, but I can't.

"Can't you do something for her?" Lili screams, tugging at

the EMT's sleeve. "Anything? What if she's dying?"

"I need you girls to get back," the EMT barks. "I need some space to treat her."

Cars swish by us on the highway. Some slow down and gawk, curious about the ambulance lights and the girl lying in the underpass, but no one stops. Tears stream down Lili's face. She spins toward me, her eyes on fire. "I can't believe you did this to her!"

"I didn't do anything!" I scream through a clenched jaw.

"Yes, you did! This is all your fault!"

The train's fading whistle drowns out Lili's words. I refuse to feel guilty for this. It wasn't like I even wanted the Twitter Twins to come tonight. How was I supposed to know Gabby was going to get so freaked she'd fall into a convulsive fit? All of a sudden, I'm so sick of the Twitter Twins I can barely breathe. "I didn't want you two along tonight," I say through my teeth. "I knew you couldn't handle it."

The red and blue ambulance lights streak across Lili's face. "You could have killed all of us!"

"Oh please." I ball up my fists. "I had it under control the whole time!"

"How were we supposed to know that?" Lili shrieks. "We thought we were going to die! You have no concept of other people's feelings! You just . . . you just treat us like toys, doing whatever you want, whenever you want!"

"Watch what you say," I warn her, aware of the medics around us.

"Or what?" Lili asks, turning to Madeline, who stands off to the side with a blank face. "You agree with me, don't you, Madeline?" Lili says. "Sutton's a user. Do you really think she gives a shit about our feelings—about anyone's feelings? Look at how she toyed with your brother! She's the reason he left!"

"That's not true!" I scream, lunging toward Lili. How dare she bring up Thayer! As if she had any idea what things were really like between us!

Charlotte pulls me back before I can tackle Lili. More medics have gathered around Gabby, and a debate has begun over whether to move her or keep her where she is. Lili turns away from us and peers over the EMT's shoulder at her sister. An oppressive, July-hot wind kicks up, blowing bits of trash along the ground. A Skittles wrapper plasters itself to Gabby's twitching legs. A cigarette butt rolls dangerously close to one of her hands.

A low, keening wail sounds in the distance: a second set of sirens. We all stand up straighter when we realize it's a police car. My heart begins to race, sweat dripping down my body.

I clear my throat and face my friends, my voice low and steady. "We cannot tell the cops what really happened. The car stalled for real, okay? This was just an accident."

Madeline, Charlotte, and Laurel look a little sickened, but Gabby's condition has weakened them. They aren't thinking of defying me anymore. And even though I violated a sacred Lying Game code, there's another set-in-stone tenet we all live by: If we ever get caught mid-prank, we stick together. When Laurel almost got busted messing with the twelve-foot holiday tree at La Encantada, we swore up and down she'd been home with us. When Madeline broke her wrist running from security the weekend we dragged the library tables into a ravine, we told her dad she'd fallen hiking. They'll forgive me for falsely invoking our fail-safe code. We'll get through this. We always do.

But Lili looks at me like I'm nuts. "You seriously expect me to lie for you?" She sets her hands on her hips. "I'm telling the cops what you did!"

"Your choice," I say calmly. "But whatever is going on with your freaky sister has nothing to do with me, and you know it. If you tell the cops—if you tell anyone—you'll regret it."

Lili's eyes widen. "Is that a threat?"

My face hardens to a mask of stone. "Call it what you want. If you tell, we'll have no reason to be friends anymore. Things will change for you, big-time, and they'll change for your sister, too." I step so close to Lili I can feel her warm breath on my face. "Lili," I say, speaking slowly so that she can understand every last word. "When Gabby wakes up, perfectly fine, and finds out that you've just made the two of you the biggest losers at Hollier, do you think she's going to thank you for doing the right thing? Do you think she's going to see you as a hero?"

Everyone is silent. Behind us, Gabby is being strapped to a stretcher. My friends shift back and forth, but I know they're not surprised. We've done this before. Lili's nostrils flare in and out.

Her eyes burn with anger. I stare back. There's no way I'll crack first.

We remain in deadlock until the police cruiser roars up in a cloud of desert dust. Two cops, one stocky with a pencil-thin moustache and the other red-haired and freckled, get out of the car and walk toward us.

"Ladies?" The redhead removes a notepad from his pocket. His walkie-talkie beeps every few seconds. "What's going on here?"

Lili whips around to face him, and for a moment, I think she's actually going to spill everything. But then her bottom lip starts to tremble. The EMTs pass us, carrying Gabby to the ambulance. "Where are you taking her?" Lili calls after them.

"Oro Valley Hospital," one of the EMTs answers.

"I-is she going to be okay?" Lili asks, her shaking voice swallowed by the wind. No one answers her. Lili catches them before they shut the back doors. "Can I ride with her? She's my sister."

The cop clears his throat. "You can't go yet, miss. We need you to make a statement."

Lili pauses, her toes pointed toward the ambulance, her body twisted back toward us. A swirl of emotions cross her face in a matter of seconds, and I can practically see her brain racing as she calculates her options. Finally she shrugs, a pure white flag of surrender. "Let them speak for me. It happened to all of us. We were all together."

I exhale.

The cop nods and turns to Madeline, Charlotte, and Laurel and starts his questions. Just after Lili climbs into the ambulance and it turns away, I feel a buzzing in my pocket. I pull out my phone and see a new message on the screen from Lili.

IF THERE'S SOMETHING WRONG WITH MY SISTER, IF SHE DOESN'T MAKE IT, I'M GOING TO KILL YOU.

Whatever, *I think. And then I hit* DELETE.

19

THE WRITING ON THE WALL

At first, Emma could only make out blurry shadows. She heard screams, but it was like they were coming from the end of a long tunnel. A hardwood floor pressed into her back. A musty, closed-up scent assaulted her nostrils. Something wet pooled on her face—she wondered vaguely if it was blood.

Soft fabric brushed up against her bare arm. Breath warmed her skin. "Hello?" Emma struggled to say. It took an enormous effort to form the words. "Hello?" she said again. "Who's there?"

A figure moved away. The floorboards creaked. There was something wrong with Emma's vision. Someone loomed nearby, but all she could see was a black blob. She heard squeaking sounds, smelled chalk dust. What was going on?

A few seconds later, her vision focused. The blob was gone. Sitting in front of her was a large upright chalkboard from an old set. Emma had passed it countless times during the party preparations today, noting that someone had written a quote from *The Glass Menagerie* on it: "Things have a way of turning out so badly." Those words had been wiped away now, and a new message had taken its place. As soon as Emma read the slanted handwriting, her blood went cold.

Stop digging, or next time I'll hurt you for real.

Emma gasped. "Who's there?" she screamed. "Come out!"

"Say something!" I yelled, too, as blind as she was. "We know you're there!"

But whoever had written the note didn't answer. And then the warm, throbbing darkness began to take hold of Emma once more. Her eyes fluttered, and she fought to keep them open. Just before she passed out again, she caught sight of the same blurry figure—or maybe *two* blurry figures—swirling their hands over the chalkboard, wiping the words clean.

The next time Emma opened her eyes, she was lying on a bed in a small white room. An instructional sheet on how to properly wash one's hands hung on the opposite wall. Another poster for how to administer the Heimlich maneuver hung over a small table that contained jars of cotton swabs and boxes of latex gloves.

"Sutton?"

Emma turned toward the voice. Madeline sat on an office chair next to the cot, her knees pressed tightly together, her fingers knotted in her lap. When she saw that Emma was awake, relief flooded her face. "Thank God! Are you okay?"

Emma lifted her arm and pressed it to her forehead. Her limbs felt normal again, not filled with sand like they had as she lay on the stage floor. "What happened?" she croaked. "Where am I?"

"It's all right, dear," said another voice. A lanky woman with dishwater-blond hair cut bluntly to her chin and a pair of tortoiseshell glasses perched on her nose swam into view. She wore a white lab coat that had the words T. GROVE and NURSE stitched on the breast. "It appears you fainted. It was probably from low blood sugar. Have you had anything to eat today?"

"A light fell from the rafters and almost hit you," Madeline said in a shaking voice. "It was crazy—it almost landed on your head!"

Emma squinted, remembering the blurry figure above her. The warning in white chalk. Her heart began to race, thudding so hard against her chest she was scared Madeline and the nurse could hear it. "Did you see someone standing over me when I was lying on the ground? Someone writing something on that chalkboard?"

Madeline narrowed her eyes. "*What* chalkboard?"

"Someone wrote something," Emma insisted. "Are you sure it wasn't Gabby? Lili?"

An expression Emma couldn't read flitted across Madeline's face. "I think you need to rest some more. Gabby and Lili were on the stage when the light fell. The custodian said it was just a freak accident—those lights are super-old." She patted Emma's shoulder. "I'm so sorry to do this, but I have to get back to the auditorium—Charlotte will have my head if I'm not there to help direct the caterers." Madeline stood. "Just take it easy, and I'll check on you when the party's over, okay?"

The bulletin board on the back of the door swung back and forth as Madeline pulled it shut behind her. The nurse murmured that she'd be back in a moment, too, and slipped out another door. In the silence of the tiny room, Emma shut her eyes, leaned back against the cot's rock-hard pillow, and exhaled.

Don't you think you should take your place now, Sutton? Gabby had said just before the ceremony began. *You're at stage left, right?* And then Lili had run back upstairs for her iPhone, right where the light was fastened. And then . . .

crash. The light hit exactly where she was supposed to be standing.

"Emma?"

Emma opened her eyes to see Ethan hovering over her, his dark eyebrows furrowed with concern. He was dressed in a worn olive-green T-shirt, dark-wash jeans, and black Vans that looked as though they'd been through a wood chipper. She felt the heat of his body as he stepped closer. He took her hand, then glanced away, as if unsure whether touching her was okay. Emma hadn't been alone with him since the art opening—since she'd rejected him.

She sat up quickly and smoothed her hair. "Hey," she croaked.

Ethan let go of her hand and dropped down on the black office chair Madeline had just occupied. "I heard a crash backstage. Next thing I know, people were calling your name. What the hell happened?"

A shudder ran through Emma's body as she told him about the light and the note on the chalkboard. When she was finished, Ethan stood up halfway, his arm muscles taut as he held his body inches above the chair. "Is the message still there?"

"No. Someone erased it."

He sank onto the chair again. "There were a ton of people backstage as soon as the crash happened. Someone would've seen all that, don't you think?"

"I know it doesn't make sense. But there was someone there. Someone wrote that message."

He gave her the same look Madeline had. "You've been under a lot of stress. Are you sure it wasn't a dream?"

"It didn't *feel* like a dream." Emma pulled the nurse's blanket tighter around her, feeling sweat from her palms melt into the rough wool. "I think it was the Twins," she said. She hushed her voice and told Ethan about what Charlotte and Madeline had said about Sutton doing something to Gabby that landed her in the hospital. Then she told him about the pill bottle Gabby had removed from the bag. "It was something called Topamax. I've seen Gabby popping pills before, but I always thought it was a party thing. Do you have your phone? I need to Google it."

"Emma," Ethan said, urgency in his voice. "Someone just told you to stop digging."

Emma sniffed. "I thought you didn't believe me about the board."

"Of course I believe you—I just hoped it wasn't true." Ethan's eyes burned a dark blue under the florescent lights. "I think it's time we put an end to this."

Emma ran her hands down the length of her face. "If we stop, that means whoever did this to Sutton will have gotten away with murder." Then she swung her legs over the tiny cot. Blood prickled through her body as she rose to her feet.

"What are you doing?" Ethan exclaimed, watching her

make her way to the filing cabinets along the wall.

"Gabby's medical history will be on file with the school if there's any type of problem," Emma whispered. She yanked open the file cabinet marked E-F and ran her fingers over the worn manila folders until she found FIO-RELLO, GABRIELLA.

Heels clacked along the hallway, and Emma froze, listening as they grew louder and then faded as they passed the nurses office. Emma pulled out Gabby's folder and saw that it was crisper than the others, as if it hadn't done the time to earn worn edges. She thumbed through the contents and let out a low whistle. "Topamax, Gabby's medicine? It's to treat *epilepsy*."

"She has epilepsy?" Ethan narrowed his eyes. "I feel like I would've heard about that."

Emma kept reading. "It says the disease was dormant until July, and that 'an incident triggered the first seizure.'" She raised her eyes to Ethan. "The train prank was in July. What if Sutton caused her epilepsy?"

"Jesus." Ethan's face paled.

Emma slipped the folder back into the drawer and guided it shut with her hip. "The Twitter Twins must have been beyond furious—maybe even angry and crazed enough to plan Sutton's murder."

Ethan's eyes were round. "You think the Twins . . . ?"

"I'm more sure than ever," Emma whispered, her

mind racing. "I'm positive Lili cut the light, too—she ran upstairs to grab her phone right before it fell. And you should've seen the way both the Twins stared at me before I passed out." Goose bumps covered Emma's flesh as she pictured it again. "They looked capable of *anything*."

My mind flashed back to the murderous look in Lili's eyes on the night of the train prank and the text she sent from the ambulance promising revenge if anything was wrong with Gabby. Thank God Emma had stepped aside before the light crashed on her head. She'd been inches away from joining me here in the in-between.

Outside, a flock of birds lifted off from a knot of bushes beneath the nurse's window. Emma paced the floor. "It makes so much sense," she whispered. "Gabby and Lili are Twitter and Facebook masters—they could've easily hacked on to Sutton's page, read that first note from me, and sent one back asking me to come to Tucson and wait at Sabino Canyon. They were with Madeline the night she hijacked me at Sabino and dragged me to Nisha's party, too. Who's to say Gabby and Lili didn't suggest the whole kidnapping thing?"

Ethan moved the chair back and forth, the caster wheels squeaking, not saying a word.

"And they're such gossip hounds," Emma went on, pausing by a big poster titled WHAT TO DO IF YOU'RE THE VICTIM OF ASSAULT. "It wouldn't look suspicious for them to skulk around, spying, listening in. *And* both of them were at Charlotte's sleepover last week. They could've snuck down and strangled me without tripping the alarm." All of Emma's nerves snapped. She was onto something big—and terrifying. "Lili and Gabby were with Sutton the night she died. It *has* to be them."

Ethan's Adam's apple bobbed as he swallowed. "So how do we prove it? How do we nail them?"

"With your phone." Emma held out her hand. Confused, Ethan dropped it in her palm. Emma pulled up the home page for Twitter and looked again at Gabby's and Lili's tweets. On August 28, they were innocuous and random: *Love my new Chanel oil blotter!* And *What are you wearing to Nisha's party? I was thinking of breaking in my back-2-school purchases.* And *Avocado burger at California Cookin', yumness!*

They sometimes shot off thirty tweets an hour. But on the thirty-first, neither of them had tweeted at all. "*That's* odd," Emma said, sinking back to the cot. "I figured they would've bragged about shoplifting with Sutton that day."

Ethan sat beside her as Emma scrolled to the most recent tweet. At ten this morning, Gabby had tweeted she'd aced the math test she never studied for.

"Humble, isn't she?" Ethan grumbled as he read over Emma's shoulder.

"This doesn't make sense," Emma said, tapping her

index finger against Ethan's phone. "Gabby made Laurel wait while she finished a tweet this afternoon right before the ceremony. So why doesn't the tweet show up on her page?" Emma's eyes widened. "Wait. What if they have secret Twitter accounts?"

Ethan looked at her as though he wasn't quite sure what she was getting at.

"It's when someone has a public account that they tell everyone about and a secondary account under a code name," Emma explained.

"Why would they bother?" Ethan asked.

"If they have stuff they want to talk to each other about that they don't want anyone else reading."

"It makes sense." Ethan's voice rose with excitement. "And it sounds exactly like something those two would do."

"But how could we figure out what they are? Would the names be an inside joke?"

"Probably," Ethan answered. "Or they could be totally random."

"Let's try fashion designers," Emma suggested. "Or maybe favorite shoe brands or movies." She called up the Twitter homepage and typed in @*rodarte*, the Twins' favorite clothing label. But that Twitter profile belonged to someone in Australia. She typed in other variations— *rodarteGirl, RodarteFan*—as well as other things the Twitter Twins liked, like Gabby's all-time favorite movie, *The*

Devil Wears Prada, or Lili's favorite band, My Chemical Romance.

They checked the Twins' Facebook pages to spark other ideas. "They have twin dogs named Googoo and Gaga," Ethan pointed out.

"Seriously?" Emma groaned and typed it in, but nothing came up—except for a lot of Lady Gaga fan pages.

They tried makeup brands, variations on Gucci and Marc Jacobs, celebs they loved, and stores they shopped at. None of them worked. Emma sat back and massaged her temples. What would *her* secret Twitter account be? A nickname no one would guess? All she could think of was how Lou, the mechanic at the garage, called her Little Grease Monkey. Or how, when she worked at the New York-New York roller coaster, some of the guys who bartended nearby not-so-secretly referred to her as the "vomit-comet hottie."

"What if Lili and Gabby's secret Twitter names are kind of embarrassing?" Emma asked. "Like something about Gabby running over Lili's foot."

"Or when Gabby got stuck in the locker," Ethan added.

Suddenly, they both looked at each other. Emma typed in @*GabbyPonyBaloney*. A profile popped up; the tiny picture was definitely Gabby. Only one girl was following her: @*MissLiliTallywhacker*.

"I can't believe it," Emma whispered. Her fingers shook as she scrolled down the page. These tweets weren't nearly as mindless. Every post she read made the room spin just a little bit faster. First, she read their tweets from August 31:

@GABBYPONYBALONEY: *Do you think we should?*
@MISSLILITALLYWHACKER: *Definitely. No turning back now. It all falls into place tonight.*

And just last week, the night of Charlotte's sleepover, when someone crept down and strangled Emma:

@MISSLILITALLYWHACKER: *She thinks we're so stupid.*
@GABBYPONYBALONEY: *She'll know the truth soon enough.*
@MISSLILITALLYWHACKER: *She'd better be careful. . . .*

And the night of Sutton's birthday party:

@GABBYPONYBALONEY: *She has no clue what's coming. I can't wait to see the look on her face.*
@MISSLILITALLYWHACKER: *Let's hope this works.*

And the tweet Gabby sent just that afternoon:

@GABBYPONYBALONEY: *Less than an hour to go. That bitch is going down.*

A locker door slammed in the hall, shaking the nursing-station walls and making the thick green contents of a big bottle of cough syrup wobble back and forth on the shelf. *That bitch is going down.* A vision of the hurtling light fixture swam through Emma's mind. She stared at Ethan. "They're talking about me."

The argument I'd had with Lili the night of Gabby's accident flashed through my mind. I'd told her she'd better keep her mouth shut, or I'd ruin her life. But maybe instead, she and her sister ruined *mine.*

"Do me a favor and email these to me," Emma said to Ethan. "All of them. I can't risk losing these like I lost the snuff film."

"Done." Ethan grabbed the phone back from Emma and started copying and pasting all of the tweets.

Muffled classical music from orchestra practice in the next room echoed through the walls. Suddenly, Emma's body ached as though she'd run back-to-back marathons. "What a nightmare," she said, slumping against the flat mattress on the cot. "Knowing there are *two* of them just makes this feel even more impossible. And were they trying to scare me? Or kill me? And if they were trying to kill me, how long before they try again?"

Ethan murmured a note of sympathy, but didn't offer any advice. "What I wouldn't give for a day off from this," Emma murmured. "A couple of *hours* off." She thought about Friday night. It was hard enough navigating broad daylight with the Twitter Twins. But dealing with a dark Homecoming dance with a haunted house theme, all by herself? She snuck a peek at Ethan. "I have an idea."

Ethan dropped his phone into his pocket. "Let's hear it."

"What if you went to Homecoming with me?" Emma gestured to the Halloween Homecoming flyer that hung on the nurse's wall. It was of a skeleton and a witch doing the tango.

Ethan took a step back. "Emma . . ."

Emma cut him off before he could give her an I-hate-dances spiel. "We could look into the Twins together. I won't have to handle everything myself. And it could even be fun. We can dress in goofy costumes, OD on the amazing cupcakes the caterer is bringing, dance—or *not* dance, if you're really opposed. We can laugh at all the people who are really into it."

Ethan's hands twisted together in his lap. "It's not that I don't want to go. It's that . . . well, I've actually asked someone else."

Emma blinked. It felt like he'd just dumped a bucket of cold water on her head, and for a moment her brain was filled with nothing but static. "Oh!" she said, a few moments too late. "Oh, well, great! Good for you!"

The look that crossed Ethan's face was comically grouchy, almost petulant. "I mean, you said you just wanted to be friends. You said you weren't interested."

"I know! I did!" Emma's voice took on the annoying chirpy quality it always got when she tried too hard to sound upbeat. "I mean, it would have been as friends. But this is totally for the better. I'm so happy for you! You'll have so much fun!"

The room suddenly felt too small to fit both of them. Emma leapt to her feet. "Um, I should go."

Ethan stood, too. "What? Where?"

"I-I should get back to the auditorium." Emma fumbled for the door. "They're still holding the party. I should help out. Plus, all my stuff is still there."

"But . . ." Ethan slung his bag over his shoulder and followed her, but Emma did not want to discuss it any further. She gave him the most carefree wave she could muster. "I'll call you later," she promised, even though she couldn't imagine doing so. She speed-walked into the hall, turned a corner, then collapsed against a bank of lockers.

The hall was quiet, the final bell of the day not yet having rung. Emma could hear her own ragged breathing. A sob rose in her throat, but she quickly swallowed it down. "You had your chance," she whispered furiously. "You made your choice. It *is* for the best."

A cackling sound floated down the hall. Emma froze, listening. There was another sharp exhalation of breath around the corner, a second triumphant-sounding snort.

A shadow spread across the floor. Had someone been watching her? *Listening?*

She sprinted down the hall, but when she rounded the corner there was no one there. When Emma breathed in, she could detect the faintest scent of coconut in the air. And when she looked down, she saw a few tiny, glittering shards of glass on the ground.

She crouched down to touch one of the pieces. The amber-colored glass perfectly matched the glass in the light fixture that had nearly shattered her skull.

20

CREEPY VAMPIRES TO THE LEFT,
STALKERS TO THE RIGHT

"Velcome!" A pimply-faced teenager in a satin Dracula cape, plastic fangs, and a penciled-in widow's peak leapt into the doorway of Scare-O-Rama, Tucson's best-stocked Halloween store. "Can I help you? You girls look good enough to bite!" When he laughed, he sounded like the Count from *Sesame Street.*

"Ew, no!" Laurel said, brushing past him. Dracula covered half his face with his cape, shunned vampire-style, and scooted away to his perch behind the counter.

It was Thursday after school, and Emma and Laurel were on the hunt for their Homecoming costumes. Truthfully, all Emma had wanted to do for the rest of the night was lie in Sutton's bed in a tight, safe ball and thank her lucky stars that the light fixture hadn't been a couple of inches to the left, but she'd finally relented after Laurel's constant badgering. The dance was tomorrow, after all—time was running out. And even if she didn't have a date, she had to attend in style. But just venturing into the world felt dangerous, like Lili and Gabby could be anywhere or do anything.

Emma kept checking their private Twitter accounts, but they hadn't posted anything new since Gabby's tweet that afternoon. She needed more on them—something concrete, unequivocal. But she'd scoured Sutton's bedroom, house, iPhone, social networking sites, two lockers, and everywhere else she could think of.

Laurel took Emma's arm and guided her to the racks of costumes cramming nearly every inch of the store. Pitchforks, sparkly top hats, slasher masks, and spiders hung on the wall. Fun-house mirrors made Emma's body look either lumpish or taffy-stretched. Predictably, "Monster Mash" blared over the stereo, and Dracula and his coworker—a tall girl stuffed into a leather bustier— bobbed along to the beat. Laurel strode up to a rack of southern belle hoop skirts and touched the faux taffeta. "I'm thinking of something retro." She tied a bonnet under her chin and posed to the right and left. "What do you think? Is it me?"

Despite her exhaustion, Emma smiled. "It's definitely you." They both collapsed into giggles. For once, Emma actually felt *close* to Laurel, almost like she was a real sister. The only thing missing here was Sutton herself.

What I wouldn't give for Emma, Laurel, and me to be shopping together right now, trying on stupid witch hats and fake noses. Having a true blood sister would change so much. Emma and I would be instant family, a different kind than I'd ever experienced. There would be no jealousy that my parents loved her more than me. We would be bound together always; I would try my hardest for us to have the best relationship possible.

Emma and Laurel sifted through Madonna cone-boob corsets, French maid outfits, and a rack of pink tutus Emma would've begged Becky to buy for her when she was four years old. A few minutes into their search, Laurel pulled out a leopard's costume and shook her head as she examined it. "This isn't right either. It needs to be *perfect*."

"It's just a dance," Emma murmured. "What's the big deal?"

There was a screech of metal as Laurel moved a cluster of hangers to the left. "Caleb really likes Halloween. And I want everything to be just right." She bit her lip.

Emma couldn't help but smile. "Do you like him?"

Embarrassment flickered across Laurel's face. "I know he tells really dorky jokes. And I know it's not so great that he's only on JV tennis. But he's so nice. We have fun together."

It took Emma a few moments to realize that Laurel was seeking her approval, apologizing for choosing a guy who might not be up to their clique's standards. "If you guys have fun together, that's what's important," she said, shooting Laurel a genuine smile. "I think he's supercute."

Laurel brightened. "Really?"

Emma nodded. "*Really.*"

The corners of Laurel's lips twitched into a relieved smile. I could tell how much Emma's words meant to her. It was the kind of encouragement I'd clearly never given her when I was around.

The next rack of costumes contained bikini tops, angel wings, hot pants, and thigh-high boots. "So, does Caleb like you back?" Emma asked.

Laurel flicked a feather on the brim of a flapper headband. "According to Gabby and Lili, he's interested."

Emma tried to keep her face neutral. She didn't want Laurel to see her flinch at the mention of the Twins' names.

Then Laurel let out a wary laugh. "Hopefully they're not lying to me as revenge for attempting to get them onstage in thongs."

At least they didn't try to drop a giant light on your head. "Do you think they've forgiven us for the prank?" Emma asked, trying to sound nonchalant.

Laurel held a blood-spattered wedding dress to her torso and nodded. "After the party kicked into gear, they said they thought the prank was really funny. I can't believe they knew we were up to something. I thought we covered our bases. Maybe we've underestimated them."

That's an understatement, I thought.

Emma ran her finger over a sequined bowler hat. "So were Gabby and Lili in the auditorium the whole time I was in the nurse's office?" The shuffling noises in the hall zipped through her mind. Those bits of glass on the floor. The eerie sense someone had been there listening, watching.

"Yeah . . ." Laurel squinted at her. "Why?"

Emma kept her gaze glued on a stack of food-themed costumes: a phallic orange carrot, a round donut with leechlike felt pink sprinkles, and a Hershey's Kiss. "I thought I saw Gabby in the hall, that's all."

Laurel grinned. "Maybe it was a ghost!" she said in a teasing, ghoulish voice, pointing to a Ghostface mask from *Scream*.

I wanted to burst out laughing; little did Laurel know the truth. But the ghost Emma heard in that hall was *definitely* not me.

Laurel assessed the bloody wedding dress once more and draped it over her arm. "This could work. So are you taking a date? Maybe someone named Alllex, perhaps?"

She stretched out the name and playfully punched Emma on the arm.

"Alex is just a friend," Emma said quickly, turning away.

"Yeah, right!"

"Seriously. Like I said, she's from tennis camp. And she's a *girl*. Short for Alexandra."

Laurel cocked her head and gave Emma a dubious look. "A girl who's *thinking of you* and *can't wait to talk*?" she asked, reciting the lines from Alex's text.

The bells to the store jingled, and a man in a pin-striped suit with two small blond boys entered. The kids ran for the rack of army uniforms and started shooting each other with the plastic machine guns. Emma watched them snake around the racks, fully aware that Laurel's expectant gaze hadn't left her face. Emma knew if she didn't give her gossip soon, she'd continue to pester her relentlessly. The more questions she asked, the more specifics Emma fabricated, the more opportunity Laurel had to catch Emma in a lie.

Emma took a deep breath and turned around. "Okay. There *is* a guy I've been hanging around with."

Laurel's eyes lit up. "Who?"

"Ethan."

"Ethan . . . who?"

"Landry." It felt strange and nerve-racking to say his name out loud.

The smile on Laurel's face was uncertain, slightly amused. "Seriously?"

Emma stiffened, feeling vulnerable. It felt like she'd whipped off the Sutton mask and Laurel was suddenly looking at *her*. "We're just friends," she said as casually as she could. "We hang out sometimes."

"But Ethan Landry isn't friends with people." Laurel still sounded incredulous. "He's Mr. I-*Vant*-to-Be-Alone."

The little boys raced around the Halloween shop as though it were a war zone. Their father slapped an Amex on the counter and gave an apologetic look to the girl in the leather bustier. "Well, I guess he's changed," Emma said.

"I suppose you'd be the perfect person to change him, Sutton." Laurel got in line to pay for the wedding dress. "You should tell everyone you're into him! It would do wonders for his popularity!"

"I don't think Ethan cares about that," Emma pointed out.

But Laurel didn't seem to hear her. "You should invite him to Homecoming!"

The earnestness in Laurel's voice tugged at Emma's heart. If she'd asked Ethan just days before, maybe they'd be going together.

"Ethan has a date already," Emma said flatly.

"So make him break it off with her!" Laurel handed a

credit card to Dracu-Dork. He slipped the dress into a yellow plastic bag without taking his eyes off Laurel. "You've done it before!" Laurel went on. "Look, Sutton, I've seen him staring at you at school. And when he showed up to your party with those flowers . . . it's obvious he's got it bad for you."

"You think?" Emma toyed with a loose thread at the hem of her shirt.

"I do," Laurel said firmly.

Emma reached out and took Laurel's hand, suddenly feeling a flood of warmth and protectiveness for her. Gabby and Lili, two girls Laurel was close friends with, might have killed Laurel's sister. Was it right to keep that from her?

Laurel looked down at Emma's fingers holding hers. "What's that for?" she asked softly.

"Laurel, I . . ." Emma started. Maybe she should tell her. Maybe Laurel deserved to know.

Sutton's sister grabbed the bloody wedding dress from the counter. "Yeah?"

There was a trusting smile on her face. Her big blue eyes blinked slowly. The words welled in Emma's throat, ready to spill forth, but then Sutton's iPhone beeped, breaking the silence. Emma peeked at the screen. It was another text from Alex. GOING FOR A CHICKEN MOLE BURRITO! JEALOUS? she wrote. Attached was a photo of Alex standing in front of Loco Mexico, a dive restaurant she and Emma had been obsessed with—they made the best guacamole in town. Emma was about to slip it back into her bag when a rusty sign next to Loco Mexico caught her eye. RAPID TOW IMPOUND SERVICES. A bunch of cars lurked behind a chain-link fence.

Alarms blared in Emma's head. *The impound lot.* Sutton's car was there. It was somewhere Emma hadn't yet looked—what if there was something in it, something specific that linked the Twitter Twins to Sutton's murder?

"Laurel," Emma said again, turning back to Sutton's sister as they made their way out of the store. "Can you take me to the impound? I think it's time to get my car."

Laurel's eyebrows shot up in surprise, as though she hadn't expected this. But then she shook her head and glanced at her watch. "I can't today. My calc study group starts in twenty minutes. Maybe tomorrow?"

"No need," said a voice behind Emma. "*We'll* take you right now."

Emma spun around, and her jaw dropped. There, standing on the curb in the blinding Tucson sunset, were the Twitter Twins.

Grinning at Emma, I thought, like a pair of lionesses that had just cornered their prey.

21

SERVICE WITH A SNICKER

"Hey, guys!" Laurel said brightly, beaming at Gabby and Lili. "That would be awesome."

"No problem!" Gabby's eyes flickered, snakelike, to Emma, then back to Laurel. There was a hint of a smile on her lips, as though she were trying to hold in a laugh. "We all know how badly Sutton needs her car back."

"Yeah, so she can stall it again," Lili added under her breath.

An eerie shiver passed through me.

Lili steered Emma to their white SUV, which was parked in the lot. "C'mon. A little birdie told me the impound closes at six."

"But . . ." Emma protested, planting her feet. "I don't have to go today. . . ."

"Nonsense," Lili said hurriedly. "We don't mind. That's what friends are for, right?"

"You guys are the best!" Laurel reached into her purse for her car keys. "Have fun reuniting with Floyd, Sutton!"

Emma glanced over her shoulder at Laurel, sure that helplessness and fear were written all over her face, but Laurel just waved obliviously. She flung the yellow plastic Scare-O-Rama bag over her shoulder and skipped toward her Jetta.

Lili opened the backseat of the SUV with a flourish. "Ladies first," she said sweetly, pointing Emma to one of the black seats inside. Emma hesitated, wondering how far she could get if she took off in a sprint.

"What's wrong, Sutton?" Gabby teased, noticing Emma's reluctance. "You all freaked out from being inside the Halloween store? Afraid another light was going to fall on your head?"

Emma swallowed hard, the words cutting her like knives. Her heart had never pounded so fast or so hard. But she told herself that the Twins couldn't do anything to her today—not when Laurel knew she was with them. Straightening her shoulders, Emma brushed her dark hair over her shoulder and called upon her deepest Sutton reserves. "No, I'm freaked out by your wardrobe choices," she snapped, eyeing Lili's mismatched polka-dot blouse and plaid skirt. "Did someone dress while under the influence this morning?"

Lili sniffed. "This month's *Vogue* says mixing patterns is in."

"I would've thought you'd know something that basic," Gabby scoffed.

"What's with the attitude today, ladies?" Emma tried to sound exasperated. "Are you two still not over that prank during your court party?"

"*Please*, Sutton." Lili opened the front passenger door. "We were over it before it even began."

Gabby nudged Emma into the backseat, which smelled overpoweringly of Skittles. The Twitter Twins climbed into the front, and Gabby started the engine. Her blue eyes met Emma's in the rearview mirror. "To the impound, right?"

Emma nodded, and the Twins exchanged a look and shared a secret giggle that turned Emma's stomach. Then Gabby steered the car out of the parking lot and made a left at the light. Lili tapped away on her iPhone. Emma could just make out the Twitter icon on the little screen. She leaned forward, dying for a peek. Was Lili writing under her secret Twitter name? Was she sending a secret missive to Gabby?

Lili cocked her head, noticing Emma. Emma

snapped her head away, pretending she wasn't looking. Lili covered the screen with her hand and smirked.
Emma pulled out her phone to check, but nothing new
was posted.

Gabby merged onto the freeway, snaking around cars
and nearly cutting off a fast-moving milk truck. "So,
Sutton. Excited for tomorrow night?" She swiveled
around and glanced at Emma, taking her eyes off the
road.

"Gabby!" Emma screamed, gesturing toward the
highway with her phone. Was Gabby even allowed to be
behind the wheel? Could people with epilepsy get driver's
licenses?

One corner of Gabby's lips lifted into a smile. She still
didn't turn around. "But, Sutton, I thought you liked to
live on the edge!"

"*Whoo, whoo!*" Lili said in a high-pitched voice, her
fingers flying over the iPhone's keyboard.

More cars honked at the SUV. Sweat began to bead on
the back of Emma's neck. She placed a hand on Gabby's
shoulder as a pickup truck swerved out of her way. "Gabby,
please!"

Finally, as Gabby was about to have a head-on collision with an oncoming Jeep Cherokee, she calmly
faced forward and wrenched the SUV back into the far
lane like they'd never been in peril at all. "*We're* really

excited for Homecoming, Sutton," she said, picking up on the previous conversation as though nothing was amiss. "It's a big night for us. You're going to die when you see us!"

Emma flinched. "Excuse me?" She grabbed the door handle, wishing she could jump out of the car.

Lili giggled. "Our *costumes* are amazing."

"God, what did you *think* we meant?" Gabby asked, snickering. The girls exchanged another glance, as though they knew how much they were freaking Emma out.

Just then, Gabby took the next exit and turned into a dingy lot. A sign on the chain-link fence read TUCSON PD IMPOUND. As they pulled in, a beefy man with a shaved head emerged from a small, nut-colored building and motioned for Gabby to roll down the window.

As soon as the car slowed, Emma unlocked the passenger door and jumped out.

"Sutton!" Gabby called. "What the hell?"

"I can take it from here!" Emma yelled back, relieved to be standing next to the worker, who had ham-sized arm muscles and a menacing tattoo peeking out from under his collar. "But thanks, guys! I really appreciate the ride!"

The Twitter Twins idled at the gate for a moment, wrinkling their noses. Then Lili shrugged and said something to Gabby that Emma couldn't hear. The two of them smiled, and Gabby threw the vehicle into reverse.

Both girls gave Emma a three-finger wave as they pulled away.

Emma waited a few beats for her heart to slow down. Then she turned to the impound worker. "I'm here to pick up my car," she said, her voice cracking.

"Come in here." The worker led Emma to the building inside the lot. "I need your driver's license and credit card."

Emma handed over Sutton's license from her wallet. The worker typed something into a dusty keyboard and stared at the screen. A wrinkle formed on his brow. "Sutton Mercer?" he repeated. "1965 Volvo?"

"That's right," Emma said, remembering the details from Sutton's police file.

The man gave her a long, suspicious look. "It says here that you picked up this vehicle nearly a month ago."

Emma blinked. "*What?*"

"It's right here. You signed it out on the morning of August thirty-first. The fine was paid in full." He twisted the monitor to show Emma the screen. She stared at a scan of the car's release form. There, at the bottom, next to the *X*, was Sutton's signature.

A memory bloomed in my mind: I *had* been here before. I remembered the leaky Bic pen that I used to sign the release forms. I remembered hearing my phone ring and feeling a jolt of happiness. But before I could get a look at the screen, the vision tunneled and blinked off.

Emma stared at Sutton's signature, that swooping *S*, the humps of the *M*. It was another clear link to what Sutton was doing the day she died, but it felt like her investigation had taken a huge left turn. Why hadn't Sutton told anyone she'd signed out the car that day? And where was Sutton's car *now*?

The man cleared his throat, breaking Emma from her thoughts. "This *is* your signature, right?"

Emma's tongue felt like it was made of lead. She wasn't sure how to answer. Should she say it wasn't and report the car stolen? But what if she did that and then the police found Sutton's body in the trunk? As soon as that happened, Emma would be arrested—without any other evidence, she was the most likely suspect in her sister's murder: the unlucky twin trying to escape a life of poverty.

"Uh . . . I guess I made a mistake," she croaked. Then she backed out of the little booth and into the blinding sunset.

The worker stared after her, shaking his head and muttering under his breath about how every kid was on drugs these days. As Emma walked out of the lot, figuring she'd call a cab to take her back to the Mercers', a flash to the right caught her eye. A figure ducked behind an abandoned old Burger King on the other side of the chain-link fence. Even though Emma had only seen a glimpse, she was almost positive the figure had dirty-blonde hair like the Twitter Twins.

They were watching my sister for sure. The only thing I didn't know was what they were planning next.

22

TWEET, UNTWEET

Just hours before Homecoming, the doorbell rang at Charlotte's house. Emma left her Diet Coke on the kitchen counter and padded through the hall to get it. She opened the door to find an older, spiky-haired, tattooed woman in a black tutu, ripped CBGB T-shirt, and worn motorcycle boots. She looked like a cross between the Bride of Frankenstein and a coked-up Courtney Love.

"Hey, sweetie!" the woman at the door cried, breaking Emma from her thoughts. She grabbed Emma's arms and kissed her on both cheeks, leaving behind vampy red lipstick prints. Emma wasn't sure if she should assume the woman knew Sutton, or if this was just the way she greeted everyone. She played it safe with a cool smile.

We'd met before—I was sure of it. A memory slithered through my mind: the woman and Charlotte's mother talking in hushed voices in the kitchen. *You know I'll kill him if it's true,* Charlotte's mom had said. But both of them straightened and smiled when I entered the kitchen, gushing with small talk about how fashionable I looked and if I thought *they* could pull off denim leggings, too. (The answer, for both, was a groaning "no.")

The woman sauntered into the kitchen and plopped two giant makeup cases down on the farmhouse table. "Okay, ladies!" she croaked in a two-packs-a-day voice. "Let's get you gory and gorgeous for Homecoming!"

Madeline, Charlotte, and Laurel cheered. It was two o'clock in the afternoon. The idea was to primp at Charlotte's, take dozens of sexy, Facebook-worthy pictures in their Halloween dresses, and then their dates would pick them up in a stretch limo a half hour before the dance. Well, everyone *else's* dates—Emma hadn't bothered to ask anyone after Ethan. She tried to play it off like going stag was the cool thing to do; Sutton probably would have.

Emma still had a lot to learn about me. The only place I went stag was the bathroom.

Charlotte's mother clonked into the kitchen on raffia wedges and gave the makeup artist an air kiss. With her perky boobs, giant Chanel sunglasses, and grass-green Juicy Couture minidress, Charlotte's mom didn't look like the rest of the mothers in suburbia, even in Sutton's upscale Tucson neighborhood. "Ladies, you remember Helene, my makeup guru," she said, chomping gum between her shiny veneers. "You're in excellent hands with her." She slung a studded bag over her shoulder and grabbed her Mercedes keys from the telephone table.

Helene pouted. "You're not staying to watch the magic?"

Mrs. Chamberlain glanced at her pink diamond-studded watch. "Can't. I've got an appointment for a Brazilian in ten minutes."

"Mom!" Charlotte covered her ears. "TMI!"

Mrs. Chamberlain gave her daughter a dismissive, you're-such-a-prude hand flutter. Emma wasn't sure which was more bizarre—that Charlotte's mother had just announced she was getting a take-it-all-off bikini wax, or that she trusted her makeup needs to Mistress of the Night Helene.

After Mrs. Chamberlain disappeared out the door, Charlotte turned to Helene. "Can I go first? I'm going as an Egyptian goddess, so I need really dramatic Cleopatra eyes."

Emma wondered if Sutton would push past Charlotte and demand to go first instead, but she didn't have the heart to do that.

"Comin' right up." Helene opened her giant makeup cases, revealing a bevy of brushes, shadows, powders, mascara wands, and curlers.

As she waited, Emma pulled Sutton's phone from her pocket and checked out the Twitter Twins' secret accounts. There was a new entry.

@MISSLILITALLYWHACKER: *The night we've been waiting for . . .*

Emma hoped Lili was just talking about her and Gabby's big night on the court.

But we both knew it meant more than that.

Madeline turned toward the fridge. "Time for refreshments," she said, winking at Emma. "Sutton, can you grab some glasses?"

Emma followed Madeline, skirting around the behemoth soapstone island, running her fingers along the eerily familiar surface. The last time she'd been in this kitchen, someone had startled her from behind and nearly strangled her. If she squinted, she could see a faint outline of the scuffmark the assailant's shoe had made on the baseboard when he or she had rammed Emma against the wall. In the oppressive atmosphere, she could almost hear the attacker's words lingering in the air: *I told you to play along. I told you not to leave.*

As Emma laid out four glasses on the island, Madeline pulled a two-liter bottle of Diet Coke from the Chamberlain's fridge and poured each glass three-quarters full. Then, raising a finger to her lips, she whipped her silver flask from her pocket and topped the drinks off with rum. Emma's nose tickled with the cloying scent.

"You're not making cocktails over there, are you?" Helene crowed, a giant blush brush in her hand. "If so, can you make me one, too, honey?"

Madeline grinned. "Sure!"

The doorbell rang again. "Sutton, can you get that?" Charlotte asked, her eyes closed as Helene swept sparkly silver powder over her lids.

Emma wandered down the long hallway lined with modernist photographs of cacti, shadows, and cloudless skies, and pulled at the ring-shaped knob of the huge door. When she saw the two girls on the porch, a hot, acidic feeling welled in her stomach.

"Hello there, Sutton," Gabby said, pushing past her. A garment bag was draped over her arm, and she wore her orange silk Homecoming Court sash across her T-shirt.

"What happened with your car? I don't see it in the driveway," Lili chirped, clomping into the hallway. She had her sash on, too.

Don't you already know? Emma wanted to ask, thinking about the lurking figure—or figures—behind Burger

King. Perhaps the Twitter Twins had taken Sutton to get her car out on the thirty-first, too. Maybe they even knew where it had ended up.

But instead, Emma told the Twins the same lie she'd told the other girls: "There was a mix-up. Those idiots at the impound lot gave the car to someone else instead. But the cops are on it."

"Hey, bitches!" Charlotte called from the kitchen before either twin could respond. "Come in and make yourself a drink. We're in a parent-free zone!"

"I don't count!" Helene let out a chuckle, which quickly devolved into a coughing fit.

Emma trailed after the Twitter Twins as they glided down the hall. "What are *they* doing here?" she murmured to Madeline as she crossed into the kitchen.

Madeline took a big swig of her rum and Diet Coke. "It was the least we could do after our botched prank."

"They should leave," Emma blurted.

Madeline wiped the condensation from her drink with a pink cocktail napkin and let out a sigh. "Sutton, don't be like that. It's not like we're going to ask them to be part of the Lying Game. Chill."

"Are you talking about us, Sutton?" Gabby practically shouted from the kitchen table, fiddling with her phone. Her voice grated on Emma's nerves, and she felt her fists ball against her sides.

"Only good things," Madeline trilled back. She squeezed Emma's wrist. "Just be nice, okay?"

Charlotte jumped off the chair. Everyone oohed and ahhed over her dramatic Cleopatra eyes, her chiseled cheekbones, and perfect alabaster skin. Madeline climbed into the chair next, topping off her drink with another tip of the flask.

"So, girls." She looked at the Twitter Twins. "Do you have dates for tonight?"

"We're both going stag," Gabby said. Her thumbs dashed over the keys on her phone at breakneck speed. "But I have my eye on someone."

"You didn't tell me that." Lili's eyebrow arched. "I do, too! Who is it?"

Gabby shrugged. "It's a secret. I don't want to say anything until I'm sure he's into me."

Lili's mouth became pinched and small. "Well, then, I'm not telling you who my guy is either."

Emma watched with curiosity. She'd never seen any tension between the two before now.

"Sutton's going stag, too," Laurel piped up, clearly trying to smooth over the sudden mood shift.

"*Really?*" Lili's beady eyes darted to Emma. "How interesting!"

"I guess we'll be spending a lot of time together if we're all going alone." The words oozed from Gabby's mouth like a threat. "One-on-one Sutton time. How lucky can we be?"

"How lucky," Emma echoed, hollow dread settling over her.

Lili reached for her phone, her fingers typing furiously. There was a chime, and Gabby glanced at her own phone's screen. The Twins' gazes darted to Emma for a split second before looking away.

The few sips of alcohol Emma had drunk burned her stomach. Pulling out Sutton's phone, she logged on to Gabby's and Lili's public Twitter sites. No new messages popped up. But their fingers were still dancing over their tiny keyboards. Occasionally they smiled, as if one had said something particularly funny.

Emma's fingers started to fly, too, calling up their private accounts. But only an error message appeared. *This page does not exist.*

Emma retyped her search, thinking she'd misspelled something, but the same error message popped up. She'd seen the page ten minutes ago. . . .

She looked up at two pairs of blue eyes. "Looking for something?" Gabby teased.

"Did you think we wouldn't notice your snooping?" Lili added.

"What are you freaks talking about?" Madeline murmured as Helene smeared gloss across her lips.

"No-thing," Lili sing-songed.

But Emma knew exactly what they were talking about. The Twitter Twins had figured out Emma was onto them, meaning something huge was going to happen tonight.

I only hoped she could outsmart the Twitter Twins before they outsmarted her.

23

THE AWFUL TRUTH

Hollier's parking lot was packed with stretch limos, town cars, SUVs, and even a couple of sports cars borrowed from parents. A banner that said HALLOWEEN HOME-COMING stretched over the front doors, and someone had placed a big lit jack-o'-lantern on the head of the statue of Edmund Hollier, the school's founder. Couples dressed in elaborate costumes walked arm-in-arm toward the gym. Homecoming had begun.

Emma lagged behind the others and shot off a quick text to Ethan. THE TTS TOOK DOWN THEIR SECRET ACCOUNTS. THEY KNOW.

Her phone buzzed immediately with Ethan's response. DO NOT GO ANYWHERE ALONE TONIGHT.

"Time to pose!" Charlotte pulled Emma toward a red carpet at the front of the gym. A line of photographers called their names, and the girls turned this way and that, flashing their sexiest smiles. Emma forced her shoulders to relax and pasted a grin on her face. The paparazzi red carpet had been her idea; she'd thought it was something Sutton would suggest. She stood next to Charlotte, who wore a glittering Egyptian headdress, a long silk toga, and gladiator-inspired heels; Madeline, who was dressed as the Queen of Hearts, in a red-and-white dress and a gleaming gold crown; and Laurel, who had donned the blood-spattered wedding dress she'd found at the Halloween store. The Twitter Twins wore costumes that accentuated their Homecoming Court sashes: Lili was the Statue of Liberty, wearing a Grecian-style dress, sandals, and a spiked crown, and carrying a LED torch that glowed red when she hit a button. Gabby was some sort of winged goddess in a similarly draped dress, nymphlike sandals, and a flower headdress. They were both in innocent white, but Emma knew better.

Emma had chosen to be a sexy version of Sherlock Holmes, complete with a checked tweed jacket, a tweed miniskirt, high Manolo heels, a detective's cap, and an angular pipe. Back at Charlotte's, the Twins had smirked pointedly and asked why she'd chosen that costume, clearly goading her. But Emma had just held their gaze and said, "Because Holmes always got his man."

The girls' dates got into the picture, too. Laurel's crush, Caleb—who *was* very cute—wore a 1920s-style pin-striped gangster suit. Noah, the guy Charlotte had asked, wore Wolverine sideburns and kept spewing *X-Men* quotes. Madeline's date, Davin, dressed as Freddy Krueger, complete with a mangled face and slasher nails. He somehow managed to look creepier than Freddy Krueger actually had. None of them wanted to go near him.

Gabby declined a paparazzi photo, too busy talking to Kevin Torres, a guy in Emma's calc class who rolled his eyes whenever anyone got an answer wrong. She draped her arm around his skinny shoulders and giggled at everything that came out of his mouth. Lili stood next to them, looking like she'd swallowed a bitter lemon. She tried several times to get Kevin's attention, but Kevin didn't take his eyes off Gabby. Emma watched them carefully, über-alert for any whispers, nudges, or random disappearances. She felt like a clock was counting down on her. Now that the Twitter Twins knew she was onto them, would they want to keep her around to play Sutton? Or was she a liability?

"Okay, people, let's move," Madeline said, ushering everyone off the carpet and into the ballroom. Thanks to

Charlotte's decorator extraordinaire, the gym, which typically smelled like old sneakers and floor wax, had been transformed into a mix between a ghoulish haunted house and a tricked-out nightclub.

Emma and the others had helped pile up the gym's bleachers and replace them with multitiered platforms containing round, black-velvet banquettes; crooked gravestones that served as high tables; burbling witches' cauldrons full of spiced apple cider and steaming hot chocolate; and wax figures of zombies, mummies, aliens, and werewolves. They'd set flickering, intricately carved pumpkins on each table, fixed gnarled-tree decals to the walls, and hung spiderwebs from the chairs. Waitresses floated past with trays of vials filled with eerie red liquid—which was actually POM Wonderful—marked with labels like DANCING ELIXIR and KISSING CURE-ALL. And at the end of the room was a craggy haunted mansion. Greenish lights flashed through the windows, and a group of girls let out shrill squeals from inside.

Suddenly Madeline clamped down on Emma's arm. "Oh my God."

She tried to steer Emma in the other direction, but it was too late. Emma had already seen what was bothering her. Garrett sat in a banquette just a few feet away. He wore a velveteen tunic, a frilly shirt underneath, and a horned Viking helmet. A blunt-tipped sword rested on the table.

And he wasn't alone.

"Hi, girls!" Nisha trilled, leaping up from the seat next to Garrett and waving happily. Her black hair had been arranged in two braids, she wore a snugly fitted corset dress, and there was a similar horned helmet sitting atop her head. She and Garrett *matched*.

"What the—" Charlotte said in a low voice. "Tell me he didn't bring *her*."

I wanted to puke. *Nisha?* That was a pretty big step down after dating me. Or Charlotte, for that matter.

Garrett looked up and saw Emma, too. His face clouded. He opened his mouth, but no sound came out. Nisha babbled for the both of them, inviting them to sit and complimenting their costumes when they didn't move. Then she eyed Emma. "Sutton, did you come here all *alone*?" she asked in a simpering voice, sounding absolutely delighted.

"Come on," Madeline urged, tugging on Emma's arm. They snaked across the dance floor, which was already sticky with spilled soda, past the DJ booth, where a few groupies leaned against the table, and into the girls' locker room. Harsh fluorescent lights shone overhead. The faint odor of sweaty socks and spilled shampoo lingered in the air.

Madeline sat down on one of the benches and took Emma's hands. "Are you okay? Do you want to leave?"

Music thumped outside. Emma searched Madeline's face, realizing Madeline thought she was upset. She wasn't, not exactly—more like confused. Did Nisha like Garrett? Was that why she hated Sutton?

Emma brushed her hair off her face. "I'm fine," she said. "It's just . . . weird."

Madeline linked her fingers through Emma's. "You're better off without him. Honestly? I didn't want to tell you this when you guys were going out, but I think Garrett dragged you down. He's sort of understated, like white bread. And you're Sutton Mercer—the *opposite* of ordinary."

Emma looked into Madeline's bright blue eyes, touched. Sutton's friends might not be perfect, but they were loyal.

"And Charlotte told me that when *she* dated Garrett, he was weirdly obsessed with the Summer Olympics," Madeline went on, snickering. "Especially women's gymnastics. Can you imagine? They're linebacker-ish gnomes!"

Thanks for telling me this when I was alive, guys.

But Emma giggled. "Yeah, maybe he wasn't worth it."

"Definitely." Madeline reached up to adjust the crown on her head. Her sleeve slipped down her arm, revealing bare skin. Emma saw four purplish bruises on the inside of her forearm in the shape of fingers.

Emma gasped. "Mads, what happened?"

Madeline followed Emma's gaze and paled. "Oh.

Nothing." She tugged the sleeve back down, her hands trembling. It got caught on her bracelet, and she struggled with it until it fell past her wrist. Then, Emma saw the pinkish burn on her hand. And the bruise on her calf. And another one on the side of her neck.

Alarms clanged in Emma's head. She'd met plenty of kids in foster care who didn't want to talk about their black eyes, the missing clumps of hair on their heads, the burns on their arms.

"Mads," Emma whispered. "You can tell me. It's okay."

Madeline's mouth formed a straight line. She pushed her pointer finger into a carved groove in the bench. "It doesn't matter."

"Yes, it does."

Girls' voices floated past the locker room. Another scream rang out from the haunted house. The second hand on the clock over the gym teacher's office made a half rotation before Madeline spoke again. "It was because of the cigarette."

"The cigarette?"

"The cigarette I was smoking out the window last Saturday. I broke a rule. I deserved it."

"Deserved it?" Emma repeated. Mr. Vega's angry face flashed in her mind. "Oh, *Mads*."

All at once, I saw a vision, too: Mr. Vega bursting into Madeline's bedroom, his face red and shiny, his voice booming. *I swear to God, Madeline, if you break your cur-few one more time, I'll break your neck!* Madeline ran down the stairs after him, and moments later I heard heated but muffled shouts. Then there was a *clang*, as though a shelf full of pots and pans clattered to the floor. I had sat there, doing nothing. Too afraid to act.

Madeline had returned a few minutes later, her cheeks streaked with tears and her eyes red. But she smiled and shrugged and pretended nothing had happened, and I didn't ask.

Emma held tight to Madeline's hands. "Was this what you wanted to talk to me about a while ago? The night you tried calling and I didn't pick up my phone?"

Madeline nodded, her lips pursed so tightly they were translucent.

"I'm so sorry," Emma said, swallowing a hard lump in her throat. "I should have been there for you." She won-dered how much Sutton really knew about all this, or if Madeline had kept it a well-hidden secret.

"I'm sorry, too," I added, even though she couldn't hear me. I had a feeling Mads and I had never discussed it before, not even that night. The phone call, the one she'd made to me the night I died, was the very first time she'd reached out. I would have answered it if I could, but I was already gone.

"It's okay." Madeline said to Emma, her voice wob-bly. "I called Charlotte. She was actually pretty awesome about the whole thing. I wanted to tell you later, but . . ." Madeline let out a bitter laugh and smoothed down the layers of her full skirt. "Believe it or not, this is nothing compared to what Dad used to do to Thayer." She peeked at Emma. "But I guess Thayer told you that, right?"

Emma's skin prickled at the sound of Thayer's name. Would Thayer have told Sutton something so personal? Had they been that close?

A whoosh came over me again. That same moment I'd seen before, of Thayer taking my hands and telling me something, trying to make me understand. Had it been about his dad?

"You have to tell someone about this, Mads," Emma insisted. "What he's doing to you is wrong. And dangerous."

"Are you kidding me?" The crown slipped down Madeline's forehead. "He'd find a way to twist this around and make it my fault. My mom would side with him, too. And it *is* my fault. If I didn't keep screwing up, things would be fine."

"Madeline, this isn't normal," Emma said forcefully. "Promise me you'll think about saying something. Please?"

Madeline stared at her hands. "Maybe."

"There are a lot of people around to support you if you do. Char, me, Freddy Krueger . . ."

Madeline raised her head and cracked a smile. "Oh God, that costume is *awful*."

"It freaks me out," Emma agreed. "I'm going to have nightmares."

"Everyone is. He thinks he looks really cool."

"Just don't let him slow-dance with you," Emma warned. "Could you imagine those slasher hands on your butt?"

The girls collapsed into giggles, nearly tumbling off the bench. A group of sophomores in matching Arizona Cardinals cheerleading costumes marched in, stopped short when they saw Emma and Madeline, and then filed back out again. That just made the two of them laugh even harder.

When they finally stopped, Emma cleared her throat and felt her smile fade. "Mads, I am here for you. I'm sorry if . . . if it seemed like I wasn't before."

Madeline stood and reached a hand out to grab Emma's. "I'm glad I told you."

"I'm glad you did, too," Emma said, giving Sutton's friend—and her friend—a hug. "We're going to figure out a way to make this better," she said. "I promise."

Lights swirled around them as they emerged into the ballroom once more. Madeline headed for the dance floor; Emma said she'd catch up with her in a minute after she got some punch. She scanned the room for the Twitter Twins, her heart jumping when she didn't immediately see them. As she walked toward the drinks table, a hand gripped her shoulder and spun her around. Dark eyes stared down on her. In the dim, orangey light, Emma could make out two faint Viking horns on the figure's head.

"We need to talk," Garrett growled. And then he pulled Emma into a supply closet before anyone could see that she was gone.

24

THE VIKING'S REVENGE

Garrett slammed the closet door. It took a moment for Emma's eyes to adjust to the dim light. Above her head was a bin of red rubber dodgeballs. To her left were soccer nets, field hockey pinnies, and extra lacrosse sticks. The tiny room smelled stale, as though it had been closed up for a while. The brightest things in the room were Garrett's Viking horns, which gave off an eerie, iridescent glow.

"What do you want?" Emma asked, trying not to get too freaked. This was just Garrett, after all. He was harmless . . . wasn't he?

All of a sudden, crammed into a dark closet and focusing

on the white of Garrett's bared teeth, even I wasn't so sure.

"I just need to ask you something, okay?" Garrett's voice was wound tight. He took another step toward Emma, nearly pinning her against the shelving unit behind her. "What's this I hear about you hanging out with another guy already?"

"W-what?" Emma stammered.

"Don't lie to me." Garrett clamped a hand around Emma's wrist. "I've heard all about it. Who is he?"

He sounded so certain, so sure of himself. Someone had told him about Ethan. "Who'd you hear that from? Nisha?"

"So it's true, then?" Garrett's breath smelled yeasty-sweet, like beer.

Emma turned away. "It's none of your business."

Garrett sighed. His grip softened a little, and his fingers began tickling the inside of Emma's palm. "Sutton, what did I do to deserve this? This summer was amazing—I know you thought so, too. You did nothing all summer but beg and beg and beg me to sleep with you, and the day I want to, you freak. Did I wait too long? Had you already moved on? Is that why you dumped me?"

"Excuse me?" Emma straightened up. "I believe *you* were the one who dumped me. You were the one who said we were done, remember?"

Garrett scoffed. "Not calling me for three days after

rejecting me when I was naked sends a pretty strong message, Sutton. Dating someone else does, too."

Emma smacked a palm to her side. "What about you and Nisha? Love your twin Viking costumes, by the way. You two make a cute couple."

"Please. I only brought her here to make you jealous."

"Too bad," Emma snarled. "It's obvious Nisha's crazy about you."

"Unlike you?" Garrett placed his rough, cold hands on the sides of Emma's face.

Emma swiped them away. "Cut it out, Garrett."

"Don't you feel anything for me? You have to feel something, Sutton." He rested a hand on her shoulder. "Don't you miss what we had?"

Emma let out a breath. "I'm sorry. I don't feel anything anymore."

Garrett stepped back and appraised Emma, shaking his head slowly as if seeing her for the first time. "So is this all a game to you? Were you stringing me along the whole time? Was it because of Charlotte? Because you had to have everything she had?"

"No! Do you really think I'm that big of a bitch?"

"Then did you do it just because you could?" Garrett went on, his face close to Emma's. His breath was making her dizzy. "Just like what you did to Thayer."

Thayer's name ripped through Emma like a knife. "I

don't know what you mean . . ." she started, choosing her words carefully. "What exactly do you think I did to Thayer?"

Garrett snickered. "You are *so* in denial, Sutton! Everyone saw that fight between you guys just before he left. He loved you. He would've done anything for you. But you stomped on his heart. Just like you stomped on mine. You *made* him run away. He's lucky, though, because unlike me, at least he never has to see you again."

Emma's mouth dropped open. But before she could ask anything more, Garrett opened the door to the supply closet, leaving Emma alone with gymnastics mats and a barrel full of baseball bats. His words hung heavy in the room, almost palpable. *He would've done anything for you. But you stomped on his heart. You* made *him run away.*

Once again, I saw Thayer shouting at me, his eyes full of conflict and emotion. *Was* it my fault that he left? What had I done to him? Was there *anyone* I'd spared?

Emma ran a hand through her hair and smoothed the folds of her tweed suit. After a moment, she stepped into the gym, nearly knocking over a tall guy dressed in a Robin Hood costume. A tall, broad-shouldered, *familiar* Robin Hood, to be exact, holding the hand of a girl dressed in a curly brown wig and an Elizabethan gown.

Emma stepped back and blinked rapidly. "Ethan?"

"Sutton . . . hey," Ethan said, dropping the girl's

hand. Emma took in her steel gray eyes, thin lips, and high cheekbones. She was familiar, too . . . *really* familiar. The last time Emma had seen this girl, she was smiling smugly as the cops pushed Emma into the cruiser in front of Clique.

"Hi, Sutton," Samantha chirped. She gestured to Ethan. "Like our costumes? I make a pretty Maid Marian to Ethan's Robin Hood, don't you think?"

Samantha was Ethan's mystery date.

25

ALMOST, BUT NOT QUITE

Emma spun and tore through the crowd, desperate to get out of the gym as soon as humanly possible. A red haze swam before her eyes. Screw keeping tabs on the Twitter Twins. She needed some air.

She barely felt her hands pressing on the double doors or the cool night air on her skin. All around her was a cruelly beautiful pink Arizona sky. Ripped ticket stubs littered the sidewalk. Someone's abandoned cat mask lay propped up against a tree. Heavy bass pulsated from inside the school, and every once in a while, there was a deafening crackle of fake thunder.

Slumping down on the bench nearest the courtyard,

Emma placed her head in her hands. She'd been the one, after all, who'd put the brakes on things. But . . . *Samantha*? The girl who'd had her arrested? It was like a slap in the face.

The doors creaked open, and music from the dance wafted outside. When Emma turned and saw Ethan, she pretended to search for something in her bag. "Where's your date?" she couldn't help but snap.

"She's . . . inside." Ethan stood over her for a moment, waiting. Emma had plopped down in the middle of the bench, but she wasn't about to shove over to make room for him. "Are you all right?"

Emma nodded stiffly. "Yep. Fine."

"I was looking for you, but I didn't see you with Madeline and the others," Ethan said, removing his Robin Hood hat from his head. It was kind of ugly, Emma noted with satisfaction. It made him look like an elf.

"Well, have a nice night." Emma knew how bitchy she sounded, but she couldn't find it in her heart to be kind right now.

Ethan's shoulders slumped. "Look. I think I know what's bothering you."

Emma looked away. "It doesn't matter." She absolutely wasn't going to talk about this.

"Sam's really nice, once you get to know her."

Emma wanted to throw her Sherlock Holmes pipe at his head. So she was *Sam* now?

"And I spoke to her about you," Ethan added. "She's willing to drop all the shoplifting charges. No juvie, no community service, no permanent record."

Emma snorted. "Was that the trade-off? You take her to the dance, she lets me walk? How nice of you. How martyrlike."

Ethan shook his head. "Is this what you're like when you're jealous?" A look crossed his face that Emma couldn't quite decipher. "You're more like Sutton than you think," he said.

"What's *that* supposed to mean?"

Ethan crossed his arms over his chest. "You told me you just wanted to be friends. *Is* that what you want?"

Inside the gym, the DJ put on a song by the Black Eyed Peas. The music sounded hollow, empty. Emma reached under her blazer and cupped her hand around Sutton's locket. "I don't know," she muttered.

Ethan lowered himself to the pavement until his face was level with hers. His eyes were soft and round. The setting sun cast sharp shadows on his cheekbones. Emma could smell his signature Ethan-ish scent, a mix of deodorant, freshly laundered clothes, and spearmint. She tried hard to keep her face impassive. She didn't want him to know what she was feeling.

"I thought that was what I wanted," Emma finally said, taking a deep breath. "It just seemed . . . easier. Safer. But now I'm not sure about anything."

Ethan stared at the back of his hands.

Say something, anything, Emma silently pleaded, closing her eyes.

"There you are."

Emma's eyes flew open. The double doors had swung wide, and a girl in a long, dark wig stood on the sidewalk. Ethan shot away from Emma like a bullet fired from a gun. "Sam," he said.

"I was looking for you." Samantha's gray eyes were cold. Her boobs looked weirdly squished in her corset. When she saw Emma, her scowl turned her pretty features into an ugly mask.

"We were just talking," Ethan blurted, moving to Samantha and taking her arm. "I was about to come in and look for you."

Samantha pivoted toward the door. "C'mon. Let's dance." She gave Emma an icy wave and pulled Ethan back into the gym. Ethan looked over his shoulder and met Emma's gaze.

A small squeak escaped Emma's mouth, but when she tried to say more, nothing came out. When they were gone, she pulled the detective hat off her head and mashed it between her hands.

Bing. Sutton's phone chimed inside Emma's bag. If it was a text from Ethan, Emma was going to throw the phone into the fountain in the middle of the courtyard.

But instead, the text was from Madeline. WHERE ARE YOU, BITCH? WE MISS YOU! YOU DIDN'T MAKE A SECRET GETAWAY WITHOUT US, DID YOU?

Another clap of thunder sounded from the gym. Emma stood up, resolute. Ethan's non-answer wasn't going to ruin her night.

She hit REPLY. ON MY WAY BACK INSIDE. After adding a tongue-wagging smiley, she hit SEND. Forget Ethan. Forget love. She had two twins to watch.

26

ONE DOWN, ONE TO GO

The next forty-five minutes passed quickly, filled with a tour of the haunted house, snarky costume-rating from one of the corner banquettes, and keeping tabs on Gabby and Lili, who made the rounds in their court sashes and spent most of the time on the dance floor as though nothing were amiss. Countless students approached Emma and the others to compliment them on a dance well done, though a notable few steered clear: Garrett, whom Emma hadn't seen since the closet incident, and Ethan, whom she unfortunately couldn't help but see chatting with Samantha—*Sam*—at one of the coffin tables. Every time Ethan glanced her way, Emma pretended she was having a fantastic time.

Finally, Emma, Charlotte, and Madeline tumbled out into the night, linking arms and laughing at the best and worst costumes of the night—dorky Amanda Donovan, who'd dressed as Mr. Peanut; John Pierce, a fabulous gay boy who always had everyone laughing, who'd come as Lady Gaga; and, of course, Davin-as-Freddy-Krueger, who'd tortured Madeline by extending and retracting his freaky knife-nails in her face all night. "I should've gone stag like you, Sutton," Madeline moaned.

Laurel appeared next, loosely holding hands with Caleb. They gazed at each other and giggled softly. When Caleb bent down to kiss Laurel lightly on the lips, Madeline whooped. "Yeah!"

"Sex goddess!" Charlotte seconded.

Laurel broke away from Caleb and shot the girls a mock glare. Emma grinned at her as she skipped toward the group, glad that she had found someone she really liked.

Madeline had parked her car in the school's lot earlier in the day in preparation for the camping expedition. As the girls headed toward the car, Gabby burst through the door, riding piggyback on Kevin Torres. Her goddess wings drooped, her floral crown was squished and tilted, but her Homecoming Court sash was still proudly in place. Kevin put her down gently on the bench, and they made disgusting cooing noises to each other.

Lili followed, also still wearing her sash. As soon as she saw Gabby and Kevin, her face stiffened, her lips puckered, and she curled her fists hard, accidentally lighting up her Lady Liberty torch. She swung a wide arc around them.

Madeline unlocked her SUV with two short bleeps. Emma climbed into the front seat next to her, while Charlotte and Laurel squeezed into the middle row. Sleeping bags, pillows, backpacks, flashlights, and an illicit bottle of vodka had been packed in the cargo space earlier that day. Very quickly, the cabin filled with the mingling odors of perfume, costume makeup, and cinnamon Altoids, which Laurel had passed around as soon as Madeline started the engine.

Just as Madeline adjusted the driving mirrors, there was a knock on the window. "Hey!" Gabby waved.

"Shit," Emma whispered. "Let's get out of here before they ask to come along again."

Madeline looked at her. "Sutton, we already invited them."

Emma's jaw dropped. "You did? When?"

Madeline shrugged. "It seemed only fair after the court prank."

"Inviting them to get ready with us was only fair," Emma said, the pitch of her voice rising higher and higher. "I don't want them camping with us!"

"Calm down." Charlotte sounded bored. "It's just one night."

Laurel looked back and forth between everyone, her cheeks still flushed from her night with Caleb. "We can't exactly uninvite them," she said. "Besides, they know where the springs are. None of us have ever been before, and apparently they're hard to find."

"The springs are hard to find?" Emma echoed weakly. Suddenly, the seat belt across her torso felt like a vise. She had to get out of here. She racked her brain for an excuse, but before she could come up with anything, Gabby wrenched open the door.

"Hey, girls!" She climbed past Charlotte and Laurel to the very back seat. Lili begrudgingly followed. When it was clear that the only available seat left was next to her sister, Lili let out a groan and plopped down, too, putting as much distance between them as she could. She gripped her Liberty torch as though it were a weapon.

Emma's skin felt hot and prickly at the nearness of the Twins. Her brain spun. Would Lili and Gabby do anything to her with the other girls around? Maybe if she played it cool—and stuck with Laurel all night—nothing would happen.

No no no, I thought desperately, willing Emma to get out of the car.

"Okay, bitches." Madeline revved the engine. "Let's get this show on the road."

Everyone whooped. "Hot springs, here we come." Charlotte draped her arms across the back of the seats.

Laurel swiveled around and looked at Lili and Gabby. "You remember how to get there, right?"

"Yeah. We just went camping there with our dad." Gabby's voice was languid and happy, as though she'd just spent hours at the spa. "He didn't want us to swim in them, but we did when he went to sleep."

"That's not true," Lili said sharply. "Dad didn't care if we swam in it."

"Yeah, he did," Gabby said. "He thought we'd drown."

"You've got it all wrong." Lili sounded really worked up. "You *always* get everything wrong."

Everyone fell silent at the razor-sharp tone of Lili's voice. "*Rrow,*" Madeline whispered.

The car rolled over a speed bump and out the school exit. Someone had draped spiderwebs over the gates and affixed devil horns to the large, many-armed cacti lining the path. Madeline turned up the winding roads that led toward the mountain. A sports car with round, xenon-bright headlights passed them going the other direction.

The girls began to chatter about the dance—Madeline and the disastrous Freddy Krueger, Laurel's burgeoning crush on Caleb. "And how about you?" Madeline nudged Emma. "You disappeared for a while. Did you find some-one fun?"

"Definitely not," Emma said quickly. She wanted to forget the whole Ethan thing ever happened.

"What did you think about the dance, ladies?" Charlotte asked, swiveling around and looking at the Twitter Twins. "Was being on the court everything you hoped for and more?"

"Of course," Gabby said automatically, lifting her sash from her chest and admiring it lovingly. "All eyes were on me. I felt like a princess."

Lili let out an irate squeak. "There were eight court girls, Gabriella. Not just you!"

Gabby shrugged. "You know what I mean."

"No, I don't think I do."

"What's wrong with you tonight?" Gabby wrinkled her nose. "You sound like Mom when you call me *Gabriella*."

A small, frustrated noise came from the back of Lili's throat. "As if you don't know?"

Everyone laughed awkwardly. Madeline cleared her throat. "Um, girls?" But the Twins ignored her.

"If you're going to be a mega bitch, maybe you shouldn't come tonight," Gabby said primly.

"You know what? Maybe I don't want to come. Maybe I don't want to spend another minute with you," Lili growled. She pointed at a Super Stop gas station at the next intersection. "Pull into there."

Madeline gripped the wheel, but she didn't put on her turn signal.

"I'm serious!" Lili screeched. "Pull frickin' over!"

Emma stiffened. Lili was more unhinged than ever.

"Whoa." Madeline set her jaw, veered into the next lane of traffic, and wheeled into the gas station. Several cars waited at the pumps. Two teenage boys in death-metal T-shirts loitered near the entrance, smoking cigarettes. Inside, Emma could see brightly colored soda bottles, racks and racks of candy, and grayish hot dogs spinning slowly on a grill.

As soon as the car slowed, Lili pushed Gabby out the back door. Then she climbed out herself, giving Gabby another shove. Gabby wheeled backward into a green trash barrel. "What the—?" she screamed.

Lili's eyes were wild. Her Lady Liberty toga was slipping, showing the scalloped, lacy edges of her bra. A bearded, greasy-haired truck driver filling his truck with diesel stared. So did the smokers by the door. "You know I like Kevin! I *told* you a million times!"

Gabby blinked her large blue eyes. "You never told me that."

"Yes, I did!" Lili stamped her foot. "You always do this to me! You knew full well I liked him. I saw you looking at me every time you guys danced. You were rubbing it in, and you know it!"

Gabby placed her hands on her hips. "Well, I like him, too . . . and he likes me back. Get over it."

"You insensitive little . . ." Lili lunged at Gabby. Madeline shot out of the car and grabbed Lili around the waist. Laurel climbed out, too, and restrained Gabby, pulling her toward a fledgling mesquite tree on the little walkway that led to the mini-mart. Emma stayed glued to her seat, unsure what to do.

The smokers by the door nudged one another and grinned. One of them called, "Cat fight!"

Lili panted hard. "I'm so sick of you," she hissed at Gabby.

"Yeah? Well, I'm sick of you, too," Gabby shot back.

Lili broke free from Madeline and pulled her iPhone from the tiny beaded clutch she held under one arm. After pressing several buttons, she put the phone to her ear.

"Who are you calling?" Gabby asked.

Lili tossed her head. "A cab to take me home. Go camping without me. I'm not going anywhere with *you*."

"Lili . . ." Gabby looked repentant. "I'm sorry, okay?"

"Yeah, Lili," Charlotte said, pushing a reddish curl over her shoulder. "You should come. You guys can work this out."

"Not anytime soon," Lili said stiffly. Then she perked up. "Hello? Yes, I need a cab, please. I'm at the Super Stop on Tanque Verde and Catalina . . ."

A stiff, dusty wind kicked up, fluttering the ends of the girls' dresses and wafting the acrid scent of gasoline into their nostrils. After Lili hung up, she walked to the front of the mini-mart and perched on the large square ice chest. The pimply smoking boys approached her almost immediately, but she gave them a death glare that sent them scurrying away.

Slowly, the girls piled back into the car. "Should we really go?" Charlotte asked.

"I hate leaving her alone like this," Laurel said.

"She'll be fine," Gabby said in a tight voice. "We're like a mile from our house—she could walk home if she wanted. She's just being a stubborn sore loser. We'll have a better time without her."

As Madeline maneuvered the car onto the highway, Emma twisted around to look at Lili one last time. She was staring at the car with unmasked fury, her crown now crumpled in her hand. A chill crawled down Emma's spine, and she said a silent *thank-you* that Lili wasn't coming on the camping trip. She could handle just one Twitter Twin. Right?

Wrong, I thought. Emma was going into the desert at night with one of my killers, and I had no idea if she'd be coming back out again.

27

A SHOVE IN THE DARK

As the car climbed higher up Mount Lemmon, the cacti gave way to deciduous pine trees, and the air thinned. The road curved up the rocky slope, offering stunning views of sparkling Tucson below.

"How much higher are we going?" Charlotte asked as they passed yet another camping spot. Several campers were parked in the lot, and a family was cooking burgers on one of the public barbecue grills.

"A little higher still," Gabby said, leaning forward between the seats.

Finally, after they passed three more scenic lookouts and made two wrong turns that forced them to reverse back down the mountain, Gabby screeched, "There it is!"

Madeline pulled the car into a flat gravel lot. A tiny wooden sign read CAMPING. Another was marked TRAILS, and a third warned WATCH FOR RATTLESNAKES.

The girls got out and unloaded the gear from the backseat. They'd climbed several thousand feet in elevation, and the air was sharp and cold. Goose bumps rose on Emma's skin. Gabby slipped out of her toga and changed into jeans and a hoodie, and the other girls did the same.

"We should probably put on sneakers, too," Gabby instructed, pulling a pair of Nikes from her bag. "The springs are about a mile hike from here."

"We're going to hike in the dark?" Emma blurted. She could barely see the scrubby trail that wound into the desert. A whistling, lonely wind blew tumbleweeds across the parking lot.

"That's what flashlights are for." Gabby pulled out a long, silver Maglite, heavy enough to bash someone's head in. When she switched the knob to the on position, nothing happened. "Huh."

Madeline and Charlotte had flashlights, too, but only one of them worked, spewing a weak, pale yellow beam onto the trail before them. "This seems like a bad idea," Emma said, her heart beating furiously. "Maybe we should come back another time."

Gabby hefted her backpack onto her shoulders. "Is Sutton Mercer . . . *afraid*?"

Emma gritted her teeth. Laurel looped her arm through Emma's. "It'll be fine," she said. "Promise."

"Let's go." Gabby's shoes made a crunching sound on the gravel as she marched toward the trailhead. Madeline pulled something out of her backpack. A flash of chrome glinted in the moonlight, and there was a sloshing sound of liquid hitting the sides of a bottle. "Here," she whispered, handing the flask to Emma. "Liquid courage."

Emma closed her fingers around the bottle and undid the top, but she only pretended to drink; she had to stay alert. The girls started down the trail, one after the other, dark shadows against a blue-black sky. Gabby's white hoodie gave off a soft glow, making it easier to keep sight of her, but the trail was narrow, and prickly cacti jutted out from all angles. Behind Emma, Laurel stumbled on a root, and Madeline's sleeve tangled in a tree branch. Gabby zigzagged the flashlight back and forth along the trail, but about five minutes after they'd started, the light died out, leaving them in complete darkness.

Everyone stopped. "Uh-oh," Charlotte said.

Emma turned around and squinted at where they'd come from, but the trail snaked over rolling hills, and she could no longer see the parking lot. She pulled out Sutton's iPhone and put it on flashlight mode, but it shed very little light. She also noticed she had no service. Her palms began to sweat. "What do we do?"

"Let's keep going," Gabby insisted. "It's not much farther. I promise."

Each of them pressed close to the girl in front of her, not wanting to get lost from the pack. "This is freaking me out," Madeline said. "Someone tell a story or something. I need a distraction."

"Two Truths and a Lie!" Laurel suggested with a nervous giggle. "We haven't played in forever."

"Fun!" Gabby said, pushing a tree branch out of the way. It snapped back and smacked Emma's jaw.

Madeline snickered. "Do you even know how to play, Gabs?"

"Uh, *yeah*." Gabby skirted around a boulder. "Just because I'm not a member of the Lying Game doesn't mean I'm an idiot."

"Could've fooled me," Charlotte muttered, and everyone giggled. Emma saw Gabby's shoulders tense as she plunged forward on the trail.

Luckily, Emma knew the rules of Two Truths and a Lie; she and Alex and a couple of other girls had played it at a sleepover. Everyone took turns making three statements: one false, two true. Everyone else had to guess which was the lie. If they guessed correctly, the statement-teller had to drink. If they guessed incorrectly, *they* had to drink.

"I'll go first," Madeline volunteered, sounding out of breath as they climbed a slope. "One: When my family went to Miami last year, I crashed a party and met JLO. Two: I had a consultation for a boob job at Pima Plastic Surgery last year. And three: I think I know exactly why Thayer left. I think I know where he is, too, but I'm not telling."

The words chilled Emma. When she swiveled around and looked at Madeline's face, she couldn't tell if she was smiling or frowning.

"The boob job has to be the lie," Charlotte's voice rang out in the darkness. "Mads has the best rack of all of us!"

"Wrong!" Madeline taunted. "The boob job is true—I made an appointment because I was flirting with the idea of double-Ds. I changed my mind, though, when I found out what the surgery was like. So drink up, Char!"

"So which one *was* the lie?" Gabby slowed down at the front of the line. "Thayer?"

Madeline shrugged. "I guess you'll never know now."

Emma fixed her gaze on Madeline. *Could* she know where Thayer was? Was she trying to protect him from someone—maybe their dad?

The liquid in the bottle made a swishing noise as Charlotte drank. "Okay. Statement one: I cheated on Garrett. Two: I think my dad's cheating on my mom. And three: I kissed Freddy Krueger in the haunted house."

"But your mom's way too hot to cheat on, Char."
Madeline sounded torn. "I'm not guessing on this one."

Emma kept her mouth shut, a thought suddenly swimming into her mind. While waiting for Sutton at Sabino Canyon, she'd seen a man she recognized from Sutton's Facebook page as Charlotte's father. He'd seemed flustered, and later, Emma found out Charlotte thought he was away on business.

But she didn't dare say it, instead maneuvering quietly around two rocks.

"Freddy's the lie!" Gabby whooped finally.

"Drink up, Gabby!" Charlotte crowed. "I was in the haunted house and felt these hands behind me. Someone spun me around and planted one right on my lips. It was totally Freddy—I saw his freaky nails. He wasn't a bad kisser, Mads."

Madeline snorted. "You can have him!"

No one asked Charlotte which one the lie was.

After Gabby drank her penalty shot, Madeline said, "Your turn, Sutton."

Emma took a deep breath and racked her brain for what she could say about Sutton. But then she had another idea. "Okay. One: I worked at a roller coaster in Las Vegas one summer," she started.

"Lie," Charlotte said automatically, cutting her off. "You've never worked in Vegas."

"You're just trying to get drunk, aren't you, Sutton?" Madeline passed her the bottle. Emma smiled to herself, but didn't bother correcting them.

They walked on. A lone coyote howled in the distance. A cactus needle scraped Emma's shin. Then Gabby turned around and looked at them from the front of the line. "Am I next? One: My sister and I cheated to get on the Halloween dance court. Two: Kevin and I made out in the haunted house right by the jar full of fake eyeballs. And three . . ." She paused for effect. Crickets chirped. "I once touched a dead body."

The wind shrieked in Emma's ears, and her heart leapt to her throat.

I shivered. Was it my body? More than ever before, I needed Emma—I needed her to nail Gabby and Lili and expose my murder. I needed them to go down for what they'd done.

Laurel sniffed. "A dead body? Yeah, right."

Blood pulsed in Emma's ears. It took everything she had to keep her feet moving forward, because if she tried to turn back, she might get lost . . . or worse.

"But if that's the lie, that means you cheated to get on the court," Madeline murmured. "You couldn't do that, could you?"

"I don't know, could I?" Gabby taunted. She twisted around and stared straight at Emma. Emma couldn't see her features, but she could tell Gabby was smirking. "What do you think I'm capable of, Sutton?"

Suddenly, the trail hit an abrupt dead end, and the girls stopped short. Instead of a hot spring burbling before them, they stood at the edge of a cliff. Pebbles cascaded over the side. The faded light showed silhouettes of criss-crossing branches below. It was too dark to tell how far of a drop it was.

A gust of wind howled along the trail, rustling dead leaves at Emma's feet, and she realized with a jolt how wrong she'd been to think she could handle Gabby. They were in the desert with no flashlights and no cell phone service. One wrong step, one stumble, and Emma would become the headline Gabby and Lili wanted: *Teen Dies in Tragic Desert Accident*. It was the perfect scenario, really. Because if Emma died out here, everyone would think Sutton Mercer met her end during an ill-fated drinking game. There would no longer be a murder to cover up, no reason for anyone to take Sutton's place. It would all just be over.

"Uh, Gabby?" Madeline shuffled her feet. "Did we take a wrong turn?"

"Nope." Gabby smacked the flashlight she was holding and tried the switch again, but it still didn't work. "The path continues on the other side of this cliff. It's a really easy jump, I swear."

Gabby pointed a few feet in the distance. A ravine

separated one side of the trail from the other.

"I'm not jumping," Emma said in a shaking voice.

"Yes, you are." Gabby sounded amused. "It's the only way to get to the springs."

A pair of eyes glowed from a tree branch above Emma's head. She made out the shape of a great horned owl.

Madeline pushed around them. "Let's just get there already, okay? I'm sick of hiking." She held on to her backpack straps and did a graceful, ballet-dancer leap over the chasm, clearing it easily. "Piece of cake!" she yelled from the other side.

Gabby let Charlotte go next, then Laurel. But when Emma tried to edge past her, Gabby stuck out her arm to stop her. "Not so fast," she said in a low voice.

Emma's stomach dropped to her feet. This was it.

"Run, Emma!" I screamed at my sister. "Get out of there!"

Across the ravine, the other girls shifted, waiting. "C'mon, guys," Madeline called out. "What's the holdup?"

Slowly, Gabby reached out and grabbed Emma's wrist. Emma flinched. What was going to happen next crystallized before her: Gabby was going to throw her over the side of the cliff. She was going to kill her swiftly and neatly in a matter of seconds, and then tell everyone that Sutton had tripped or stumbled. A new headline formed in Emma's head: *Girl Gets Away With Murder—Twice.*

All at once, something broke loose inside Emma's body. She wasn't going to die—not tonight. "Get away from me!" she cried, shoving Gabby backward.

Rocks cascaded beneath Gabby's feet. Gabby's mouth made a small O. There was a scrambling sound, and her arms wheeled in the air for balance. Time seemed to slow down. Gabby's sneakers slipped beneath her as though she were skating on ice. She grappled for something to steady herself, but the only things around her were thin tree branches and razor-sharp cacti. A startled screech rang out in the darkness. There was a deafening *swoosh* of rocks, another shrill wail, and then Gabby was falling.

"Gabby!" Madeline cried, rushing to the edge of the cliff.

"Oh my God!" Charlotte screamed.

A single wail punctuated the air. A series of crashes sounded, a body smacking against tree branches, jutting rocks, sharp cacti. And then, agonizing moments later, there was a crash, a clear but distinct sound of a heavy falling object finally hitting bottom.

28

WALLED IN

Emma's stomach lurched like she was about to throw up. "Oh my God." She stared at her hands as though she didn't recognize them. She hadn't just pushed Gabby. It *couldn't* have been her. She was a *nice* girl, Emma Paxton, not capable of violence, even if the person she'd hurt was about to hurt her.

"Jesus, Sutton!" Charlotte pressed her hands to her head. "What did you do?"

"Gabby?" Laurel's voice echoed in the rocky ravine. "*Gabby?*"

"She isn't dead." Madeline's voice shook. "She can't be. She's okay down there."

Emma peered over the ravine. She couldn't see the bottom. She looked at her hands again, and they began to tremble. All at once she felt horribly disgusted with herself. Who had she *become*? "I didn't mean . . ." she sputtered. "I didn't think . . ." Tears began to roll down her cheeks.

"What the hell happened?" Charlotte demanded. "Did you push her?"

"No! She grabbed me, and I . . ." Emma cried, the words coming out in a combination of a moan and a sob. "I didn't think she'd . . ." But she couldn't say anything more. *Had* it been an accident, or had her fears and anger gotten the best of her? Had she pushed harder than she thought? Guilt sloshed through her veins. This had to be a mistake. A dream. A nightmare. But then she remembered grabbing Gabby's taut shoulders and pushing her away. Fresh, terrified tears swarmed her eyes.

"Haven't you put Gabby through enough, Sutton?" Charlotte screamed. "What if she's hurt?"

"I told you, I didn't mean to do it!" Emma shouted, her head spinning. She squinted through the darkness to the bottom of the ravine. Gabby *had* to be there, alive, fine. This wasn't how things were supposed to go. *She* wasn't supposed to be the villain—Gabby and Lili were, for killing Sutton! She was just defending herself! But Sutton's friends wouldn't buy that. Neither would the cops—not without proof of what the twins did.

"Someone call nine-one-one," Laurel yelled.

Emma looked helplessly down at Sutton's phone. "There's no service out here!"

"What are we going to do?" Madeline shrieked.

Laurel pointed to a dark, narrow path that led down the mountain, practically overgrown with cacti, brambles, and shrubs. "We have to get to her. We have to see if she's okay."

Laurel bushwhacked through the brush and started down the slope, using her cell phone as a dim flashlight. Emma leapt over the ravine and followed them. Cactus spines poked her arms, insinuating their way under her skin, but she felt impervious to the pain. *It was an accident*, Emma repeated over and over to herself, but a tiny voice inside her kept crying, *Was it?*

"Gabby?" Laurel called out.

"Gabs!" Madeline screamed.

No answer. A chilly wind gusted, piercing through Emma's thin sweater.

"What if she's unconscious when we get to her?" Laurel sobbed. "Does anyone know CPR?"

Charlotte clutched a tree branch that looked moments away from snapping with the weight of her grasp. "How will we be able to call an ambulance? What if she's having a seizure?"

"The doctor said her medicine would prevent that,

right?" Laurel said, sounding completely unconvinced.

"What if she forgot to take it today?" Madeline asked, her voice shaking.

Charlotte crept carefully down the path, avoiding a spear-shaped rock that jutted from a patch of dirt.

Again Emma tried an outgoing call on her cell phone. The other girls did, too, but no one could get a signal. *Crack*. Emma stopped short and looked around. "Gabby?" she called hopefully. No answer.

The girls kept going. After another ten minutes of stumble-walking down the steep slope, they finally arrived at the bottom of the ravine. It looked like a dried-out riverbed, the sides walled in by craggy black rock, the bottom smooth and sandy. The air was so calm that it felt like they were beneath a dome. Stars twinkled dimly in the sky. Muddy moonlight leached through gray clouds. They were absolutely hidden here. They could die and never be found.

Just like I had. In fact, this seemed like a perfect place to hide my body. I waited to feel a tingle of recognition, a cosmic message that it was here. . . .

"Gabs?" Madeline screamed. "Where are you?"

"She's not here, guys." Charlotte slumped to a rock on the other side of the riverbed. "We must be in the wrong spot."

Emma blinked into the bluish darkness. As far as she

could tell, there was nothing on the ground. Certainly not a body. A cold, clammy feeling overcame her, and she sank to her knees. All at once, she couldn't breathe.

Madeline stood over her. "Are you okay?"

Emma nodded, then shook her head. "I . . ." But she couldn't get the rest of the words out.

"She might be in shock," Laurel said.

"Jesus," Charlotte whispered, as if this was all they needed.

"We should split up to look for Gabby," Laurel suggested. She gestured to her right. "I'll go that way."

"I'll go left," Charlotte said.

"I'm going back to the car," Madeline said. "Or as far as I need to go to get cell service to call nine-one-one. Sutton, don't move, all right? Just sit still. We'll come back for you."

Everyone headed off in opposite directions. Emma watched until their dim shapes disappeared in the distance. The air whipped quietly around her. Pebbles rained down the side of the mountain. Slowly, the crushing feeling on her chest began to abate. She gulped in air and rubbed her hands together. She couldn't just sit here. She had to look for Gabby. "Hello?" she called out. Her voice echoed slightly.

Suddenly, Emma heard a thin, small sound to her right. She stood up straighter, alert. "Gabby?"

Next came a choppy inhalation of breath. And then, there it was again: a tiny moan.

"Gabby!" Emma's body filled with hope. She spun around, trying to locate the direction of the noise.

Another moan. Emma walked toward a wall of rocks on the side of the ravine. "Gabby?" she called. "Is that you?"

"*Help*," a hoarse, weak voice cried.

It *was* Gabby. Emma scanned the empty ground, shining Sutton's phone on the rocks until she found a narrow opening a few feet up that she otherwise would've mistaken for an animal burrow. She peered inside the dim, black space and listened hard. Her heart simultaneously lifted and broke when she heard another faint, desperate cry from deep inside. "Help!"

Emma had found Gabby, all right. She was trapped.

29

THE DARKEST PLACE IN THE WORLD

Emma peered into the tiny opening. "Gabby!"

The rocks must have shifted when she fell, walling her inside. She stepped back and blinked into the darkness. "Laurel? Charlotte?" No one answered.

Another weak cough emerged from inside the cave. Emma tried 911, but her phone refused to dial out.

The temperature had dropped at least ten degrees since Emma had descended into the gulch, but sweat ran down her face and back. She assessed the opening again. There was a space in the rocks just wide enough for a body to slip through. She could do it. She *had* to. She was the one who'd shoved Gabby off the cliff. Even though Gabby had killed Sutton, Emma wasn't a killer, too. She had to make this right.

"I'm coming, Gabby," she called.

She dropped her backpack to the ground and rolled up her sleeves. Taking a deep breath, she hoisted herself up to the small hole and wriggled through. The inside of the space smelled musky, like an animal. The rocks felt slick and cold on her skin. Her shoulders bent inward, her arms out in front, feeling the way. Her hip bones ground against the sides of the tiny tunnel as she moved forward a few feet.

"Gabby?" she called. Her voice sounded so loud inside the cave. "Gabby?" she tried again. But Gabby didn't answer. Had she passed out? Had she had another seizure? Was she dead?

Tiny pebbles fell on her head with even the slightest provocation as she squirmed forward. Dust clogged her lungs. At one point, she glanced over her shoulder and could barely see the tiny crack she'd slithered through.

I crawled along with her, the small, confined space feeling like a coffin with the lid closed.

"Gabby?" Emma cried again. Her knees banged on a rock. Her shoulders squeezed through two tightly compacted boulders, and she emerged into a wider pocket inside the cave where she could almost stand. "Gabs?" Still no response. Where had she gone? Had Emma's ears played tricks on her?

Suddenly, a loud *boom* filled the air. Dust whipped across her face and up her nose. A loud whooshing sound roared in her ears. Pebbles pelted Emma's back and head and ran down her shirt. *It's an avalanche*, she thought, covering her head and flattening herself to the bottom of the tunnel.

The noises continued for a few moments more. When they petered out, Emma carefully raised her head and looked around. Dirt swirled everywhere. She squinted in the direction she'd come. The hole she'd climbed through was *gone*. She was walled in.

"Oh my God," I whispered.

Panic rose in Emma's chest. "Help!" she screamed, but her voice didn't seem to carry, bouncing off the close, thick walls. "Help!" she cried again, but it was no use. No one called out from the other side. Why weren't Sutton's friends back by now? Why didn't they hear her?

She looked into the wider opening again, pricking up her ears for another one of Gabby's moans. "Gabby?" she whispered, looking right and left. Her heart pounded so loudly in her head she feared its vibrations might cause another landslide. Her eyes began to play tricks on her, forming shapes she knew weren't there. A chair. A seated figure. A tennis racket propped up against the rocks. Her head spun; she had to be losing oxygen in the sealed space.

And then a cold, strong hand grasped Emma's wrist.

Emma screamed out. She tried to wrench free, but the hand wouldn't let go. The flicker of a dim flashlight illuminated the lower half of a girl's face. "G-Gabby?" Emma stammered.

The figure in front of her smiled. But those weren't Gabby's lips. Emma drew in a breath. Was that . . . ?

"Hi, Sutton," said the girl, followed by a maniacal giggle. "Glad you could drop in."

The dank air chilled the back of Emma's neck. Her free hand dug into dirt and rocks to steady herself. "Lili?" her voice quivered. "W-what are you doing here?" Hadn't they left her at the Super Stop station? Hadn't she refused to come?

"Come on, Sutton." Lili cackled. "You know the answer to that, don't you?"

The words sliced through Emma's chest. All at once, she understood what was going on: Gabby and Lili's fight, Gabby's fall, Lili's moans inside this cave, even the walls crumbling down around Emma—all of it had been orchestrated by Gabby and Lili as a way to get Emma in here alone. They weren't mad at each other. Gabby wasn't hurt. The Twitter Twins knew Emma would crawl into this cave to rescue the girl she'd thought she'd pushed—because she wasn't Sutton, because she would feel terrible about what she'd done. And now, they had her right where they wanted her. They *had* warned Emma, hadn't they? Countless times, countless ways. *Keep being Sutton. Say nothing. Stop sleuthing. I mean it. Or you're next.*

She'd fallen right into their trap.

"Please." The word spilled from Emma's lips. Her body bucked and her head spun; she thought she might throw up. "Can't we talk about this?"

"What's there to talk about?" Lili asked in a low voice.

"Please let me go," Emma begged, trying to pull away. Lili gripped her tightly. "I screwed up, Lili. I'm sorry. But I won't do it again. I promise."

Lili made a *tsk* noise with her tongue. "I warned you, *Sutton*. But you didn't listen." She shifted on the rocks, edging closer to Emma. With a swift, violent motion, Lili grabbed Emma by Sutton's necklace, just as she'd done that night in Charlotte's kitchen. Emma kicked with all her might, banging her knee on the rocks over her head, feeling blood run over her shin. She tried to scream, but Lili had clapped a hand over her mouth, and it only came out as a muffled gurgle. Lili pulled at the necklace, stretching the chain tight against Emma's throat. Emma began to cough, flailing her arms and legs, thrashing with all her might. Lili pulled harder, the chain cutting into Emma's skin.

"Please!" Emma croaked, barely having enough air to cry out. Her lungs screamed, and she desperately tried to inhale. Lili giggled.

Suddenly, there was a prick of pain at the side of Emma's neck, and the necklace broke free. The heavy locket released from the chain and dropped down the front of Emma's shirt, landing in the waistband of her jeans. Lili's eyes blazed. Her teeth were bared in a crocodile smile. A vein stood out on her forehead, and she leered at Emma with hatred and vengeance. It was the face of a killer. *Sutton's* killer . . . and hers, too.

I wanted Emma to run. I wanted her to fight. But instead, I steeled myself for the worst. Suddenly, the strange snapping sensation I always got when I was about to relive a memory whipped through me like a freight train. I saw bright, whirling lights. Widened eyes. A girl on a gurney. The word EMERGENCY glowing in red on top of a porte cochere. My nose tickled with the scent of antiseptic and sickness. My ears tingled with the sounds of moans—maybe my own.

And just like that, I fell headfirst into another memory. . . .

30

THE AFTERMATH

The emergency-room waiting area is crowded with people: sick babies screaming, a greasy guy in a hard hat with the mother of all splinters in his fleshy, dirty thumb, a bunch of old people who look like they're already halfway in the grave. The five of us sit upright in our chairs, not leafing through old magazines, not watching the lame-ass local news on TV, just staring at the double doors that divide us from the emergency room and Gabby.

By the time we arrived at the hospital, Gabby had already been taken into the treatment area. The only thing the nurses told us when we burst through the doors was that we had to wait, and they pointed us to the seating area where Lili was already pacing.

Mr. and Mrs. Fiorello arrive, leaving me terrified Lili's going to tell them what really happened. She doesn't. Instead, she clutches them, sobbing into their chests. They sit a few chairs away from us, fidgeting, staring at paperback books without turning the pages. Mrs. Fiorello has curlers in her hair, and Mr. Fiorello is wearing shoes that look suspiciously like bedroom slippers. Then again, it is almost one in the morning.

About a half hour into the wait, Lili jumps up and approaches one of the triage women behind the thick panes of glass. Mrs. Fiorello follows her; Mr. Fiorello leans his head back on the chair and closes his eyes. When the woman tells Lili she can't see her sister for the fifth time, Lili screams, "What if Gabby's dead? What if she needs my blood?"

Laurel bursts into tears. Madeline bites off the last of her manicure. Charlotte keeps making these gagging, puffed-cheeks faces like she's about to throw up.

"I'm sorry," I say quietly to them, knowing that they're all privately thinking that I'm a huge bitch. "I didn't know this would . . ."

"Just shut up about it, okay?" Charlotte hisses, digging her nails into her thighs. "Don't make me regret not saying anything to the cops."

A balding, middle-aged male doctor in blue scrubs and a surgical cap emerges through the ER doors, spies Lili and her mom, and walks to them. Mr. Fiorello and the four of us jump up and rush to their side. My stomach churns. The doctor's face is drawn, as though he's about to deliver bad news. He clicks and unclicks a pen and twists his mouth. "You're Gabriella Fiorello's family?" he asks.

Lili's parents nod. Mr. Fiorello wraps his arms around Mrs. Fiorello and Lili's shoulders, pulling them tight.

"Gabriella had what's called a grand mal seizure," the doctor says. "It's when the electrical activity over the surface of the brain is altered. She's a little shaken up, but she's resting now and is doing just fine."

Lili's eyes are round. "She's fine? But why did she have a seizure?"

On and off goes the pen with nonstop clicks. "A seizure can be caused by an infection, but we tested her blood, and she showed no signs of infection. It can also be caused by a brain tumor, but we've done an MRI to rule out that possibility. More than likely—"

"What about fear?" Lili cuts him off.

The doctor's eyebrows shoot up questioningly.

"Can a seizure happen out of fear?" Lili asks. "Like if someone really, really scared her?" She turns and looks pointedly at me. I shrink down a little in my shoes.

"That's very unlikely," the doctor says. "We think Gabriella has epilepsy. She's probably had it since birth, but the disease can lay dormant in people for a long time before manifesting itself. Why it chose tonight to rear its ugly head, we'll never know."

"Epilepsy?" Lili repeats, looking like she doesn't believe him. "But . . . that's, like, a serious disease! Only freaks have epilepsy!"

"Lilianna." *Mrs. Fiorello shoots Lili an irritated look.*

"That's not true," *the doctor says gently.* "Epilepsy is very manageable. Many patients who have it don't ever suffer a grand mal seizure again. But to make sure, Gabriella will have to be on medication for the rest of her life. We're lucky she didn't have a seizure when she was driving a car, or when she was somewhere alone. It's great that all five of you were with her and knew to call an ambulance."

I sneak a peek at the others, wondering if they're going to speak up. The ambulance wasn't called because of Gabby, after all, but because I'd stalled the car on the tracks. But no one says a word.

The Fiorello parents nod, taking this in, and thank the doctor. He gestures to the swinging white doors. "You can go see her now if you want. She's a little sleepy, but she's been asking for you."

We shove through the ER doors, pass a nurses' station and a couple of empty beds, and find Gabby on a small cot in a curtained-off cubicle. She's dressed in a faded, polka-dotted hospital gown, and her face is pale and drawn.

Lili runs to Gabby and throws her arms around her, making the bedsprings squeak. "I'm so glad you're okay," *she whispers, her voice choked with tears.*

"I'm totally fine," *Gabby says, looking exhausted but okay.*

After she hugs her parents, she gives us a small smile. "Hey, guys."

We each hug Gabby. Her body feels so tiny under the thin

hospital gown. Then we hug each other, all of us filled with relief and gratitude and nervous energy. Lili even hugs me, squeezing me tight. "Mark my words," she murmurs into my ear. "The prank might have ended okay, but Gabby and I are going to get you. You aren't going to know when, you aren't going to know where, but we'll get you back one way or another."

I wave my hand dismissively. The Twitter Twins, pranking me? Right. I'm no longer that scared, needy girl from the waiting room. I'm Sutton Mercer again, the girl everyone looks up to. The girl everyone fears. The girl who gets away with everything.

"I'd like to see you try," I challenge.

Lili doesn't blink. "Game on, Sutton."

"Game on," I answer back.

31

CLEVER LITTLE BITCHES

"Please," Emma whispered as Lili loomed close, her body weak from Lili's choke hold and the lack of oxygen. "Please don't hurt me."

"Say goodbye," Lili growled.

Emma closed her eyes and pictured all the people she would say goodbye to. Ethan—she'd never even gotten to kiss him. She never realized exactly how much she *wanted* to kiss him until right now. Madeline, Laurel, and Charlotte—no more laughing with them, no more gossiping. It struck her, suddenly, that these were people she knew in Sutton's life, not hers. Was there anyone who would miss her from when she was Emma? Who did she have who would mourn *her*? Even Ethan couldn't grieve for Emma in public. He would have to know her as Sutton Mercer, not Sutton's secret twin. And Alex didn't know she was pretending to be Sutton, wouldn't realize that it was Alex's friend who was now dead.

Sutton's face, a face so identical to hers, flared in her mind. She'd wanted to know Sutton more than anything else in the entire world. And she'd wanted to solve this for her sister, to put this horrible crime to rest. Who knew what would happen now. *I'm sorry, Sutton*, she thought. *I tried my best.*

I know, Emma. I tried to place my hand over my sister's to comfort her, to let her know I was right there.

The cave was tomb-silent. Lili leaned down so her lips were next to Emma's ear. And then, quietly, joyfully, she whispered, "*Gotcha.*"

Her hands went slack from Emma's neck. When Emma opened her eyes, Lili was giggling hysterically. "Gotcha!" she cried again, louder this time, as though she were calling to someone.

Rocks began to shift, and suddenly, the big boulder that had walled Emma in disappeared. A bright flashlight shone into their faces. "Gotcha!" another voice cried from outside the cave. Emma shielded her forehead and stared at the willowy blond. Was that . . . Gabby?

Emma scuttled out of the cave. As soon as her feet hit

solid ground, Gabby cuffed her playfully on the shoulder. "You were so scared! We got you so good!"

Madeline, Charlotte, and Laurel appeared behind Gabby, contrite looks on their faces. Emma's heart raced, and she gasped for air. "Did you guys know about this?"

Laurel smiled sheepishly. "We found out at the dance."

Emma gaped. She turned to Lili, who was climbing out of the cave, then back to Gabby. She tried to settle her nerves with a deep breath, but it caught in her throat. "How long had you been planning this?" she sputtered.

The Twitter Twins exchanged a glance. "Lili and I scoped this place out a couple of weeks ago on a camping trip with our dad," Gabby admitted. "And then when you invited us to go camping, we put everything into action."

Lili grabbed Gabby's flashlight and shone it up the ridge. "There's a ledge just below where Gabs fell. She jumped there after you pushed her." She put *pushed* in air quotes. "I made lots of noise down here to make it sound like she'd had a bad fall."

"So you were here the whole time?" Emma asked.

"Yup. I only pretended to call a cab," Lili said. "I hid my car in the back of the Super Stop earlier today."

"Oh, and we weren't really fighting about Kevin, by the way," Gabby said with a grin. "Lili isn't into him."

Lili made a face. "He smells like smoked salmon."

"He does not!" Gabby's plump lips pursed.

Lili shrugged and turned back to Emma and the others. "When you guys left, I drove here and hid at the bottom of the ravine—there's another parking lot nearby that got me here much faster. Once I knew Gabby pretended to fall, I climbed into the cave"—Lili pointed at the rocks—"which we actually made. Wait 'til you see it in the daytime. It looks *so* fake and cheesy."

"Lili waited for you guys," Gabby went on, proudly rocking back and forth on her heels. "And then, when Sutton climbed in, I came out from my hiding place and walled you in together." She wiggled her hands in front of her face as if to say *Spooky.*

"You should have heard Sutton!" Lili's eyes gleamed. "She was begging for her life! It was priceless!" Lili shone her flashlight on her iPhone. "I got a recording of it. We can *all* hear Sutton. *'Please! Don't hurt me, please! Can't we talk about this?'*"

Gabby grinned at Emma. "You've been freaked for weeks, waiting for us to prank you. I swear you were going to pee your pants when we drove you to the impound the other day."

Lili wagged her finger at Emma. "I told you we were going to get you back for that car-stalled-on-the-tracks prank."

"Speaking of which, did you like our little choo-choo charm?" Gabby flicked Lili's charm bracelet and it jingled. She turned to the others. "We sent Sutton a little present at the country club a couple of weeks ago. A little reminder that we weren't even yet."

"So it was you," Emma said, more of a statement than a question.

"Of course it was us." Lili grinned. "Who else would have?"

Gabby giggled. "Who knew the unflappable Sutton Mercer could get so frightened?"

Everyone turned and looked at Emma, waiting for her response. Her heart was still thrumming fast. Her blood coursed with adrenaline. Just moments ago, she'd believed this was the end. She could have sworn Gabby and Lili were Sutton's killers and the case was solved. But now, everything felt turned upside down. This was all just a prank? There was no malice, no murderous revenge? Her relief mingled with the sinking realization that once again, she had no idea who had killed Sutton.

But for the first time in weeks, I relaxed. Emma was safe—for now. Gabby and Lili just wanted to be in our clique. My killer was still out there, but the five girls who stood staring at Emma—thinking she was me—weren't killers. They were my friends.

Finally, Emma straightened up and took a deep breath. "You definitely got me," she admitted. "It was a good prank."

"It was an *awesome* prank," Charlotte agreed. "How did you think of it? Did you guys have help?"

"Believe it or not, the idea came out of our tiny brains," Lili pointed just above her ear. "We've told you a million times, we have tons of ideas for pranks. But you snobs didn't listen, so we decided to take matters into our own hands."

Charlotte crossed her arms over her chest. She glanced at Emma. "I think this might've been the best prank *ever.*"

"Much better than the train tracks," Madeline piped up.

"Better than the snuff film, too," Laurel added. "And even better than what Sutton did to . . ." She peeked at Madeline and shut her mouth.

Gabby and Lili turned to Emma. They looked so hopeful and eager, two puppies desperate to impress the alpha dog. All at once, Emma felt for Gabby, for all she'd been through.

I felt badly for Gabby, too. But more than that, I felt embarrassed. I'd callously brushed off her seizure. I'd insisted, over and over, that no one dare tell what *I'd* done, like I was the most important person in the room. Was it possible I'd treated my murderer cruelly like this, too? Had I crossed the wrong person, someone who'd sought revenge with more than just a prank? Someone who'd paid me back by taking my life?

Finally, Emma cleared her throat. "I know I said there was only room in the Lying Game for four people, but I think we can make an exception."

"Maybe even *two* exceptions," Charlotte added.

Laurel nodded.

The Twitter Twins clasped hands and jumped up and down as if they'd just won *American Idol*. "We knew it! We knew you'd let us in!"

"I suppose we have an induction ceremony to perform," Charlotte announced. "Your official entrée into the Lying Game."

"You'll get to pick executive titles," Madeline said. "I'm Empress of Style. Sutton's Executive President and Diva."

"I want to be Mistress of Awesomeness," Gabby piped up immediately, as if she'd been thinking about this for a while.

"I'll be High Princess," Lili chimed in.

"There are a bunch of rules, too," Charlotte said. "Which includes no lying during games like Never Have I Ever and Two Truths and a Lie." She fake-coughed out the name *Gabby* into her palm.

"I didn't lie!" Gabby protested. "I told two truths! The false one was the dead body. I would never touch something *dead*." She shuddered.

Madeline shifted onto one hip. "So you cheated to get on the Homecoming Court?"

Lili made a small, embarrassed *eep*, but Gabby shrugged. "Guilty as charged. We hacked into the site and voted for ourselves hundreds of times. Told you guys we're smarter than you think."

"I guess you are." Emma hiked her backpack higher on her shoulder. "I don't know about you, but I've had enough camping for one night. I think the hot springs can wait for another day."

"Let's get the hell off this freaky mountain." Madeline grabbed Gabby's flashlight and shone it on the trail. "You know the way back, right?"

"But of course!" Gabby trilled.

As they started up the ridge, another thought popped into Emma's mind. She pulled Gabby aside. "It *was* an awesome prank. But, um, next time? Maybe don't cut a light fixture quite so close to my head."

Gabby stopped. Even in the blue-black darkness, Emma could see consternation wash over her face. "You mean that light in the auditorium? We didn't do that! God, Sutton! We're not insane!"

Then she moved ahead of Emma, her long ponytail swishing. Emma stood still a moment, a cold realization vibrating all the way down to her fingertips. Of course Lili and Gabby hadn't cut that light to fall on her. Someone else had.

My killer.

32

THE MOMENT WE'VE BEEN WAITING FOR

Bzzz. Bzzz.

Emma opened her eyes and looked around. She was lying on a sleeping bag on the floor of the Mercers' family den. The blue light of the muted TV flickered across the room, bags and containers of Thai takeout lay abandoned on the coffee table, and several dog-eared copies of *Us Weekly* and *Life & Style* were facedown on the carpet. The time on the cable box said 2:46 A.M. Charlotte, Madeline, and Laurel slept beside her, and Gabby and Lili were curled up near the fireplace, their brand-new Lying Game membership cards still clutched in their hands.

Bzzz.

Sutton's phone glowed next to Emma's pillow. The screen said ETHAN LANDRY. Emma was immediately alert.

Emma slid out of the sleeping bag and padded into the hall. The house was eerily still and dark, the only sound the rhythmic ticking of the grandfather clock in the foyer. "Hello?" she whispered into the phone.

"*There* you are!" Ethan cried on the other end. "I've been calling all night!"

"Huh?"

"Didn't you get my messages?" Ethan sounded out of breath, as if he'd been running. "I need to talk to you!"

Oh, now *you want to talk to me,* Emma thought, glancing out the window. A familiar red car sat at the curb. She dropped the curtain and pulled her T-shirt down so that it covered her stomach. "A-are you outside Sutton's *house?*"

There was a pause. Ethan sighed. "Yeah. I was driving around, and I saw Madeline's car in your driveway. Can you come out?"

Emma wasn't sure how to feel about Ethan sitting outside the Mercers' house in the middle of the night. If it had been anyone else, she would've thought it was slightly stalkerish. At least he'd used the phone this time, instead of pebbles. "It's three A.M.," she said frostily.

"Please?"

Emma ran her finger around the lip of a bowl on the hall table. "I don't know. . . ."

"Please, Emma?"

The area around Emma's temples began to ache. Her muscles were stiff from squeezing into the cave. She had no energy to play hard to get right now. "Fine."

The lights on Ethan's car died as Emma padded across the yard. "Why didn't you answer my calls?" he asked when she stepped off the curb.

Emma peered at Sutton's iPhone. Sure enough, there were six messages and missed calls from Ethan. She hadn't noticed them before—she'd been having too much fun with Sutton's friends, giving Gabby and Lili makeovers, drinking Kahlua shots, playing *Dance Dance Revolution*, and, of course, inducting Gabby and Lili into the Lying Game.

"I was busy," she answered, a hard edge to her voice. "I figured you were busy, too."

Ethan squared his shoulders and opened his mouth, but Emma held up her hand to stop him. "Before you say anything, it's not Gabby or Lili. They aren't who I thought they were." She was careful to use *I* instead of *we*, like it was her investigation only, not both of theirs.

Ethan frowned. "What happened?"

Emma took a breath and told him about the night. "It was just a prank," she concluded. "I mean, Gabby and Lili were definitely mad about the seizure thing, but they aren't Sutton's killers. All they wanted was to be part of the Lying Game."

Ethan leaned against the door of the car. A few houses down, a dog let out a lonely howl.

"They didn't drop that light on my head either," Emma went on, a shiver trailing along her spine. "I think Sutton's real killer did."

"But Gabby and Lili made so much sense. You said yourself Lili went back upstairs to retrieve her phone just before the light fell."

Emma shrugged. "Maybe the killer noticed that, too, hoping I'd suspect Gabby and Lili because of what Sutton did to them." She winced, thinking how she'd taken the bait. Even if Gabby had only fake-fallen, even if it was all a ruse, Emma had still lashed out in anger. What if things had gone wrong and the force of Emma's push had really killed her? She'd never felt so out of control.

Ethan shifted his weight and coughed into his fist. "The reason I've been trying to get ahold of you is that Sam told me something really . . . strange. At the end of the night, she got kind of fed up and asked what I was doing hanging out with someone like Sutton. She was like, 'I heard Sutton Mercer hit someone with her car and almost killed them.'"

"What?" Emma shot up. "Who?"

"I don't know. She wouldn't say. Or maybe she didn't know."

Emma squinted. "Had you heard anything like this before?"

Ethan shrugged. "Maybe it's not true."

Emma's heart pounded. Who could Sutton have almost killed with her car—and *when*? How could she not have known something so huge? "Maybe it *is* true," she said hesitantly. "I went to the impound to pick up Sutton's car earlier this week . . . but it wasn't there. Sutton signed it out . . . *on the thirty-first.*"

"The night she died?" Ethan's Adam's apple bobbed nervously.

"Yes. Not a single one of Sutton's friends knew she'd picked up the car." Emma tied her hair in a tight knot. "What if she had a reason not to tell anyone she picked it up? Maybe this rumor about her almost killing some- one with her car is true. Maybe she tried to run someone down on the thirty-first."

"Whoa, whoa, whoa." Ethan waved his hands across each other. "You're jumping to conclusions. Sutton wasn't always nice, but she wasn't a killer."

"Yeah," I wanted to add. Now Emma thought I was a hit-and-run kind of girl?

Emma took a deep breath. Maybe she *was* letting her imagination run away with her. "Still," she said. "We need to find Sutton's car. We need to figure this out."

"So it's *we* again, is it?" Ethan asked, smiling. "I'm allowed to be part of the investigation after all?"

Emma stared into the distance over his shoulder. "I

guess." But embarrassment and rejection still pulsed inside her. This was what scared her about getting too close to someone: all the mixed signals, all the misinterpreted gestures, all the emotions that became overamplified because something big was on the line. It was so much easier to steer clear of all that. It prevented so much potential pain.

"I'm sorry about Sam," Ethan said, reading her thoughts. "But she really is just a friend."

"I don't care," Emma said quickly, trying to look like she meant it.

"Well, I *want* you to care." Ethan's voice cracked. "I mean, I want you to care that we're not together."

"You can go out with her if you want. It's obvious she likes you."

An amused laugh escaped from Ethan. "I highly doubt she likes me after tonight. I spent the whole time asking questions about you, avoiding you, coming to talk to you in the parking lot, or obsessing over whether or not you were okay."

Emma winced at the memory. "Yeah, but then when she came looking for you, you jumped up in a heartbeat. You ditched me."

"She was my date!" Ethan raised his palms to the air. "I had to be polite! And even after I went back to her, I just asked more questions. At the end of the dance, she was like, 'I'm not the girl you want.' And it's true."

Emma snuck a peek at him. A sincere, earnest look flooded Ethan's face. "I know you have your doubts," he continued softly. "But I can't let you go. I can't stand by and just be friends."

He reached over and took Emma's hands. A tingly sensation snapped through Emma's insides. As she stared into Ethan's bright, loyal eyes, the tightly closed fist inside of her slowly began to open. Screw all her baggage. Screw worrying about getting hurt or emotions clogging up the investigation. Ethan was the most amazing guy Emma had ever met. What was the point of living if she didn't take some risks every once in a while? And maybe, just maybe, this was something Sutton would have wanted for her, too, if she were still alive: to go after Ethan, even if the prospects were scary, even if she was putting herself out on a limb. Sutton would encourage her to go after what she wanted anyway.

Of course I would. Of course I *was*.

Leaning forward, Emma brushed her lips softly against Ethan's. Ethan slid his hands up to her shoulders and kissed her more deeply. Emma's whole body sparked and came alive. Their mouths fit perfectly together. Her head started to spin. For the first time in her entire life, Emma just let go.

"*Yes!*" I cheered next to them. It was about time!

Snap.

Emma broke from Ethan, her heart shooting to her throat. She whirled around to see if one of the girls had followed her outside. But the front porch was still and unoccupied. No one lingered by the garage. *Snap.* Emma grabbed Ethan's hand. "Do you hear that?"

The sounds were coming from the house across the street. It was situated at the top of the hill, but something scuttled in the small ravine at its base. Emma tilted her head to the side, listening. "Did you see anyone when you drove up?"

"No." Ethan stood slightly in front of Emma, shielding her. He clutched tightly to her hand. "Maybe it's whoever lives there."

"At three in the morning?" Emma whispered.

"Maybe it's just someone on a walk," Ethan suggested. "Or . . ."

Footsteps crunched closer. Twigs snapped. A leaf crackled. Emma squinted across the street, petrified. She heard a slight cough . . . and smelled a faint whiff of coconut sunscreen.

Her hand flew to her mouth. She thought of the elusive figure that had loomed near Ethan and Emma on the tennis courts and on the bench outside the gallery. The squeak of sneakers as someone darted around the corner outside the nurse's office. All those times she'd felt like someone was watching her. . . .

"Ethan," Emma said nervously. "I have to get out of here." She ran across the Mercers' lawn with Ethan close on her heels. A figure stepped up the ravine, but Emma still couldn't see who it was. This suddenly felt like a nightmare; all she wanted was to wake up. Her movements felt slow and languid, like she was trying to slosh through mashed potatoes. She lunged across the final few feet of the driveway. Her hand was on the door, turning the knob. Once she was inside, Ethan spoke through the wood. "Lock the door," he said, his voice shaking.

Emma punched the lock and chained the bolt. Breath shuddered through her chest as she watched Ethan sprint to his car, gun the engine, and take off down the street.

Emma collapsed onto the Mercers' staircase, clutching her knees to her chest. Someone had been out there. She paced into the den, only slightly comforted by the sight of her friends sleeping, completely unaware of whoever was lurking outside. Emma's eyes flickered across the room, taking in the objects that'd become so familiar—the porcelain cactus, the framed photo of Sutton and Laurel at the Grand Canyon, the ikat-print ashtray that sat on the coffee table, even though no one in the family smoked.

A shadow moved across the porch light and cast an outline against the drawn blinds. Emma froze. This couldn't be happening. She pressed her body flat against Sutton's navy-and-white striped sleeping bag. She'd locked the front door, but what about the rest of the house?

Emma lay still, listening to the sounds of her friends breathing, counting their inhales and exhales. Moments turned into minutes. She scrunched her toes against an itchy wool throw blanket and counted to one hundred before jumping up, hopping over Laurel and Charlotte, and padding back into the hallway. The marble was cold against her bare feet as she crept up the steps. She needed to lock the window in Sutton's room—the one that was so easily accessible by the oak tree outside. She might not be able to reach the lowest branch from the ground, but anyone over six feet could.

At the top of the steps, she peered into the shadowy doorway at the end of the hall. Her feet inched across the carpet. She clutched Sutton's thin pajama pants and tried to slow her breathing as she stepped into the darkness of Sutton's room. Goose bumps rose on her bare arms as a cool breeze swirled around her body.

The window was wide open.

Moonlight spilled across Sutton's light blue sheets and the glossy magazine next to her bed. Emma took a small step backward and thudded into something warm and hard. She tried to scream, but the sound was muffled against the hand that suddenly wrapped over her mouth. Another hand was on her waist, pulling her body tight and holding her still no matter how hard she tried to break free.

"Shhhh." Warm breath tickled her ear. "It's me," a low voice growled.

The guy's voice resonated through me like an electric shock. From it cascaded a series of images, disjointed and brief. Sneaking away from a party and kissing in the desert. Finding a letter in my locker that was so heartfelt it made my knees weak. And then, yet again, that memory in the court-yard: him saying something to me, and me shouting back, *As if I'd ever want to be with you? You're nothing but a loser!*

And then a final memory wriggled to the surface, so short and sharp it was nothing more than a synapse: car headlights shining on his face. His eyes widening with fear, his arms thrashing in front of his body. And then . . . *boom*. Contact.

The hands loosened their grip and spun Emma. Her body went rigid. She took a second to process the hulking boy with dark hair, blinking, deep-set hazel eyes, high cheekbones, and deep Cupid's bow lips. That face. She knew that face. She saw a secretive boy in the pictures in Madeline's house. A smirking boy whose face was plastered on bulletin boards across town and haunted all those *Have you seen him?* Facebook posts. And now, here he was, smiling a strange, jagged smile, the kind of smile that hinted that he knew absolutely everything about her—including exactly who she wasn't.

"Thayer," Emma whispered.

EPILOGUE

A MOMENT IN TIME

As I stood in my old bedroom, staring at the boy who'd just climbed through my window, time just . . . *stopped*. The wind quit gusting outside. The birds fell silent. Emma and Thayer froze in their places, too, immobile as statues. Only I continued to move and flutter and think, getting my bearings and collecting my thoughts.

I tried to hold on to the flood of Thayer memories like they were a life raft at sea, but just when I thought I had my arms securely around them, they slipped away and sank deep down once more. Was it true that Thayer and I had shared something together—something real, something big? Those emotions I'd felt seemed so true, so *raw*, more momentous than anything I'd felt for Garrett or any other boy. But what if the memory of the headlights in Thayer's eyes was true, too? Had *I* hit Thayer? Was that rumor true?

Something even more frightening occurred to me. Was I, right this moment, staring into the face of my murderer?

After what I'd remembered, I hated to think that Thayer could be my killer, but I'd learned a thing or two about my tricky, dead-girl brain: I couldn't trust each individual memory, only the whole picture. What first seemed like a terrifying kidnapping had ended up being merely a dangerous prank, after all. A near-death had resulted in weary laughter, with everyone fine. Who was to say that the next glimpse of Thayer I saw undid those true-love feelings I had for him? Who was to say I hadn't died his bitter enemy?

It was impossible to know how I'd left things during my last few days on earth—whom I'd loved, and whom I'd hated. And it was impossible to know whom Emma should trust . . . and whom she should run from.

I stared into Emma's wide, glassy eyes. My sister was more terrified than I'd ever seen her. Then I turned to Thayer, peering into his lazy, self-assured face. Suddenly, something came to me about him that I'd long buried. This guy was a charmer. A hypnotizer. He could wrap you around his finger just as well as I could, convincing you that every word out of his mouth was true.

So who was the better liar? Me . . . or him?

Be careful, I wanted to tell Emma. Sure, she had a brand-new boyfriend, but something told me that Thayer was the type of guy who could sweep her off her feet before she even knew what hit her. I had a feeling Emma was about to embark on a new kind of Lying Game with Thayer. But in this little club of two, the stakes were a matter of life or death.

A loud *tick-tick-tick* sounded across the room, the second hand on the bean-shaped clock on my wall suddenly moving again. The curtains fluttered in the window. And as I turned back to Emma and Thayer, time had unpaused for them, too, thrusting my sister into her next moment with Thayer.

A boy I might have once loved. A boy I was now almost certain I couldn't trust. A boy who might have killed me.

⌐⌐ ACKNOWLEDGMENTS ⌐⌐

As usual, *Never Have I Ever* couldn't have happened without a dedicated and creative team. Thanks so much to Lanie Davis, Sara Shandler, Josh Bank, and Les Morgenstein at Alloy Entertainment for their time and care with this project. A huge shout-out to Kristin Marang and Liz Dresner for your awesome web promotions and skills, and to the fantastic editorial team at HarperTeen, Farrin Jacobs and Kari Sutherland. Sequels are sometimes hard, but I think this one went swimmingly thanks to all of you!

Also kudos and much praise for Katie Sise—I am so happy for your help. Love to my family, Shep, and Mindy (paparazzi princess), and to Ali and Caron, who love newborn lambs and talking about food as much as I do. Love to Joel for always putting up with me when I write these books (and for putting up with me in general). Much appreciation to all of the readers, bloggers, librarians, booksellers, festival organizers, and everyone else in the reading community who has reached out to me to help promote this new series. All of you know who you are, and all of you are awesome! And for all you readers, yet another reminder: *Never Have I Ever* is a work of fiction, and I dearly hope none of you emulate the club's sinister and often dangerous pranks. I hope you enjoy reading about Sutton's spooky coven, but please don't try any of her tricks at home!

Finally, a huge, exciting thank-you to Andrew Wang and Gina Girolamo at Alloy LA for developing these books for TV, Chuck Pratt for writing an amazing *Lying Game* pilot, to Alexandra Chando for playing such a convincing and loveable Sutton and Emma, and to everyone else working on the show henceforth. You all are amazing for believing in the books, and I can't wait to see the series when it airs!

Read on for a preview of
THE LYING GAME
book three

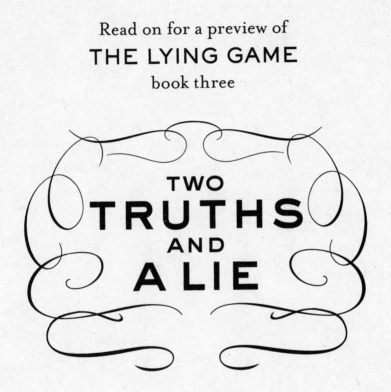

TWO
TRUTHS
AND
A LIE

If anyone had peeked through my window, they would have thought it was just a normal slumber party, a festive night that involved popcorn, manicures, and six gorgeous girls from the most exclusive clique at Hollier High giving each other makeovers, sharing juicy gossip, and plotting their next prank for the Lying Game. My iPhone had dozens of photos of past sleepovers that looked exactly like it: a shot of my best friend, Madeline, holding up a picture of a model with fringe bangs and asking if the look would flatter her heart-shaped face; one of my other besties, Charlotte, sucking in her cheeks to apply the new shade of blush she'd bought at Sephora; one of my adoptive sister, Laurel, snickering at a D-list celeb in *Us Weekly*; and plenty of photos of me, Sutton Mercer, looking like the glamorous, powerful "It girl" I was.

But on this particular night, something was different . . . and five out of the six girls didn't even know it. The girl my best friends were laughing with, the girl they thought was me . . . *wasn't*. Because I was dead. My BFFs were talking to my long-lost twin, Emma, who'd taken my place.

I'd died a month ago and was now perched somewhere between the land of the living and the great beyond, watching my life continue, but with Emma as the star. Everywhere she went, I went, like we were still sharing the same womb. Bizarre, right? I didn't think the afterlife would be like this either.

That night, I watched as my twin sister sat among my friends. Her legs were curled beneath her on the plush white sofa in the exact same way I used to sit. Her heavy-lidded eyes sparkled with my favorite silver MAC shadow. She even laughed the same way I did—loud, staccato, and a bit sarcastic. Over the past month she had perfected my mannerisms, answered to my name, and worn my clothes, all with the aim of being me until my murderer was exposed.

The worst part? I didn't even *remember* who killed me. There were whole chunks of my life that had been wiped clean from my mind, and I was left wondering who I'd been, what I'd done, and who I'd pissed off so much that they'd murdered me and then tricked my sister into assuming my identity. Every once in a while I would get a sudden flash of lucidity and a whole scene would snap into brilliant clarity, but the moments before and after it? Complete blanks. It was like getting a few random screen-grabs from a ninety-minute movie and trying to make sense of the entire plot. If I wanted to find out what had happened to me, I would have to rely on Emma . . . and hope that she caught my killer before my killer caught her.

There were some things Emma and I had figured out: My friends all had alibis for the night I died. As did Laurel, meaning they were all cleared. But there were so many suspects left. A particular one lingered in both our minds: Thayer Vega, Madeline's estranged brother, who'd skipped town last spring. His name kept popping up, and rumors swirled that he and I were somehow involved. Naturally, I couldn't remember a thing about Thayer himself, but I could tell *something* had happened between us. But what?

I watched as my best friends giggled and gossiped and began to wind down. By 2:46 A.M., the lights were low, and each girl's breathing was slow and deep. The iPhone I'd sent hundreds of texts on before I'd died suddenly chimed, and Emma's eyes sprang open as though she were expecting the message. I watched as she checked the screen, frowned, and tiptoed out of the house and across the yard. Ethan Landry, the only person who knew Emma's true identity—apart from my killer, of course— stood waiting for her by the curb. And there, in the moonlit driveway, I watched as they talked, hugged, and shared their very first kiss. Even though I no longer had a body, a heart, I still ached all the same. I would never kiss anyone again.

But then footsteps crunched nearby. Emma and Ethan flew apart worriedly. I was yanked behind Emma as she rushed back inside. I glanced over my shoulder just before she slammed the door, and I saw Ethan running into the night. Then, a shadow passed across the front porch. I could hear Emma's shallow, nervous breathing. I could tell she was scared. With another jolt, I was tugged along as she ran toward the stairs to make sure my bedroom window was locked.

When she and I reached the landing, we both caught a glimpse of the inside of my old bedroom. The window was indeed open, and standing in front of it was a familiar-looking boy. The blood drained from my sister's face as she took in his features. I let out a scream, but it faded noiselessly into the ether.

It was Thayer Vega. He leveled a smirk at Emma that said he knew all of her secrets—including exactly who she *wasn't.* And I could tell, in an instant, that whatever it was he had meant to me in life was wrapped up in mystery—and danger.

But no matter how hard I tried, I couldn't remember what that danger was.

∾ 1 ∾

SHE'S SEEN HIM

"Thayer," Emma Paxton said, staring at the teenage boy in front of her. His mussed hair looked black in the darkness of Sutton's bedroom. His cheekbones were prominent above his full lips. His deep-set, hazel eyes narrowed sinisterly.

"Hey, Sutton," Thayer said, drawing the name out.

A nervous chill ran down Emma's spine. She recognized Thayer Vega from his missing person posters—he'd vanished from Tucson, Arizona, in June. But that was long before Emma had made the trek to Tucson to reunite with her long-lost twin sister, Sutton. Long before she'd received an anonymous note saying that Sutton was dead and that Emma had to take her place, and tell no one . . . or else.

Emma had scrambled to figure everything out about Sutton on the spot—who her friends were, who her enemies were, what she liked to wear, what she liked to do, who she was dating. She'd come to Tucson simply to find a family member—a foster child, she was *desperate* for family, *any* family—but now she was mired in solving her sister's murder. It had been a relief to rule out Sutton's closest friends and sister, but Sutton had made a lot of enemies . . . and any number of people could have been her killer.

And Thayer was one of them. Like so many other people in Sutton's life, what Emma knew about him she'd cobbled together from Facebook posts, gossip, and the Help Us Find Thayer website his family had created after he'd skipped town. There was something dangerous about him—everyone said he'd been mixed up in some kind of trouble and had a horrible temper. And according to the rumors, Sutton had something to do with his disappearance.

Or maybe, I wondered, staring at the wild-eyed boy in my room, *Thayer had something to do with mine*. A memory popped into my head. I saw myself standing in Thayer's bedroom, the two of us locked in a bitter stare-off. "Do what you want," I spat, wheeling toward the door. Thayer looked hurt, then his eyes flashed with anger. "Fine," he snapped. "I *will*." I had no idea what the fight was about, but it was obvious I'd really pissed him off.

"What's the matter?" Thayer assessed Emma now, crossing his arms over his toned, soccer-player chest. His knowing expression was identical to the one in his MISSING poster. "Scared of me?"

Emma swallowed hard. "W-why would I be afraid of *you*?" she asked in the toughest voice she could muster, the one she used to reserve for butt-grabbing foster brothers, borderline-personality foster moms, and creepy guys loitering in the dodgy neighborhoods she'd grown up in after our biological mother, Becky, ditched her. But it was all a front. It was almost 3 A.M. on Saturday. Sutton's friends, who were downstairs for a post-Homecoming sleepover, were fast asleep. So were the Mercer parents. Even the family's huge Great Dane, Drake, was snoring away in the master bedroom. In the eerie calm, Emma couldn't help but think of the note she'd received on Laurel's car her first morning in Arizona: *Sutton's dead. Tell no one. Keep playing along . . . or you're next.* And the strong, terrifying hands that had strangled her with Sutton's locket at Charlotte's house a week later, threatening her once again to keep quiet. And the imposing, shadowy figure she'd seen in the high school auditorium just after an overhead light fell inches from her head. What if Thayer was behind all that?

Thayer smirked as though he was reading her mind. "I'm sure you have your reasons." And then he leaned back and stared at her like he could see right through her—like he was why she was here, pretending to be her dead sister.

Emma looked around, assessing her options for escape, but Thayer grabbed her arm before she could put any distance between them. His grip was hard, and she let out an instinctive, piercing scream. Thayer clamped a hand over her mouth. "Are you insane?" he growled.

"Mmm!" Emma moaned, struggling to breathe through Thayer's suffocating hold. He was standing so close that Emma could smell his cinnamon gum and see the tiny freckles that dotted the bridge of his nose. She struggled against him, panic welling in her chest. She bit down hard on his hand, tasting earthy, salty sweat.

Thayer swore and stepped back, letting Emma go. She spun away from him. His elbow crashed into a sea-green vase on Sutton's bookshelf. It tipped over, plummeted to the ground, and shattered into dozens of tiny pieces.

A light flipped on in the hall. "What the hell was that?" a voice called. Footsteps sounded and, seconds later, Sutton's parents burst into the room.

They moved to Emma's side. Mrs. Mercer's hair was mussed and she wore a baggy yellow nightshirt under a robe. Mr. Mercer's white undershirt was messily tucked into blue flannel pajama bottoms and his hair stood out straight from his head in silver-flecked spikes.

As soon as the parents noticed the intruder, their eyes widened. Mr. Mercer inserted himself between Emma and Thayer. Mrs. Mercer wrapped a protective arm around Emma's shoulders and pulled her close. Emma sank gratefully into Sutton's adoptive mother's embrace, rubbing the five angry marks that had popped up on her skin where Thayer had gripped her.

I had mixed feelings about my parents protecting Emma from Thayer. Were they simply worried because she'd screamed . . . or was it because of something more sinister about Thayer himself, something they knew about him from a past run-in?

"You!" Mr. Mercer bellowed at Thayer. "How dare you? How did you get in?"

Thayer just stared at him, a hint of a smirk on his face. Mr. Mercer's nostrils flared. His square jaw was set menacingly, his blue eyes blazed, and a vein stuck out on his temple, visibly throbbing. For a second, Emma wondered if Mr. Mercer assumed Sutton had invited Thayer into her room and was mad that his daughter let a boy in at three in the morning. But then she noticed the way Mr. Mercer and Thayer were crouched, as if ready to fight. It felt like something dark and hate-filled hung in the air between them, something that had nothing to do with Sutton at all.

More footsteps pounded up the stairs. Laurel and Madeline appeared in the doorway, having come from the den where the sleepover was taking place. "What's going on?" Laurel grumbled, rubbing her eyes. Then she caught sight of Thayer. Her light eyes opened wide and she covered her mouth with trembling fingers.

Madeline was dressed in a black camisole and her black hair was pulled back in a perfect bun even though it was the middle of the night. She elbowed her way between Laurel and Mrs. Mercer. Her mouth fell open. She reached out for Laurel's arm as if she might fall to the ground in shock.

"Thayer!" Madeline's voice was shrill, her expression an odd mixture of anger, confusion, and relief. "What are you doing here? Where have you been? Are you okay?"

The muscles in Thayer's arms flexed as he balled his fists. He glanced around at Laurel, Madeline, Emma, and the Mercer parents like he was a wounded animal wanting to flee his attackers. After a beat, he spun on his heel and bolted in the opposite direction. He shot across Sutton's bedroom, hoisting himself out the window and shimmying down the oak tree that served as an escape hatch from Sutton's room. Emma, Laurel, and Madeline flew to the window and watched Thayer scramble through the darkness. His gait was uneven—he favored his left leg with a pronounced limp as he moved across the grass.

"Get back here!" Mr. Mercer screamed, racing from

Sutton's bedroom and banging down the stairs. Emma scampered after him, with Mrs. Mercer, Laurel, and Madeline following behind. Charlotte and the Twitter Twins staggered out from the den, looking sleepy and confused.

Everyone gathered around the open doorway. Mr. Mercer had run halfway across the yard. "I'm calling the cops!" he shouted. "Get back here, damn it!"

No answer came. Just like that, Thayer was gone.

Photo by Daniel Snyder

SARA SHEPARD is the author of the #1 *New York Times* bestselling series Pretty Little Liars. She graduated from New York University and has an MFA in Creative Writing from Brooklyn College. Sara recently moved back to Philadelphia's Main Line from Arizona, where her new series, The Lying Game, is set.

For exclusive information
on your favorite authors and artists,
visit www.authortracker.com.

Don't miss a single scandal!

EVERYONE IN ULTRA-EXCLUSIVE ROSEWOOD, PENNSYLVANIA, HAS SOMETHING TO HIDE . . .

DISCUSS THE BOOKS AND THE HIT TV SHOW AT **WWW.PRETTYLITTLELIARS.COM.**

CHECK OUT **WWW.PRETTYLITTLELIARSBOOKS.COM** FOR SERIES GOSSIP, GAMES, AND GIVEAWAYS.

HARPER TEEN

An Imprint of HarperCollins*Publishers*

WELCOME TO THE NEW AMERICA

Don't miss a single page of the forbidden love and extraordinary adventure in the Eve Trilogy.

Visit TheEveTrilogy.com to follow Eve's journey.